KATE ELLIS

Kissing the Demons

PIATKUS

PIATKUS

First published in Great Britain and the US in 2011 by Crème de la Crime,
An imprint of Severn House Publishers Ltd
This paperback edition published in Great Britain in 2024 by Piatkus

1 3 5 7 9 10 8 6 4 2

A CIP catalogue record for this book
is available from the British Library.

ISBN 978-0-349-44094-1

Typeset by Palimpsest Book Production Ltd., Falkirk, Stirlingshire, Scotland.
Printed and bound in Great Britain by Clays Ltd, Elcograf S.p.A.

Papers used by Piatkus are from well-managed forests
and other responsible sources.

Piatkus
An imprint of
Little, Brown Book Group
Carmelite House
50 Victoria Embankment
London EC4Y 0DZ

An Hachette UK Company
www.hachette.co.uk

www.littlebrown.co.uk

Kate Ellis was born and brought up in Liverpool and studied drama in Manchester. She is the award-winning author of the Wesley Peterson detective novels as well as the Joe Plantagenet mysteries and the Albert Lincoln trilogy set in the aftermath of the Great War.

Kate has won the CWA Dagger in the Library Award for her crime writing. She has also twice been shortlisted for the CWA Short Story Dagger and been longlisted for the Theakston's Old Peculier Crime Novel of the Year Award.

Visit Kate Ellis online:

www.kateellis.co.uk
@KateEllisAuthor

Praise for Kate Ellis:

'A beguiling author who interweaves past and present'
The Times

'Clever plotting hides a powerful story of
loss, malice and deception'
Ann Cleeves

'Haunting'
Independent

'The chilling plot will keep you spooked
and thrilled to the end'
Closer

'Ellis skilfully interweaves ancient and contemporary
crimes in an impeccably composed tale'
Publishers Weekly

By Kate Ellis

ONE

Death arrived at the party dressed in the traditional way. Long black robe; monkish cowl pulled forward to half-conceal a skull face with cavernous eye sockets and grinning yellow teeth.

Death was tall, as one would expect, and in his bony right hand he carried a long plastic scythe – the real thing would have been hard to get hold of and much too conspicuous. And Death didn't want to face any awkward questions.

Nobody took much notice as he stalked up the wide stairs, almost tripping up on the threadbare carpet. When he reached the landing he stood for a few moments, leaning on the banisters to survey the mortals below.

The ground floor of thirteen Torland Place was packed and all the time costumed newcomers were arriving in the hall carrying glasses and bottles. Some stopped to talk with animated gestures; some had the far away look of beer-goggled youth; and others were making their way to the living room where, through the open door, partygoers were attempting to dance with varying degrees of success.

Then Death spotted his target – a girl in flimsy white with sequinned fairy wings. He watched as she wove her way through the crowd, slightly aloof, like a being from another world. She had pale hair and large green eyes and she possessed a virginal quality that seemed out of place in that alcohol-fuelled atmosphere. She stopped by a doorway and stood alone, oblivious to the raucous laughter and loud music around her. Separated from the rest of humanity.

Death studied her. The Maiden, he thought. Death and the Maiden. But he knew her real name. It was Petulia. He mouthed the word. Petulia.

He saw her take a step towards a young man with dark curls and a face straight out of a Renaissance painting who was dressed in a white coat with a stethoscope slung around his neck. Death appreciated his beauty – which would fade as all beauty fades with time – and watched as he raised a can of lager to his lips, looking as though he'd prefer to be elsewhere; as though he found the squalid rented house with its smell of sweat and stale beer beneath him. The Maiden's steps faltered, as though she'd suddenly sensed the protective force field of sophisticated boredom that surrounded her quarry.

Then she turned away, her eyes searching the hallway for somebody – anybody – who might be a sympathetic companion. Death knew how she felt. He had experienced the loneliness of crowds so many times. It was hell on earth.

He looked at his watch. It was two in the morning and people were beginning to drift away from the party, still clutching beer bottles and half-full wine glasses. Death too had had his fill of the too-loud conversation, the couples copulating on cheap duvets in the shabby bedrooms and the preening mortals dancing clumsily on beer-sticky floors. But he hadn't had his fill of the house. He could never tire of it because he felt at home there. As if the very walls knew him and welcomed him in.

It was almost time to go. Death watched as the Maiden disappeared into the kitchen. She looked tired but she was still awake and sober enough to dodge away from a large boy in rugby kit whose exploratory arm had started to snake around her slim waist.

If Death had been made otherwise, he would have harboured fantasies about claiming her soft pale body for himself. But life and love were none of his concern.

The Maiden was the one. And one day very soon Death would claim her.

When DCI Emily Thwaite set out that Saturday morning the Yorkshire weather couldn't make up its mind what to do. It had promised sunshine first thing. Then the clouds had gathered in the sky like youths on a street corner, threatening showers and possibly worse.

She reached her office on the first floor of the modern police headquarters at the back of the railway station, took off her thin raincoat and hung it on the stand. She had drunk far too much the night before and she still had a nagging headache. But if your new neighbours offer you their hospitality and constantly top up your wine glass, it would be churlish and mealy mouthed to refuse – or so she'd reasoned at the time.

She walked over to the small mirror that hung on the wall and looked at herself, noting the dark rings beneath her eyes and the fine red tracery marring the white surrounding her pupils. The wages of sin – or at least the wages of a good night on the Cabernet Sauvignon. She delved into the depths of the roomy bag which hung from her shoulder, pulled out her hairbrush, dragged it through her thick blonde curls and wiped a microscopic smudge of dirt from her nose. She'd do, she thought, running a finger round the ever-tightening waistband of her trousers. She'd signed up to the gym in the new year but the burdens of work and family meant that she hadn't had time to go. One day, perhaps. One day.

Saturday morning wasn't the best time to be summoned into work, what with the children to be ferried to ballet and swimming. But the Superintendent had called her at home first thing, saying that he wanted to speak to her urgently on a delicate matter so she'd had to delegate those precious, looked forward to tasks to her husband, Jeff. Sometimes she feared that she was a lousy mother. But with a job like hers, the occasional bout of benign neglect was unavoidable.

Suddenly she saw a shadow out of the corner of her eye, partially blocking out the daylight that filtered in from the outer office. She tipped the hairbrush back into her bag and fixed a professional expression to her face but when she looked round she was relieved to see Joe Plantagenet leaning on the door frame. His thick black hair looked tousled, as if he'd just got out of bed after a restless night. Perhaps he had, Emily thought. It was a long time since he had spoken to her about his private life and, although she was a naturally curious soul, she didn't like to ask, even though there were times when she was desperate to know. There were so many questions she'd have liked to put to Joe if only she had the courage . . . or the blatant cheek. She'd always been known for her direct approach when she'd been in Leeds CID. Maybe working in Eborby was making her soft.

'Has the Super told you what he wants to see us about?' Joe asked.

'All he said is that it's delicate – whatever that means.'

Joe smiled. He had a slightly crooked smile, a smile which

spread to his blue eyes. 'Well, we won't find out standing around here, will we?'

He stood to one side and allowed her to walk out of the CID office ahead of him. As it was a weekend and there were no major investigations in progress, there were only a handful of officers on duty. But if something bad happened, all that would change.

Emily walked down the corridor to the Super's office, aware of Joe following close behind. When they came to the office door, they stopped and exchanged looks. Joe raised his hand and knocked.

A deep voice growled a 'come in' from the other side of the door. Joe stood back and let Emily go first, whether out of politeness or reluctance, she wasn't quite sure.

She smoothed her hair and pushed the door open, her heart beating fast. She had a vague inkling that whatever she was about to hear would be bad. The Super didn't do routine on a Saturday morning.

'Come in, Emily,' the Super said, his voice as smooth as the rather expensive wine she'd consumed last night. He gave her a businesslike smile and turned to Joe.

'Do sit down, both of you. As I said to DCI Thwaite, something's come up that could be of a rather sensitive nature.'

Emily caught Joe's eye. 'What sort of thing, sir?'

For a few seconds the Superintendent sat there in silence, as though the extreme delicacy of the matter, whatever it was, had rendered him speechless. When he eventually spoke his voice was hushed, as though he didn't want to be overheard. 'It concerns something that happened twelve years ago.'

Emily leaned forward. It was well before her time – before Joe's too, come to that. 'What was that, sir?'

Another silence. Whatever this was, it had certainly got the Super worried. Then he spoke again. 'Two fifteen-year-old girls went missing. The last confirmed sighting of them was in Bearsley. Some kids were playing near a patch of woodland known locally as Dead Man's Wood and they saw the two girls entering the trees. This was around seven thirty one summer's evening. The two lasses were never seen again. There was a massive search, of course, but . . . There was a lot of speculation at the time.' the Super continued. 'One theory had it that they'd run away to London and another that they'd been abducted and taken miles away. A necklace belonging to one of the girls was found about ten yards into the wood. The clasp was broken as if it had been torn off. A handkerchief was found a few feet away from the spot – an expensive linen one. We announced it at the time . . . said we wanted to eliminate the owner from our enquiries.'

'I take it this handkerchief was embroidered with a distinctive pair of initials?' said Emily, instantly regretting her flippancy.

The Super gave her a cool smile. 'I'm afraid not.'

'Pity,' she heard Joe mutter.

'So did the investigation team think it was dropped by the killer?'

'Without bodies we can't be sure that there was a killer, can we? But nobody came forward to claim the handkerchief so we can only assume . . .'

'That the owner had something to hide.'

The Super sat back. He picked up a pencil and began turning it over and over in his fingers. He was a large man, Emily thought; tall and bald with the build of a rugby player. But his hands were surprisingly long and sensitive. She would have expected great paws with sausage fingers.

'That's the trouble, Emily. The handkerchief was bagged up and kept by Forensic. There were slight traces of DNA – semen, apparently.'

'Bit of hanky-panky in the woods, then?' she said.

'Perhaps.' The Super hesitated. 'Traffic division arrested a man for a motoring offence a couple of weeks ago. His DNA was run through the computer as a matter of routine and . . .'

There was a long pause and Emily wished he'd get to the point.

'As you know, we can extract DNA from tiny samples now and the lab people found a match. The sample on the handkerchief matches those of the individual the traffic officers arrested.'

'Has this individual got a name?'

This was the question Emily had been about to ask but Joe had got in first.

The Superintendent thought for a while before answering which only fanned the flames of Emily's burning curiosity. Whoever it was, it had got the Super rattled. The possibility that it was the Chief Constable himself flashed through her mind, only to be dismissed when she visualized the ostentatiously upright man. But many a Dr Jekyll had turned into a Mr Hyde given the right circumstances and provocation. She sat forward and waited and she noticed that Joe had assumed an almost identical posture.

'That's why I said it was rather delicate,' the Super said in hushed tones. 'It's actually Barrington Jenks . . . MP for Eborby and Under Secretary of State in the Justice Department.'

Emily's lips formed an 'oh'. She looked at Joe. He had slumped back in his seat and it was difficult to tell what he was thinking.

'Well, he's not above the law,' Joe said quietly. 'He'll need to be interviewed.'

'I realize that, Joe. But I think a bit of discretion . . .'

'He's at home this weekend – spending time in his constituency. Perhaps if you both paid him a discreet visit . . .'

'I don't think we need to waste any time,' said Emily. 'We'll go now.'

The Superintendent looked a little alarmed. 'I can't emphasize enough that this needs careful handling. Jenks has friends in some very high places.'

'If he raped and murdered two young girls, he'll soon be making new friends in some pretty low ones,' said Joe.

The Superintendent gave him a worried look and turned his attention to Emily. 'I'm trusting you to handle this with tact.'

'Naturally, sir,' said Emily.

She was relieved when Joe stood up. She wanted the interview to be over. She wanted to corner Barrington Jenks MP and ask him some awkward questions.

'Let's go and see Jenks now,' she whispered to Joe as she closed the Super's door.

'Maybe we should bring ourselves up to date with the case first.'

Emily sighed. She knew he was right. She'd just have to curb her natural impatience.

Petulia Ferribie often cursed her parents for giving her such an outlandish name. It was usually abbreviated to Pet but she hated that too. It held the suggestion that she was some kind of plaything – something to be picked up or put down on the whim of an owner. When people – men in particular – saw her sweet face, elfin figure and blonde hair, they tended to make assumptions that were completely wrong. Perhaps wearing the white fairy costume at the fancy dress party last night had only served to perpetuate those assumptions. Maybe it had been a mistake but it had been the only thing available at the time.

But what did it matter? All those boring, self-obsessed students were of no interest to her anyway. She found their relentless pursuit of binge drinking and casual sex so immature. And as for her irritating housemates, they'd seemed fine when they'd met last year in the hall of residence. Caro, Matt, Jason and Pet – the Gang of Four, they'd called themselves. But once they'd moved into number thirteen everything had turned sour. Maybe it was just that she'd grown up after the first year. Or maybe it was the house itself that had changed everyone. She hated the place. It always seemed to be cold in there and something about it made her uncomfortable, as though she was never quite alone even when her housemates were absent. Since they'd moved in the previous September she'd found it hard to sleep, as though there was a presence in the shadows of her room, watching, wishing her ill.

She carried on past the soaring cathedral, its carved stone west front glowing in the weak sunlight. Walking quickly, she darted into one of the narrow medieval streets that radiated like tentacles from the great church. It was only March but the tourists were out in force, attracted by history and the recent spell of fair weather. Pet had come to hate tourists meandering along, taking photographs, looking for places to fuel up with food and drink, gawping at the cathedral and the rest of Eborby's myriad attractions with the slow awe of primitive tribesmen faced with their first aeroplane. They were nothing but a nuisance to people who actually lived there.

Pet wove her way through the crowds on Jamesgate, swearing under her breath. If she didn't get a move on she'd be late. And she wanted to see the main event. He would be there, taking part. And maybe he would see her.

Suddenly she spotted Jason standing in the doorway of an empty shop. He was strumming on his guitar and his dark curls flopped forward to conceal his pale, almost feminine face. She made no move to acknowledge her housemate;

instead she averted her eyes as though he was an embarrassment to her.

Everyone in the house had treated Jason coolly since he'd
failed his exams last summer and been thrown off his course.
And here he was busking in the street, practically begging like
some tramp.

To her horror he looked in her direction, stopped in mid
song and raised his hand. She looked away but her escape
route was blocked by a couple, entwined and aware only of
each other. She felt like shouting at them, hitting them on their
smug backs to make them shift. But instead, she dodged round
them and half walked, half ran out of the shade of the overhanging upper storeys and out into the watery spring sun.

She could hear music somewhere ahead. The sharp primitive
sound of shawm, crumhorn and hurdy-gurdy over the swaying
beat of the tabor. It was the sort of music that made Pet want
to dance, although she resisted the temptation as she had no
inclination to make a fool of herself.

She looked round to check that Jason hadn't decided to
follow her and was relieved that there was no sign of him.
Jason might be good looking but he was a loser and of no
interest. Not like the man she hoped to see that morning.

The appetizing aroma of hot dogs and fried onions wafted
from a stall in the far corner of the crowded square and Pet
realized she was hungry. But she had no time to eat. At eleven
o'clock the Waits, early music's representatives at the Eborby
Music festival, were due to make their way to Stone Street,
Eborby's widest thoroughfare. During the course of its history
Stone Street had always been a gathering place and the scene
of numerous public executions. But history didn't concern Pet.
Her passion was music. At university she studied piano and
violin and she considered it a blessing that all the time spent
in necessary practice in her department kept her away from
Torland Place.

She pushed her way to the front of the crowd and stood
staring at the musicians. They were dressed in red tunics with
brown hose and soft leather boots; everyday dress in Eborby's
heyday during the reign of Richard III. The musician playing
the hurdy-gurdy with such concentration was taller than the
others, with dark hair that had begun to whiten at the temples.
She'd half expected him to look ridiculous in his medieval

outfit – like most of the people at the party last night had looked in their fancy dress – but somehow he didn't. He looked like some king's minister or great lord. How could Ian Zepper have looked otherwise?

She stared at him, willing him to notice her. He didn't look in her direction. But she didn't give up hope; there was still time.

The Eborby Waits began to make their way out of the square, the crowd following like rats behind the pied piper. Pet waited and brought up the rear, not realizing that she would never reach Stone Street that day. Or any other.

Death was watching her, hidden in the anonymity of the crowd. The knife was ready, concealed in a pocket, the blade warmed by his body.

He would cover her eyes when the time came to silence her forever. There were demons in their eyes; he'd known that from the first day Grace had looked at him with all that mocking contempt. And demons had to be destroyed.

TWO

Joe looked at his watch. It was eleven o'clock and the concert in Stone Street would soon be starting: he'd seen the posters dotted around the city and taken note. Early music always reminded him of his first meeting with Kaitlin: her choir had sung a Palestrina mass in the church where he'd been posted as a trainee priest and afterwards they'd started talking about music and life. That momentous meeting had made him realize that he'd been fooling himself. He hadn't been cut out for the celibate life. His vocation had been a terrible error of judgement.

Kaitlin had entered his world like a cleansing tornado. Then just as suddenly she was gone, killed in a chance accident just six months after their wedding. Sometimes he envied his boss, Emily Thwaite, her apparent domestic bliss – although he knew that she too had experienced periods of turbulence. Nobody ever has a completely calm voyage through the world from first cry to final breath. In his job he knew that only too well.

The parents of Jade Portright and Nerys Barnton certainly hadn't had it easy for the twelve long years since their daughters' disappearance. Time might have led to a sad, numb acceptance but the pain of such a loss never went away. And now the whole affair was to be dug up again like a stinking corpse. Unhealed wounds would be picked at again until the raw pain returned anew. In Joe's experience cold cases were always like that.

Any tentative plans he had to sneak off to the Stone Street concert would have to be put on hold. He still had three thick files to plough his way through because he needed to be armed with all the available facts before he faced Barrington Jenks MP.

'Well?'

He looked up. Emily Thwaite had just parked her ample backside on the corner of his desk and she was looking at him expectantly.

'Well what?'

'You've been reading the files – what happened?'

'Nothing much, as far as I can tell. Two friends – Jade Portright and Nerys Barnton – went into a small patch of woodland commonly known as Dead Man's Wood behind a row of Victorian houses in Bearsley.'

'I know where you mean.'

'Did anyone see the girls go into the wood?'

'Some kids were taking a short cut on their way to the swimming baths and they saw them behind the houses, heading for the trees. One of them knew Jade because she was a friend of his older sister and he said they were walking quickly, as if they were going there for a purpose. In other words it didn't look like a casual summer evening stroll.'

'They'd arranged to meet someone?'

'That was never established. And after the kid saw them going into the trees they were never seen again.'

'Any evidence of violence?'

'Only the necklace belonging to Jade – a small silver locket. The clasp was broken which could indicate some sort of struggle but, on the other hand, I suppose it could have become caught on something. The handkerchief was found a couple of yards away. And there were signs that the ground had been disturbed.'

'By the girls putting up a fight?'

'Not necessarily. It might have been a courting couple or . . .'

'And now Barrington Jenks's DNA puts him at the scene?'

'But not necessarily at the same time as the girls.'

Emily's eyes shone. Joe knew she was hooked. 'How long after the girls vanished was the woodland searched?'

'They were last seen around seven and the parents reported them missing just before midnight after they'd checked that they weren't with friends. Next morning, as soon as the kid told his mum where he'd seen the girls, the woodland was fingertip searched. It had rained till around five on the day the girls disappeared then the sun came out. Forensic said the handkerchief hadn't been exposed to rain so . . .'

'Whoever owned it was there between five that day and the following morning.'

'The same time as the abductor.'

Emily frowned. 'We don't know there was an abductor, Joe. All we know is that the girls were never seen again. They might have run away to the bright lights. I believe Kings Cross is full of northern kids who think the streets of London are paved with gold. I blame Dick Whittington myself.'

Joe didn't answer. He had started delving into a small cardboard box that had been brought up with the files. Inside was an evidence bag containing the broken locket. He held it up to the light and, as he stared at the thing through its veil of plastic, he felt a wave of deep sadness. It was a cheap little bauble but it had probably been precious to Jade Portright. It was always the small things that got to you.

He put his hand into the box again. The only thing left inside was a video tape. A dog-eared white sticky label clung to the side bearing the legend 'Jade and Nerys – summer 1999'. Joe put it on the desk in front of him and looked at it, suddenly disturbed by the prospect of seeing the missing girl as a smiling, living human being . . . and imagining her parents' pain.

'We'd better have a look at it,' said Emily quietly, picking up the tape. Somehow Joe knew she shared his misgivings. She was a mother herself. She would be able to imagine exactly how it felt to lose a precious child.

They walked down the corridor to the AV room in silence.

Normally the room would be occupied by some unfortunate
Detective Constable assigned to trawl through hours of CCTV
footage after having drawn some proverbial short straw. But
today Joe and Emily sat there while the screen flickered into
life.

For anyone who knew how the story ended the images were
heart-rending. Two girls in their mid teens, giggling at the
camera. Wearing swimming costumes in some suburban
garden, wading through a younger sibling's paddling pool and
splashing each other with cold water, screaming with glee.
Then, suddenly coy, as they remember they're being filmed,
covering their youthful, semi-naked bodies with towels and
shooing away the camera.

The girl wearing the locket was presumably Jade. She had
lanky limbs and her pretty features weren't yet fully formed,
even though there was something knowing about her eyes, as
though she was only too aware of her burgeoning sexuality.

Her friend Nerys, in contrast, was small and dark with
darting brown eyes that suggested intelligence and mischief.

'Poor little cows,' Emily said, almost in a whisper.

Joe said nothing. He couldn't find the words.

'Let's go and have a word with the Honourable Member of
Parliament for Eborby,' she said.

After seeing those images of the missing girls, Joe suspected
that tact and delicacy weren't going to be in the forefront of
their minds during the visit.

In spite of his distinguished name, Joe Plantagenet usually did
his best to avoid the Great and the Good. In his experience
their expensive shoes usually concealed feet of very dirty clay.
But he didn't share this thought with Emily on the drive out
to the village of Colforth, ten miles north of Eborby.

It was four o'clock now and Joe hoped they'd find Barrington
Jenks MP at home. Emily hadn't wanted to telephone ahead
to warn of their arrival. She'd always favoured the element of
surprise.

Colforth was the sort of picturesque North Yorkshire village
visitors flocked to see. Pretty stone houses, pubs of the cosy
traditional kind and a babbling stream running by the main road,
traversed by several small stone footbridges. This was holiday
country with its fair share of wealthy residents inhabiting

converted barns sold off by canny farmers feeling the financial pinch.

Barrington Jenks' place was in the centre of the village: a fine Georgian double-fronted house that had been home and workplace to the local doctor in times gone by, until a new medical centre had been built and the doctor moved to something more modest. Emily brought the car to a graceful halt outside the house.

'Your turn to do the talking,' she said as Joe rang the doorbell.

The front door opened to reveal a small Filipina woman in her twenties. She was remarkably pretty . . . and she looked terrified as she stood aside to let them in. She flitted silently up the elegant Georgian staircase, thickly carpeted in a rich shade of cream and some time later a man appeared on the landing. He was dressed in casual trousers and an open-necked shirt but he had the mildly harassed look of a man who had just dressed in a hurry.

Joe watched him as he descended the staircase and saw his expression change to a mask of quiet confidence. He was a tall man with thick, well cut silver grey hair, a slight tan and a smooth face. He reminded Joe of a male model in one of the old-fashioned catalogues his mother used to browse through.

Joe did the introductions and Jenks shook hands with long-practised warmth.

'So sorry to have kept you waiting. I've just got back from Eborby and I've been in the shower. Dinner tonight with the Lord Lieutenant,' he said, leaning forward confidentially. 'Now what can I do for you, officers?'

It was Emily who spoke. 'It concerns your arrest for a motoring offence, sir.'

'Please, come through.' He led them into the kind of drawing room Joe had only seen before on visits to stately homes. This one was smaller scale, of course, but it was all there; the Persian rugs, the swagged silk drapes, the expensive art hanging on the hand-printed wallpaper and the antique furniture.

They were invited to sit and Joe tried to make himself comfortable on a Regency sofa. Emily took a chintz-covered armchair and it looked as though she'd made the best choice.

'I'll ring for tea,' Jenks said, walking over to the fireplace and pulling an embroidered rope.

'Thank you,' Emily muttered. She caught Joe's eye and gave him a slight nod.

Joe cleared his throat. 'Er . . . you gave a DNA sample when you were arrested, sir.'

'That's right,' Jenks said, making himself comfortable in a leather armchair facing Emily. 'An interesting experience. For the first time in my life I actually knew what it felt like to be a criminal,' he said as though the whole thing had been staged rather than real – like a Prime Minister pulling a pint for the cameras.

Joe glanced at Emily, wondering how to broach the subject of Jade Portright and Nerys Barnton. Then he decided on the direct approach.

'As a matter of routine the DNA sample you provided was run through our computer . . . compared with samples from past crime scenes.'

The MP assumed an expression of polite, innocent interest. 'Really?'

'A match was found.'

Jenks's eyes flickered for a split second but the expression didn't change. He waited for Joe to continue.

'Twelve years ago a handkerchief was found near the scene of a suspected abduction. There was semen on the handkerchief. The lab found a DNA match to the sample you gave.'

Joe looked at Emily. She was sitting quite still, her eyes fixed on the man in the armchair opposite, hardly daring to breathe as she awaited the reply.

'That's impossible,' he said after a long silence.

'You haven't asked where the handkerchief was found,' said Emily.

'Very well. Where was it found?'

'In a small patch of woodland behind some houses in Bearsley . . . suburb of Eborby. Known to the locals as Dead Man's Woods.'

Jenks mouthed the name and then his face lit up with relief. 'I used to live near there and I occasionally walked my dog in those woods. Now if that's all . . .'

'Do you remember two girls who went missing in 1999? Their names were Jade Portright and Nerys Barnton. They were fifteen years old.'

'Yes. I remember. As I said, I lived in Eborby at the time

and there was a lot of publicity about the case, but I assure you . . .'

'You still haven't explained how your handkerchief came to be lying a few feet away from a necklace belonging to one of the missing girls. The necklace had a broken clasp, as though it had been pulled off her neck in a struggle.' Joe looked him in the eye. 'You see why we have to question you, sir?'

'Of course. You're only doing your duty.' Jenks had assumed a cooperative citizen expression. 'I'll try to answer your questions as best I can, that goes without saying.'

'So can you explain how the handkerchief came to be in Dead Man's Wood?' Emily asked sweetly. 'And I ought to tell you that the girls were last seen around seven on a Saturday evening in June. It had been raining just before then and the woods were searched first thing the following morning. According to the lab the handkerchief hadn't been there when it rained.'

There was a long period of silence while Jenks considered his answer.

'I must have dropped it when I walked my dog.'

'There was an appeal for anyone who'd been in the area around that time to come forward. You never came forward.'

'That's because I hadn't seen anything suspicious. If I had, I would have told the police immediately.'

'So you admit that you were there that night?'

'It was a long time ago. I really can't remember.'

'And the semen on the handkerchief? How did that get there? Did you meet someone in the wood? Is that why you didn't come forward?' Emily inclined her head and waited for the answer.

Joe could almost see the man's mind working, wondering how much he could avoid telling them. As a politician, he was accustomed to evading awkward questions but this time there was no escape.

Jenks finally sat up straight, his face open and honest. 'Very well, I'll tell you the truth. But you must assure me that what I say stays within these four walls. I know it's twelve years ago but I really don't want my wife to be hurt by a silly indiscretion.'

'Go on,' said Joe quietly, leaning forward, ready to take the man's confession.

Jenks slumped forward so that his head was only a couple of feet away from Joe's. He played with his wedding ring nervously, no longer the powerful man in control.

'I didn't come forward at the time because I was embarrassed. You see, I met this woman . . . well, more of a girl really. She was a student and I bought her a few drinks in a bar in town and she asked me back to her place. I'd been on my own – my wife was down in London with the children and . . . foolishly I went and . . .'

'And?' Emily was impatient to hear the rest of the story.

'Well when we got to her place her housemates were there and obviously I didn't want to be seen so . . .'

'So you suggested a bit of alfresco sex?' said Emily.

'She suggested it actually. She said it was a warm night so why didn't we go into the wood. I said it would be damp because it had rained that afternoon but she said . . .' He swallowed hard. 'She said she'd been a Girl Guide and was always prepared. She took a sleeping bag and plastic ground sheet from her room, you see, and she laid it on the ground. I had the impression she'd done that sort of thing before and . . .'

Emily was about to interrupt but Joe raised a warning finger and waited for him to continue. The man was obviously finding the confession difficult and Joe felt a modicum of sympathy. We've all done things which, in hindsight, cause us shame and embarrassment – but not all of us have to relive them in a formal statement to the police.

'Anyway,' Jenks continued. 'When we'd finished she asked for a hundred pounds – said it was towards her studies.'

'And you paid up?'

'I didn't have much choice. I walked with her to the cash point and withdrew a hundred and fifty. The extra fifty was for myself, of course . . . but she said she'd take the lot.'

'And you didn't argue?' Joe could see amusement in Emily's eyes as she contemplated yet another case of a man rendered helpless and foolish by his primal urges.

Joe didn't wait for an answer. He produced photographs of the two missing girls from his inside pocket and passed them over to Jenks who held them by the edge as if they were contaminated.

'When you were in the woods did you see anything of those girls?'

'Sorry. I don't remember seeing anybody.'

'What was the name of the girl you were with? We'll need to speak to her to confirm your story.'

'She said her name was Jasmine but I'm not sure if that was her real name. She was tall and blonde. That's all I can remember.'

'She told you she was at the university? What was she studying?'

Another shake of the head. 'Sorry. Don't know.'

'And her address? You said she took you to her house – where was it?'

'It was near the wood – big tatty Victorian semi. Student house. I remember it was number thirteen – Jasmine made a joke of it: unlucky for some, she said, but not unlucky for me. The house next door was immaculate – I remember that. The wood was just behind the garden I think. We didn't have to walk far.'

'You wouldn't know her surname by any chance?'

Jenks shook his head. 'Please tell me this won't go any further,' he said. 'I've always played on my happy family man image and this could finish me.' He looked up at Joe with pleading eyes.

But Joe wasn't making any promises.

Then Jenks spoke quietly, head bowed. 'I want to consult my solicitor.'

Caro was keen on house meetings. A natural bureaucrat, she had taken charge of the various rotas – cleaning, taking out bins, shopping – but she had encountered only frustration for her pains, as her housemates lacked her innate sense of order.

She had called a meeting for Saturday tea time – before the housemates went their separate social ways – and now she sat at the head of the kitchen table, surveying the chipped blue melamine surface with its ingrained coffee rings, as she hoped to one day sit in pride of place in some lofty London boardroom.

She glanced at her watch. 'Where's Pet?'

'I haven't seen her since she went out this morning,' said Matt.

Caro began to twirl a strand of her short dark hair in her fingers, twisting it into a tight corkscrew curl then letting it unwind. Pet irritated her with her fey smiles and cunning helplessness. Men liked her, of course, but Caro saw through all the artifice. And it had all got worse since they moved into number thirteen. Things that had seemed like minor eccentricities in hall were now magnified to major character flaws.

'What about you, Jason?' She looked at the young man sitting furthest away from her. He looked bored as he leaned back dangerously in his chair. Caro was almost ready to scold him, to point out that if he tilted the chair any more, he would fall over and break it . . . and Cassidy, the landlord would take the cost of a replacement off their deposit. But she stopped herself. But when he took out a worn tobacco tin and started to roll a cigarette she felt she had to speak. 'We agreed, Jason. No smoking in the communal areas. What you do in your own room's your own business but . . .'

'OK, OK,' Jason said wearily returning the tin to his pocket. 'And I saw Pet in town this morning when I was busking. I don't know whether she saw me but she shot off bloody quick.'

'Where was this?' Matt asked. He sounded worried.

'Jamesgate.'

'She said she was going to the Music Festival,' said Matt quietly.

'Then she probably met someone from her course there. I say we get on with the meeting without her.' She consulted the sheet of paper in front of her and looked round the table expectantly before moving on to the important topic of cleaning rotas.

And it wasn't until six, when Pet still wasn't answering her mobile, that Caro began to feel uneasy.

THREE

There was still no answer from Pet and Matt turned his mobile phone over and over in his hand. Where was she? What was she doing?

'I'm going out.'

Jason stood in the doorway, armed with his guitar. His face looked pale, although he seemed to be his usual arrogant self.

'Where are you going?'

'Down into town to give one of my alfresco concerts – got to earn a crust now I'm one of the Great Unemployed. If I'm lucky I'll catch the punters on their way to their expensive troughs – alright for some.'

Jason's self-pitying attitude was starting to annoy Matt. It was his own fault he'd failed his exams and not bothered turning up for the resits. Jason was bright and if he'd spent less time smoking weed and partying he would have stood a chance. But Matt was in no position to preach.

'Tracked Pet down yet?'

Matt shook his head. It was almost six o'clock. But she was a grown woman.

'I shouldn't worry about her. She'll be tucked up in someone's bed.'

'She's not like that,' Matt snapped in reply.

A knowing smirk appeared on Jason's lips. 'I'll be off. See you later.'

When Matt heard the front door bang, he picked up his phone and tried Pet's number again but still no luck. It really wasn't like her not to say if she was going to be away this long. And she always kept her phone switched on. Always.

He was just wondering what to do next when he heard a key turning in the front door lock. Typical of Jason to have forgotten something, he thought. And then he experienced a sudden rush of hope that perhaps it was Pet.

He heard footsteps on the bare wood floor of the hallway and the landlord appeared in the doorway. Andy Cassidy was in his thirties; tall with a shaved head and a muscular body. His pristine black T-shirt showed off a pair of tanned arms decorated with an assortment of tattoos; mostly Chinese. Matt often wondered what they meant – or if some Chinese wit had told him the characters represented something heroic or spiritual when they really said something derogatory.

'How are you doing?' Cassidy said smoothly. He liked to be thought of as one of the lads. Matt knew that he had been a student himself once upon a time – until he had abandoned a graduate traineeship at a well-known supermarket for the world of property development. 'I hear you had a party last night.'

'Surprised you weren't there.' Matt saw Cassidy swing round

as Caro entered the room. 'Don't worry, there was no damage if that's what you're worried about.'

Andy Cassidy looked Caro up and down appreciatively. 'No worries when you're here, Caro. You've got them well trained, eh.'

Caro pressed her lips together. 'You should give us notice when you want to visit.'

Cassidy shrugged apologetically. 'Sorry. I was just passing and I thought I'd pop in. No harm in taking an interest, is there? Where's the lovely Pet?'

Matt turned away. Cassidy made it so obvious he wanted to get into Pet's knickers; always trying to talk to her; always asking after her when she wasn't there.

'We don't know,' said Caro. 'I take it you haven't seen her?'

'Why should I have seen her?'

'She's often said that she's bumped into you around town.' She looked the landlord in the eye. 'I wondered if you were following her. You can get put inside for stalking, you know.'

'I've never had to stalk anyone in my life.'

Caro caught Matt's eye and she gave him a wink. She loved winding Cassidy up.

'I'm surprised you lot are in on a Saturday night.'

'Never heard of student debt?' Caro said sharply. 'Anyway, we're recovering from the party.' She looked at Matt. 'Some of us have got hangovers. So are you here for the pleasure of our company or . . . ?'

Cassidy's face suddenly became solemn. 'Actually, guys, I'm thinking of selling the place. Recession and all that. In fact I'm expecting a mate of mine any moment. I told him about the place a while ago and he's keen to take it on. He's an estate agent and he's going to give it the once over. Sorry and all that but you'll be moving on soon anyway, won't you?'

It was true that they were all fixed up with somewhere else in the next academic year. Matt had arranged to share with someone on his course, Caro was moving in with a friend and Pet was moving into a flat in her tutor's house with another music student. As for Jason . . . Matt wasn't sure.

Matt was about to say that number thirteen hadn't been a happy house but the words seemed a little silly and sentimental.

To men like Cassidy houses didn't have characters of their own – they were machines to produce income.

'This really isn't on,' said Caro. 'You should have made an appointment.'

'It's the only time Ethan's free. I promise you won't even know we're here.'

'It's still not acceptable . . .'

But before Cassidy could say anything more the doorbell rang.

'That'll be Ethan.' Cassidy gave Caro a nervous smile. Matt suspected that he was a little scared of her. She had that effect on some people.

When Cassidy hurried out to answer the door, Caro turned to Matt, a scowl on her face. 'Bloody cheek. We could complain, you know.'

Matt sighed. 'I don't suppose it'll affect us.'

'It will if he has queues of people traipsing through the place while we're trying to revise. We'll have to be firm. By appointment only. I'd better see what Cassidy's up to.'

But at that moment Cassidy appeared on the threshold. Another man stood behind him; he was average height and slightly built with short dark hair and a long thin face, the sort that doesn't stand out in a crowd. He was around the same age as Cassidy, but unlike the landlord, he wore a smart grey suit.

'This is my mate, Ethan McNeil. I don't think you've met.'

Matt nodded to the newcomer.

'Mind if he looks round in here?'

The question was rhetorical. McNeil stepped into the room, his grey eyes taking in every feature. He said nothing but made notes on a clipboard he was holding. Matt noticed that his handwriting was small and neat as his cheap ballpoint pen moved fast across the paper.

'Seen anything of your neighbour recently?' Cassidy asked this question every time he visited. When they'd first moved in he'd said he'd been trying to persuade Mr Quillan to sell him the house next door. But now he planned to dispose of number thirteen Matt wondered why his interest was continuing.

'We're on nodding terms but we hardly have neighbourly chats over the garden fence. Why are you so interested if you're selling this place?'

'Next door's in good nick – might be a sound investment if I can get it at the right price.'

So Cassidy was after a bargain. Ever the businessman. Or maybe there was something else behind his desire to get rid of the place.

It was eight o'clock and as Joe crossed the bridge over the river the crowds were out in force; locals making for the bus stops after a Saturday afternoon spent shopping and tourists who walked at a slower pace taking in Eborby's sights and sounds. He passed an Italian restaurant and the wafting scent of warm garlic reminded him that he was hungry. He hadn't eaten since one when he and Emily had grabbed a couple of sandwiches and now he promised himself a takeaway. A Saturday treat.

He was hardly aware of passing the cathedral. All he could see in his mind's eye was that image of Jade and Nerys and he found himself scanning the faces of women he passed for a resemblance.

Was there a chance that those two girls were still alive? Probably not but he knew that stranger things had happened.

He walked through Vicars' Green and on to Gallowgate, turning left at the National Trust tea shop, now closed for the evening. As he passed beneath Monks Bar his foot made contact with a discarded chip paper and he found himself facing the main road where the buzz of traffic jerked his thoughts back to reality.

His flat was close by, housed in a small reclaimed brick building huddled in the shadow of the city walls. Joe liked waking up each morning and seeing the grey medieval walls through his bedroom window. And he liked feeling close to the heart of things.

He unlocked his front door and flicked on the hallway light to banish the silent gloom. The place smelled a little stale because he hadn't had a chance to clean for over a week. Maybe he should get someone in, he thought. But he knew he'd never get round to arranging it.

The letter that lay on the hall floor bore an Eborby post mark and a hand written address. The writing looked so familiar that his heart began to thud but he told himself that lots of people formed their letters like that. And besides, Kaitlin died years ago. A fall down cliff steps in the West Country had ended their short marriage. The sea had taken her away and smashed her body on the vicious rocks until she was hardly recognizable. From that day on he had hated the sea.

He tore the envelope open and drew out a single sheet of paper inside, crisp, white and neatly folded. He opened it out and read the short message.

'King's Head. Seven o'clock, Sunday. K.'

He stared at the paper, his hands shaking a little as he clung tightly to the note, denting the pure white paper. For a few moments he stood there, trying to make some sense of what he was holding, before carrying the paper into the living room and letting it fall on to the coffee table. On second examination he could see that the writing was similar to Kaitlin's, perhaps, but not identical. He took a deep, calming breath and considered the contents of the note. He had no plans for Sunday evening – or for any evening that week, come to that. But that didn't mean that it was wise to keep the appointment.

The flat was too silent. He could hear his own breathing and the clock ticking away the seconds on the mantelpiece so he decided to put the television on. At that moment he needed life. He needed company.

After phoning in his order for an Indian takeaway and prizing the top off a bottle of Theakstons ale, he picked up the telephone, wondering whether to call Maddy. They'd promised to keep in touch after all. He muted the TV and dialled the number but there was no answer. Maddy would be out, enjoying her new life in London. He suddenly felt a wave of emptiness and shut his eyes.

He drained the bottle and opened another. When he was half way through it and the anaesthetizing effect of the alcohol had begun to seep into his tired brain, he returned to the hall and rummaged in his briefcase. He had arranged for the video tape of the two missing girls to be transferred to DVD so that he could take it home and watch it without distraction. At least the puzzle of their disappearance would fill the empty hours.

He returned to the living room and slid the DVD into the machine underneath his TV. After a while Jade Portright and Nerys Barnton appeared on the screen, laughing and fooling around for the camera. Self-consciously posing, their eyes flicking towards the lens as though they were concerned about the impression they were making for posterity.

Joe forced himself to concentrate. Had Barrington Jenks had anything to do with their disappearance? Or had he been telling the truth about his encounter with the mysterious Jasmine who may, or may not, have existed outside Jenks's imagination? Tomorrow he and Emily would visit the address Jenks had given them – number thirteen Torland Place where Jasmine was alleged to have lived – but, if it was a house rented out to students, he didn't hold out much hope of anyone remembering her. Twelve years was a very long time in the transient world of student accommodation. But it had to be followed up.

He put a cushion in the small of his back and leaned back in the leather armchair, his eyes still focused on the TV screen.

He reached for the remote control and paused the image. Then he rewound it a few frames. His initial impression was proved correct. There was a slight movement in the bushes in the background, a screen of greenery planted at the bottom of Jade's garden to give the Portright family a modicum of privacy in suburbia. And when the bushes parted slightly he could just make out a shadowy shape which may or may not have been human. At first he thought it might have been an animal, the family dog, perhaps – whatever it was was too large for a cat. But there was something furtive about the way the greenery parted slightly and then slowly returned to its former state. As though someone was keeping watch and had shifted to get a better view.

He took the DVD out of the machine and took another swig of Theakstons. On Monday he'd get the image enhanced and then there was just a chance they'd discover who, if anyone, had been watching those two missing girls.

It was Saturday night but somehow none of the students at thirteen Torland Place felt like making the effort to go out in search of entertainment so Matt gathered the cans of beer and the half-full wine bottles left over from the party and laid them on the living room table.

Caro stretched out on the sagging sofa while Matt sat on a dining chair feeling awkward. Jason came down last, attracted to the prospect of a drink like a moth to a flame, perched himself on the edge of the table and began to empty the left over bottles with an earnest concentration of one intent on inebriation.

The conversation was sporadic. Since they'd moved into the house and the camaraderie of that first year in hall of residence had vanished, they'd tended to circle around each other like suspicious cats. After a while they stopped talking altogether. Until Jason broke the silence.

'You know we've always said this house is spooky? Why don't we have a seance? It'll be a laugh. And we can finish off this booze while we're at it,' he said, reaching for a can of lager.

'No way,' said Caro, irritated.

'You're not chicken are you?' Jason began to make clucking noises and Matt took a swig of lager, resisting the urge to give his housemate a punch.

Caro looked at Matt for support but he merely shrugged and Jason seemed to take this for consent.

'Where's that Scrabble game? We can use the letters. Come on. If there is something dodgy about this house we might find out what it is.'

Soon Jason had organized everything with uncharacteristic efficiency. He arranged a circle of letters on the table and placed an upturned glass in the centre while Caro watched, tut tutting from time to time and refusing to have anything to do with it. The adult watching the children at play.

Jason lit a couple of candles that stood, half used, on the mantelpiece and switched off the light, making ghostly whoops. Matt sat opposite him, a little uneasy at being swept along with Jason's enthusiasm. But it was all nonsense, he told himself. So what was the harm?

Jason lowered his voice. 'Is there anybody there?'

'Oh for heaven's sake . . .' said Caro from the comfort of the sofa.

But Jason took no notice of her. He repeated his question.

Then suddenly the glass twitched beneath their fingers and began to move in a straight line towards one of the plastic letters. O. Then B, then E.

'You're pushing it,' Matt said with a nervous giggle.

'I'm not.' It could have been Matt's imagination but he thought Jason's confident bluster had gone.

'Play nicely, children,' said Caro as if she was bored with
the whole thing.

'Shut up,' Jason snapped. 'It's spelling something out.'

Caro stood up, her attention captured at last.

The glass suddenly began to move at speed so that the two
touching fingers almost lost contact. And when it had finished
spelling out the name 'Obediah Shrowton' it shot off the table
and smashed into pieces on the floor by Caro's feet.

At eleven thirty there was still no sign of Pet.

Matt knew that he wouldn't be able to sleep. As well as
his increasing unease about Pet's absence, he kept thinking
of the seance. Obediah Shrowton seemed a strange name to
come out of someone's imagination, but there, alone in his
room, he felt reluctant to consider the alternative explanation.
At first he'd been sure that Jason had been pushing the glass
but then he'd seen the look of disbelief on his face and felt
the force tearing the glass away from his finger. Something
had happened that neither of them could explain and it was
only Caro who remained sceptical – but then her finger hadn't
been on that glass.

He picked up his mobile phone and tried Pet's number again.
The action seemed futile but at least he felt he was doing
something. Caro had agreed that if she wasn't back by Sunday
night they should report her missing but she had said, with
her characteristic reasonableness, that if she had decided to
go off with some friends or some new lover for a few days,
reporting her absence officially would only make them look
stupid. He hadn't argued. His head told him Caro was right.
But some inner voice still whispered that something bad had
happened . . . that things were getting beyond Caro's ordered
control.

He held the phone to his ear, expecting to hear the usual
disembodied voice telling him to leave a message on Pet's
voice mail. But when he heard the ringing tone, he sat up
straight, holding his breath. The phone was switched on. Maybe
Caro's unimaginative assumptions had been correct after all.

The tone stopped.

'Hi. Pet? Where have you been? We've been worried about
you.'

Matt was quite unprepared for the sound on the other end

of the line. The almost incoherent and terrified words 'please' and 'no' followed by a faint, muffled yelp, like an animal in pain.

Then the line went dead.

FOUR

E mily groaned and turned over as she heard her husband, Jeff, get up and make his way downstairs. He was going to get breakfast as he always did on a Sunday. She told herself she was a lucky woman . . . although sometimes it didn't feel that way.

She could hear noise downstairs. The boys had switched the TV on and were probably sitting, mesmerized on the sofa munching on something unhealthy. But she had neither the time nor the inclination to do anything about it.

She lay there going over everything she had to do that day. After what she considered to be her well-deserved lie in, she would meet Joe and they would call at the address Jenks had given them for Jasmine, his alibi. Jasmine, unless they had a remarkable stroke of luck, would be long gone but there was always a chance that someone, an elderly neighbour or a landlord perhaps, would be able to provide a clue to her whereabouts. And if that failed they'd try the university first thing on Monday.

She put her hands behind her head and lay there with her eyes closed. Jeff had opened the window so she could hear church bells ringing in some distant tower. She had always liked Sundays – until police work took over and Sunday became a day much like any other. But at least today the case they were working on lacked the usual urgency. Those two girls had been missing for twelve years so it would hardly be a race against time to find them.

When the phone on the bedside table began to ring she looked at it with distaste for a few moments before picking it up.

'Oh bloody hell, Joe, what do you want?' she said as soon as she heard the voice on the other end of the line. 'I'm having a nice lie in here. Can't it wait till later?' She knew Joe well enough by now to know that he wouldn't take offence . . . unlike some.

'Someone's just called the station to report a missing person. Female student at the university.'

'Can't uniform deal with it?'

'Wait till you hear the address.'

'Go on,' said Emily, suddenly alert.

'Thirteen Torland Place. The address Jenks gave us for Jasmine.'

Emily swung round so that her feet met the floor and stood up. It was time to get dressed.

'What did you want to go and do that for?'

Jason's lips had arranged themselves into a sneer but Matt stood his ground. They stood facing each other either side of the kitchen table while Caro positioned herself at the end, looking from one to the other like a tennis umpire.

Matt opened his mouth, trying to think up an answer. Since the strange call, the cut off cry of pain, he had lain awake worrying about Pet, the scenarios in his tired brain becoming ever more dire and disturbing, and at eight thirty that morning he had rung the police to report her missing. Now, over tea in cracked mugs and barely tanned white toast, he felt that perhaps he'd been a little hasty. But Jason annoyed him so he stood his ground.

'I think she's in trouble,' he said, glancing at Caro whose expression gave nothing away.

Jason's full lips twitched upwards in a knowing smirk. 'I reckon she's with some new bloke. What you heard was probably a cry of pleasure. She probably rolled over on to her phone and it got switched on by accident at the moment of ecstasy.'

Matt squared up to his opponent. 'Pet's not a slapper.'

Jason gave a knowing chuckle and Matt resisted the urge to punch him in the mouth.

'Shut up. You're like a pair of fucking kids,' said Caro, the umpire. 'Does it matter whether or not Pet screws around? The question is, is she in trouble at this moment?'

The answer was silence. Both Matt and Jason knew Caro was right. If Pet was in any sort of danger, the last thing she needed was for her housemates to be bickering about the niceties.

Matt spoke first. 'Well I've reported her missing now and they've got her details. They said it was too early to worry but then I said it was really out of character and I told them about the phone call and said it sounded as if she was being hurt. They said someone would call round.'

'Probably some uniformed plod with a notebook,' said Jason. 'They won't do anything.'

Matt felt his fist clenching but he told himself to let it go. He found it hard to believe that he'd actually liked Jason in their first year in hall of residence. He'd liked Caro and Pet as well. They'd all got on so well. Until they'd moved into number thirteen and everything had started to fall apart.

'Anyone fancy a beer?' Jason said, making for the fridge.

'It's too bloody early.' Caro stared at him. 'And where's your share of the electricity bill? You promised to transfer the money into the house account.'

Jason raised a grubby hand. 'I told you before, I've got a bit of a cash flow problem at the moment but I'll ring my dad tonight. He'll pay up. No worries. Since he left mum for the tart, he's been very generous with the readies.'

Caro grunted. They'd all heard the saga of Jason's parents' broken marriage and his father's infatuation with a younger woman at work. He'd moved in with the woman and had assuaged his tender conscience by throwing cash at the problem. This hadn't gone down well with his wife and three teenaged children and Jason had no qualms about turning the situation to his advantage.

'Well I need that money by Tuesday.'

She was about to leave the room when Jason spoke. 'I think we should look up Obediah Shrowton on the Internet . . . see if he existed.'

'OK, if it'll stop you going on about it.'

Without a word Caro marched out of the room and returned half a minute later carrying a laptop case. She cleared the table of breakfast debris, took the computer out of its protective case and placed it carefully on the Formica surface.

When the thing had woken up she typed in the name Obediah Shrowton and waited, the others huddling round her in anticipation.

Matt watched the words appear and he heard Caro swear softly under her breath.

Obediah Shrowton was a murderer. In 1896 he killed five people at a house in the Bearsley district of Eborby. And he lived at thirteen Valediction Street. Wherever that was.

'Well at least it isn't here.'

The young woman who opened the door of thirteen Torland Place had short dark hair and the businesslike manner of someone who normally wears a suit to work. Today she was wearing neatly ironed jeans and a plain white T-shirt but she was the sort who would never really master the casual look.

Emily held up her warrant card and recited her name. Joe watched the young woman's face and saw that she had merely raised her eyebrows in mild surprise. No worry, no panic. It was almost as though reporting a missing person was a routine matter, something that happened every day.

'Well, I must say you're very quick off the mark,' she said. 'I didn't expect such good service. My name's Caro Smyth, by the way.' She stuck out her hand and Emily shook it. Joe was rather surprised to see that the nails were ragged and bitten; somehow they didn't fit with the efficient persona Caro presented to the world. But we all have our hidden side. 'You'd better come in. I told Matt that it was far too early to involve the police but he seems really worried. I think she's just met someone and gone off for the weekend but . . .'

'So you share this house with the missing girl, Petulia Ferribie?'

Caro was about to lead them inside but she turned and focused her intense gaze on Joe, looking him up and down, as though assessing his suitability for the task. Joe guessed that she didn't have a high opinion of men; Emily, being one of the Sisterhood, had received no such examination.

'That's right. There are four of us. This way.'

Joe looked around. He had known many places like it during his student days in Manchester: large semi-detached houses built in the last decade of the nineteenth century with high ceilings, and shabby paintwork. Like many student houses he had seen, someone had made misguided alterations in the nineteen sixties, ripping out original features and installing cheap coloured bathroom suites and hideously coloured chipboard kitchens on the smallest possible budget. At one time these measures would have been termed improvements but now nobody pretended any more.

Caro opened the first door on her right. 'The police are here.' She announced. She didn't sound too happy about it. But, Joe thought, few people do.

They followed her into the room. A young man was sitting at an old, bulbous legged table, drumming his fingers nervously on the stained wooden top. He was medium height with short ginger hair and had the pale, slightly puffy look of a student who survived on lager and pizzas with too little exercise. He stood up as they came in, fingering the hem of his washed-out T-shirt nervously.

'I'm Matt Bawtry,' he said, his voice a little high pitched. 'I reported Pet missing. Nobody's seen her since yesterday morning and . . . Well, it's out of character. She's never gone off like this before.'

Joe heard a muffled snort from the direction of the doorway and turned to see another young man enter the room. He wouldn't often have described a man as beautiful but this one could have served as a muse for any variety of Italian Renaissance artists with his dark curls, warm brown eyes and flawless, slightly tanned complexion. He wore skin tight jeans and a thin cotton shirt and underneath the mask of cynical bravado, Joe sensed an underlying tension.

'Did I hear someone say the word "police"?'

Emily turned to face him. She looked unimpressed. 'And you are?'

'I'm Jason Petrie. I live here. I assume you've come about Pet. Matt's panicking. She'll be back as though nothing's happened . . .'

'Mr Bawtry said her absence was out of character,' said Joe.

Jason shrugged.

'How long have you known Petulia?' Emily addressed the question to all three of them.

It was Caro who answered. 'About eighteen months. We met in our first year when we were all in Dewsbury Hall – that's at the university. We decided to get a house together and . . .'

'I take it you're all students?'

'Apart from Jason,' said Matt. 'He failed his exams. Dropped out.'

Jason gave a wry smile and inclined his head.

'What do you do now?' Joe asked.

'Good question,' said Caro under her breath.

'Bit of busking. Bit of bar work to make ends meet. I get by.'

'And he's got a rich daddy with a guilty conscience,' said Caro with a hint of bitterness. 'OK for some.'

'Actually I've got an audition on Tuesday – playing guitar with a jazz group,' said Jason. He sounded a little defensive. 'They get regular gigs at weddings and hotels and . . .'

'You never mentioned that,' said Caro.

'Why should I?'

'Oh fuck off,' said Caro. 'I just wish you'd grow up.'

The vehemence of Caro's words surprised Joe. There was hostility in this house. He could almost smell it.

Emily took charge of the situation. 'Let's get back to Petulia, shall we? When did you last see her?' She looked at Matt expectantly.

'We had a party on Friday night. Fancy dress. Pet was floating around dressed as a fairy or something. I didn't see her the next morning but then I slept in till lunchtime.'

'Was she with anyone at the party?'

Matt shook his head. 'She was just wandering about on her own. I thought she looked a bit lost.' He looked regretful, Joe thought. Perhaps he'd have liked to have been with Pet himself.

'She was probably bored,' said Jason. 'I know I was. What idiot invited that rugby crowd anyway?'

When Matt didn't answer Joe suspected a guilty conscience.

He gave Caro a businesslike smile. 'And you, Caro? When did you last see her?'

'The Saturday morning after the party. She was going into town. The Eborby Music Festival was on and there was an outdoor concert of early music. Pet's a music student and she's into that sort of thing.' She paused. 'Actually she seemed quite excited about it . . . which isn't like Pet. Maybe there was going to be an added attraction – something more interesting there than a load of flutes and lutes.'

'A man?'

'Well, she's not interested in women,' Caro said, sounding slightly disappointed. 'And like Matt and Jason said, she certainly wasn't with anyone at the party.'

'And you?' Joe was suddenly curious.

'What about me?'

'Were you with anyone at the party?'

She was suddenly on the defensive. 'I don't see that that's relevant.'

'Oh come on, Caro,' said Jason. 'You were draped around that rather butch girl from Media Studies.' Caro was about to open her mouth but Jason continued. 'And for the record I borrowed a white coat and stethoscope from a medic mate of mine and Matt here went as a cowboy. Such imagination.'

'What are you all studying?' Joe asked.

'I'm doing Accountancy and Business Studies,' said Caro. 'Matt's electrical engineering and, as I said, Pet's studying music.'

'And I was wrestling with the finer points of the Metaphysical Poets before I was chucked off my course,' said Jason. 'English.'

'I did English at Leeds,' said Emily, hoping to establish a rapport.

'Then you followed the path of Dogberry and Verges?' said Jason with a smirk.

'We're not all "foolish officers",' she answered quickly.

Jason looked rather surprised that she'd picked up so quickly on Shakespeare's description of his two inept law enforcers from *Much Ado About Nothing*. Surprised and a little deflated.

'You don't seem very worried about Petulia, Jason? Why is that?'

Jason shrugged. 'Caro's just told you she was excited about that concert or whatever it was. I was out busking – entertaining our illustrious tourists – and I saw her making for Stone Street where this festival thing was being held. At a guess she'll have been meeting someone who wasn't at the party. That's why she'd been looking so pissed off in her little fairy costume.'

'What about the phone call? Tell us again what you heard.'

Everyone looked at Matt as he told them about the strange call from Pet's mobile, stumbling over his words as if rendered

suddenly nervous by his rapt audience. When he'd finished
Jason chipped in with his salacious interpretation of events
but Matt shook his head vigorously.

'And what time was this exactly?'

'Eleven thirty last night. I've been trying ever since but I'm
just getting voice mail.'

Joe and Emily exchanged looks. If necessary they could
pinpoint where the phone had been when it had been answered
so strangely. But Joe hoped it wouldn't come to that.

They kept the conversation going, finding out all they could
about Pet, about her background, her friends and her lovers.
Not that there had been many of the latter, according to Caro
who seemed the most dispassionate of the trio.

Then Joe asked whether they had Pet's home address. Caro
shook her head. There was a stepmother, she said, but there
was no way Pet would have gone to her because she detested
the woman. There were no brothers or sisters and her father
was in Dubai. Pet didn't talk about her family much. In fact
she hardly mentioned them at all.

When Joe asked if they had a recent photo of Pet, Caro left
the room and returned a minute later with a photograph. Joe
took it from her and studied it. There were four people in the
picture: Caro, Matt and Jason and, at the edge of the group
was a girl with fine blonde hair tumbling to her shoulders.
She was small with perfect, almost feline features. But despite
her beauty, she had a rather vacant look, as though her mind
was somewhere else.

'Mind if I keep this?' he said.

Caro shrugged. 'Help yourself.'

Joe tucked the picture carefully into his wallet. Perhaps Caro
was right. Perhaps Pet had just gone off for the weekend with
some new lover she wanted to keep from her housemates. But
Matt was sure that was out of character so maybe he was right
to worry. If she didn't turn up soon he'd want to speak to Jason
again as he was apparently the last of the group to see her –
Joe almost mentally added the word 'alive' but it was far too
early to fear the worst.

He caught Emily's eye. It was time to ask their next question
– the original reason for their visit. Emily gave him a small
nod. She was leaving it to him.

'I know this is a long shot,' he began. 'But have you heard

of a young woman called Jasmine who lived at this address about twelve years ago?'

As expected, Jason gave a dismissive grunt. 'You're joking, aren't you. We would have been about eight.'

'I realize that but I imagine you can put me in touch with your landlord.'

'He won't be able to help you,' said Caro. 'He only bought this place three years ago. And twelve years ago he would have been at uni.'

'Where?'

Matt looked up. 'Here in Eborby. He stayed and went into property development.'

'Then we'll need his contact details,' Emily said.

Caro wrote something on a sheet of paper and handed it to Emily who stood up.

'If Pet turns up, inform us right away.' she said, making for the door.

Joe followed her, looking around, thankful for once that his own student days were over.

The visit to Petulia Ferribie's student house had taken Joe's mind temporarily off the strange letter from 'K' he'd received in the post the previous day but now, as he followed Emily up the crazy-paved garden path of the house next door to number thirteen, it pushed its way to the forefront of his thoughts. There was only one certain way to discover the identity of 'K' and that was to keep the appointment. He was tempted to share his problem with Emily but he decided against it. This was something he'd have to deal with himself.

He stood a little behind Emily as she rapped firmly on the door of number fifteen Torland Place. In contrast to its neighbour, here the paintwork was fresh and the windows, with their Roman blinds, sparkled clean in the weak spring sunlight.

The door swung opened to reveal a woman in her late twenties. She had a wide mouth, shoulder length blonde hair and her jeans and loose floral top showed off her slim figure to best advantage.

But her attractive face was marred by the angry scowl she aimed in Emily's direction. 'We're not interested,' she said, preparing to shut the door in the DCI's face.

But Emily held up her warrant card and introduced herself and the scowl turned into a worried frown.

'What is it? What's happened? Is it Rory?' The words came out in a rush.

He saw Emily's expression soften. Finding two police officers on the doorstep was enough to make any law-abiding person fear the worst, especially if a loved one is away from home.

'It's nothing to worry about Mrs . . .'

'Quillan. Jackie Quillan.'

'We'd just like to ask you some questions about the house next door. How long have you lived here?'

'Two years.'

Joe saw the look of disappointment on Emily's face.

'Do you know where we can find the previous owner?'

Jackie Quillan nodded. It looked as if they were in luck. 'We bought the house from my husband's uncle. He couldn't manage any more so he went into sheltered accommodation. We were coming back up to Eborby to live so it seemed like the ideal arrangement.'

'Where can we find him?' Joe asked, notebook at the ready.

Jackie recited an address in the suburb of Pickby, not far from Emily's own home. 'What's all this about? Why do you want to see him?'

'It concerns something that happened twelve years ago. We're trying to trace a young woman who lived in the house next door. Number thirteen.'

'There are new students in there every year so you're going to have your work cut out.' She held the door half open, as if she was anxious to shut it and get rid of them.

'Do you know the students who live there now? There's a girl called Petulia Ferribie?' Joe asked.

The answer was a shake of the head. 'I don't know their names. They don't communicate much. Are you going to see Uncle Norman then?'

'Yes. We'll pay him a visit. Just routine. I don't suppose there's anyone else in your house who might have had more contact with the students next door?' Emily asked hopefully.

'There's only me and my husband and we've hardly said a

word to them. High fences make good neighbours, so they
say. And so do thick walls.' She gave them an insincere smile
and made to shut the door.

'Don't take too much notice of anything Uncle Norman
tells you. He gets confused,' she said before the door swung
shut in their faces.

'The lady doth protest too much, me thinks,' Emily muttered
as they made their way back to the car.

'You've got a suspicious mind,' Joe said, flicking the remote
control that opened the car doors. 'Where next?'

'Let's go and spoil the landlord's Sunday lunch.' She sighed.
'Ever get the feeling you're wasting your time, Joe?'

'Frequently.' At that moment Joe longed to be in some cosy
town centre pub with a Sunday roast and a pint of Black Sheep
to wash it down with. 'Fancy lunch at the Star?'

Emily looked at her watch. 'I'm tempted but we'd better
see the landlord first.' She paused. 'I think those students were
worried about something other than the missing girl. There
was an odd atmosphere in that house, don't you think?'

'And it backs on to the woods where Jade and Nerys were
last seen.'

'You're right, Joe. That house is the epicentre for something
but God only knows what it is.' Emily gave him an enigmatic
smile. 'So let's go and see this landlord and then mine's a
roast beef and large Yorkshire pudding.'

She climbed into the driver's seat and set off, exceeding the
speed limit by ten miles per hour.

Obediah Shrowton. Matt mouthed the name. It was a name
from another era, conjuring a picture of a whiskered patriarch
in a starched collar and forbidding black. Stern, humourless
and mildly malevolent. He couldn't leave it alone. But what,
if anything, was the connection between Obediah Shrowton
and the hectic transient lives they led at Torland Place? If he
dug deeper it might start to make sense.

He sat in his room, overlooking the wood where the skeletal
branches of the trees had acquired a green mist of buds. There
was something unsettling about those trees. They leaned
together as though they were sharing some nasty secret and
at night when the wind blew they whispered like conspiring
ghosts. He'd always liked trees; they represented the fun of

climbing and the beauty of nature. But Dead Man's Wood was different somehow. And he didn't know why.

He'd already discovered the bare facts of the Shrowton case but it was time to find out more. After clicking on a variety of websites eventually he struck gold. Obediah Shrowton's full biography, laid out neatly and easy to read.

He balanced his laptop on his knee and stared at the text. Obediah Shrowton had been an upright citizen of Eborby, employed in the City Treasury. He went to work in the Town Hall each day and was respected by the small army of clerks under his command.

In 1889 at the age of thirty-two he had married a girl called Violet Nicksen. Violet was the daughter of a clergyman from near Sheffield and she had been working as a governess in Eborby when the couple had met at a church event. They settled in the Bearsley district and Violet gave birth to five children, only two of whom survived infancy. The children who hadn't survived were buried in St Aiden's churchyard, their little graves marked by the most costly headstones their parents could afford.

Then one day – an apparently normal day in April 1896 – Obediah had come home from work and proceeded to slaughter his wife, his two young children, the nursemaid and the cook. He had taken an axe from the garden store – probably like the crumbling brick outbuilding that stood near their back door – and hacked his victims to pieces. Newspapers at the time had called it a scene of butchery and carnage. This was probably an understatement.

Obediah had denied any involvement, claiming that he'd returned home and been greeted by a scene of unimaginable horror. A postman who had been delivering the evening post investigated the open front door and discovered the gruesome tableau of dismembered bodies and Shrowton sobbing on the hall floor with a bloody axe in his hand. Later Shrowton had claimed he'd been too shocked to report the deaths immediately to the authorities and this went against him at his trial. The jury hadn't believed his story and he was hanged for his alleged crime at Eborby jail in October 1896.

Matt picked up his mobile phone and tried Pet's number again. Somehow he felt a little better now that the police were aware that she might be in danger – almost as if the burden was now shared – although he hadn't felt that the pair they sent had taken her disappearance seriously enough. They'd seemed more interested in someone called Jasmine who'd lived in the house many years ago. Still, they had both been senior detectives. At least they hadn't sent a brace of probationers.

He knew he had work to do for university but he found it hard to concentrate. He typed Torland Place into the search engine. A number of sites came up and his eyes scanned the results. Then one in particular caught his eye and he clicked on it.

Valediction Street, it said, was renamed Torland Place after the gruesome murders of five people at number thirteen.

'Shit,' he whispered, his heart beating so fast that he could almost hear it in the heavy silence.

FIVE

The landlord, Andy Cassidy, lived near the centre of Eborby in an elegantly proportioned Georgian house just off Boothgate. The original Georgian sash windows were freshly painted and the swagged drapes at the windows were the sort that cost a fortune. The front door, flanked by a pair of healthy bay trees, was painted sage green. All in the best possible taste. Joe wondered how much he charged the students for the privilege of living in the relative squalor of Torland Place – probably too much.

After Joe had raised the lion head knocker and let it fall twice, they both waited, ID in hand, to interrupt Andy Cassidy's Sunday. After half a minute the door opened slowly. The man in the doorway wore a black T-shirt, jeans and an impatient expression as he folded his tattooed arms defensively. 'I'm in the middle of something. What is it?'

But when he glanced down at the warrant cards and realized they weren't there to convert him or sell him something, his manner changed and a worried frown appeared on his face. Joe had seen the transformation hundreds of times before and it almost made him pity Jehovah's Witnesses and door to door salesmen. 'Sorry. I thought you were . . . Is something the matter?'

'Nothing to worry about, Mr Cassidy,' said Emily. 'May we come in?'

'Yeah, sure. Come in.' Cassidy sounded a little distracted, as though he was going through all the possible reasons they could be calling in his mind.

He led them through to an elegant drawing room. A tempting smell of Sunday roast hung in the air and it made Joe feel hungry. He made himself comfortable on a soft leather sofa and Emily sat opposite him. She caught his eye – she wanted to do the talking.

'Which property is it? I've got fifteen properties in Eborby. And nine in Leeds.' As he sat back in his seat Joe thought he looked rather pleased with himself.

'It's thirteen Torland Place,' said Emily.

'What about it?' There was a wariness in his voice. 'Actually that's one of the places I'm getting rid of. With the recession there's quite a few bargains to be had so I'm buying some apartments in the new Gungate development which means that I need to release a bit of capital.'

Joe sensed Cassidy was comfortable talking about business – and it meant he was putting off the moment when the conversation turned to more sensitive matters. But Emily came straight to the point.

'You have a tenant called Petulia Ferribie at Torland Place.'

He frowned, as if trying to recall the name. 'I can't be sure without looking at my records, of course, and they're all in my office.'

Joe didn't believe a word of it. Cassidy knew the name alright. There had been a momentary flash of recognition in his eyes when Emily had said it. Recognition and something else perhaps.

He took the photograph Caro had given him from his wallet and handed it to Cassidy. 'That's her on the left.'

'Yeah. I've seen her around.'

'It seems she's gone missing.'

'I was round there yesterday and nobody mentioned it.' For the first time during the interview he looked uncomfortable.

'So you've no idea where Petulia Ferribie might be?'

Cassidy shook his head. 'Sorry. Wish I could help.'

'Were you at the party they had on Friday night?' Joe asked.

'People don't tend to invite their landlords to parties, more's the pity,' he said with a smile, more relaxed now.

Suddenly the smell of roasting meat seemed stronger and, as Joe visualized the succulent joint, crispy roast potatoes and fluffy Yorkshire pudding, he wondered about the cook. He heard clattering dishes in the distance but, in his experience, most wives and partners can't resist seeing who's at their door. Unless Cassidy had so many business visitors that curiosity had died years ago.

'That smells good,' he said.

'Anna's from Poland but makes a mean Sunday roast.'

Joe saw Emily frown at this sudden display of overt sexism. 'You're married?'

'Not exactly,' Cassidy said with a sly grin. Somehow Joe suspected that the arrangement might not altogether be to Anna's advantage.

'Can you tell me who owned the house before you? We're trying to trace the whereabouts of a student who lived there twelve years ago.'

'Good luck,' said Cassidy with a dismissive grunt. 'I bought the place three years ago from an old guy called Quillan who lived next door. He owned both houses and rented out number thirteen. He's sold up since. Probably wanted to ensure a bit of comfort in his old age.'

'What can you tell us about Mr Quillan?' Emily asked.

'Not much. He was an old bloke like I said. Kept himself to himself.'

'Married?'

'He lived alone as far as I could see.' He stood up. 'Look, much as I'd love to sit and chat all day, my dinner'll be ready soon and I'm meeting some friends later.'

Joe saw that Emily was pushing herself out of her seat reluctantly. Andy Cassidy's sofas were uncommonly comfortable. You get what you pay for.

Cassidy began to make for the front door and they followed. There was probably little more they could learn here. Although Joe suspected that he knew more than he was saying.

If Pet didn't turn up safe and well soon, they might just have to pay her landlord another visit.

* * *

Emily sat in the lounge bar of the Star and examined her watch. Two o'clock. She'd promised to be back by two thirty at the latest and she knew she should really ring Jeff to tell him she'd be late. But somehow she couldn't face listening to a catalogue of domestic woes.

She kept telling herself that Jeff was great with the kids and she couldn't possibly survive the job without him. But there were times she needed to think, unencumbered by the realities of everyday life, of lost school-books and sibling squabbles. And now was one of those times.

After draining a large glass of red wine she looked at Joe. 'I'd better call Jeff and tell him I won't be back for lunch.'

'Don't feel too bad. It's a while since we've been on the Sunday shift.'

Emily tried to smile. Joe's words hadn't done anything to make her feel less of a rat. And the fact that she was sitting in one of Eborby's historic city centre pubs, waiting for Sunday lunch with all the trimmings with a good looking colleague added to her weight of guilt.

'Can't be helped,' said Joe. 'The Super wants this Barrington Jenks business dealt with at the highest level and apparently that means us. Another drink?'

'Thanks, Joe. I bloody need one.'

When he'd gone to the bar she fished her phone out of her handbag and called home. Jeff didn't sound pleased. Sarah was asking for her and he had to take the boys to football that afternoon which would mean dragging his reluctant daughter there too. Emily said she'd be back as soon as she could, careful to make no firm promises.

Joe returned bearing drinks and the news that the food wouldn't be long. Emily was glad because the smell from the kitchens was starting to tantalize her empty stomach. She'd tried to lose weight so many times but her hearty appetite was her greatest enemy, always waiting to tempt her like her own personal demon.

When the dinners arrived the young waiter set the plates down in front of them with an exhortation to 'enjoy'. Emily clasped her knife and fork and tucked in and it wasn't until she was half way through that she looked up at Joe and noticed that he seemed a little preoccupied with a faraway look in his blue eyes.

'Something the matter?' she said, her mouth still half full.

He hadn't intended to mention the letter he'd received but he suddenly felt a need to share his dilemma with someone. He took it from his pocket and pushed it over the table towards her. 'This came in the post yesterday.'

Emily put her knife and fork down and peered at the letter. 'Who's K?'

'I've no idea. I've been going through all the people I know but I can't think . . .'

Emily watched his face. 'But you've got your suspicions?'

He shook his head.

'Come on, Joe. You're a lousy liar – must be all that time you spent in that Seminary.' For some reason she could never forget that he had once started training to be a priest. Perhaps, she thought, it set him apart from all the other men she knew. Perhaps it intrigued her, although she would never have admitted it.

He looked up at her. 'If you must know the writing's very like Kaitlin's . . . my late wife's.'

Emily stared at him in silence for a few moments. The words had shocked her. She knew the bare bones of the story about how Joe had lost his wife but he never mentioned her. She had always assumed that her loss was something he'd rather forget.

'You think someone's playing a joke? If they are, it's a bloody unfunny one, if you ask me.' She had been about to use the word cruel but on second thoughts that sounded a little overdramatic. 'Are you going to keep the appointment?'

'Have you a better suggestion?'

'Do you want some moral support?' She didn't know why she offered but it seemed like the right thing to do.

He smiled. 'You haven't seen your kids all day. I think going out tonight would be pushing things a bit with Jeff, don't you agree?'

Emily didn't reply.

'Thanks for the offer anyway,' he said flashing her a smile. 'Do you think we've got any chance of finding this Jasmine?'

Emily shrugged. 'Jasmine might not even be her real name.'

'We need to talk to Norman Quillan. And hope he was the kind of landlord who did more than just collect the rent.'

'The interfering type, you mean?'

'Keep your fingers crossed,' Joe said, turning his attention to the meal in front of him.

Matt needed to share his unsettling discovery with his house-mates. He needed them to know that Torland Place had once been known as Valediction Street and its name had been changed because of the notoriety of the very house they lived in. Maybe sharing the knowledge would render it harmless. Or, on the other hand, it might give the horror fresh life.

He knew Jason was out busking – or earning a crust as he put it – and Caro was working in her room upstairs so when he heard a crash downstairs the sudden noise made him jump. Then he took a few deep breaths. Perhaps Pet had returned. Perhaps she was down there safe and sound. But somehow he didn't feel inclined to investigate.

He felt annoyed with himself for letting the house affect him like this. He needed a distraction and he was almost glad when he looked up and saw Caro standing in the doorway.

'You OK, Matt? You look stressed.'

Matt turned his face away. 'I'm alright.'

'You're an idiot calling the police, you know. Pet'll be furious when she comes back.'

'They had this address anyway,' Matt said defensively. 'They were looking for someone who used to live here.' He hesitated. Maybe Caro would understand after all. 'I've been doing more research on the Internet. This place was . . .'

But Caro interrupted, rolling her eyes. 'Just because of that stupid seance? Jason was pushing the glass.'

'Obediah Shrowton used to live here . . . in this house. This is where he murdered all those people.'

Caro gaped at him for a moment before she spoke. 'You are joking?'

'They changed the name of the road because of the notoriety. Torland Place used to be Valediction Street. It was this house, Caro. It happened here. Can't you feel it? Since we moved in we've been at each other's throats. There's something bad here.'

He'd expected a sarcastic response but Caro stood there staring ahead. 'You're making it up,' she said half-heartedly.

'Look it up yourself.'

She swore under her breath and Matt watched her face,

satisfied for once that she was taking him seriously. This was the first time Matt had seen the normally cool Caro show any emotion. He found it rather unsettling. But it confirmed that the whole thing wasn't in his head.

He heard the front door open and bang shut and a few seconds later Jason was standing there, guitar case in hand. 'What's up?'

'Matt's been doing some research.' Caro said softly. 'Torland Place used to be Valediction Street. Obediah Shrowton lived here. This is where he murdered all those people. Did you know about this?'

'No way. I had no idea. How could I?' His mouth widened into a grin. 'This is great. We can open up the place to ghoulish tourists. People love that sort of thing. The Jack the Ripper tours in London are huge business. We're sitting on a gold mine, my friends.'

'Piss off, Jason,' said Caro, looking as though she was on the verge of tears. 'Its not funny.'

Jason shrugged his shoulders. 'I'm going to check out Pet's room,' he said.

Caro straightened herself up. 'What the hell for? You've no right to go poking around in her room. Even if she isn't here, she's got a right to privacy.'

'Keep you knickers on, Caro. There might be something that'll tell us where she is.' Jason began to make for the door.

But Matt blocked his exit. He didn't like the thought of him going through Pet's things any more than Caro did.

'We should leave it to the police.'

'They were more interested in that previous tenant . . . Jasmine or whatever her name was. Maybe Pet is Jasmine. Maybe she's been living under a false name.'

Matt picked up his phone and tried Pet's number again. Sometimes Jason pushed things too far.

Barrington Jenks put the phone down and poured himself a single malt. He deserved it. Needed it. Since that visit from the two police officers yesterday he had felt under a considerable amount of strain and stress was something he could do without. His wife, Tamsin, was down in London. They had agreed long ago not to interfere too much in each other's lives. But Tamsin would be angry that he'd been so indiscreet.

Damage limitation was the only way forward. But first he had to know how far the police had progressed in their investigation. He sank back into the armchair and the velvet cushions moulded themselves to his body as he sipped the golden liquid which slid down his gullet like smooth fire, relaxing and warming.

Closing his eyes, he took his mind back to that evening twelve years before. It had been one of those typical summer days of sunshine and sharp showers. He had stopped for a drink in a bar and he'd seen her with her short skirt and silky hair. Their eyes had met and she'd given him the come on. So obvious. The speed with which he'd responded to the invitation almost suggested that he'd been looking for such an encounter. Maybe he had but it was something he hadn't acknowledged at the time.

Perhaps he'd found it odd that Jasmine was studying at the university until he'd remembered stories in the newspapers about students selling their bodies to make ends meet. Some, apparently, almost saw it as a blow for feminism – using men's weaknesses as a means to make some money. Jenks had always thought these women were deluding themselves but when he recalled that encounter twelve years ago, he began to wonder. Jasmine had certainly been in control back then.

He yawned. He had been up late the night before at the Lord Lieutenant's dinner, going through the motions of polite conversation like an actor on a stage. He was used to such occasions and the games people played – the thin veneer of warmth and the subtle jostling for position – but last night he had found the pretence exhausting.

He took another sip of whisky and pressed his stomach with his free hand. Sometimes the discomfort was almost unbearable but he was reluctant to consult a doctor. He had to maintain the illusion of youth. He had to appear invincible . . . even to himself.

With a groan he put the glass down on the side table, missing the coaster. Just when he thought it was all over, it had started again. And now he had to sort it out and ensure Jasmine's discretion.

He hauled himself out of the armchair and as he straightened up his body he felt like an old man. The ache in his stomach was growing worse. Perhaps it was an ulcer, he thought. Or something more serious. As he made his way upstairs he caught sight of himself in the mirror on the landing, saw that his face had a grey look and he suddenly felt afraid. Sickness had never featured in his life to that point. When his mother had become infirm he had put her in an expensive nursing home and never visited her again. He had never had time for weakness.

He stumbled into his bedroom and sat on the bed for a while, staring at the telephone. Then he stood up and opened the drawer where he kept his old diaries and address books. After rummaging for a while he found what he was looking for: the number without a name beside it. Her number. He picked up the telephone receiver and dialled, and as the ringing tone droned in his ear, he could hear his heart pounding against his ribs. This was something he had vowed never to do. But it was necessary. If the police found her first it could ruin everything. They had to get their story straight.

He heard a breathless voice on the other end of the line. Either Jasmine had been hurrying to answer the phone or he had caught her in the throes of passion. His mind supplied all sorts of scenarios in those few moments, some mundane, some exotic. Somehow, knowing Jasmine, the exotic or erotic seemed more likely.

'Hello.' The deep, throaty voice sent an unexpected thrill of excitement shooting through his body.

'Jasmine? It's me. Barrington.' He closed his eyes, imagining her reaction. 'Look, I've had a visit from the police.'

SIX

Sunday afternoon is the traditional time for visiting relatives and Joe wondered whether they would have to battle with an army of Norman Quillan's devoted family to gain his attention. Perhaps, Joe thought, his nephew and his wife would be there, doing their familial duty. But ideally he wanted to talk to the old man alone without any distractions.

Emily was uncharacteristically quiet as they drove. Joe wasn't sure whether she was thinking about the case or wallowing in guilt about abandoning her children on a Sunday. He knew it was the aspect of the job she found hardest to deal with. But she usually managed fine.

'Let's hope he remembers something about this Jasmine,' she said as he swung the car into a tree-lined drive. 'The sooner we can confirm Jenks's story, the better.'

'Did you believe him?'

'He was very convincing. But then a lot of people would say that he tells lies for a living so he's bound to be good at it by now. What do you think?'

Joe parked the car and they got out. Viking Court was a fairly new development of sheltered retirement flats, low-rise and neat. Emily observed that the flats here probably didn't come cheap. And she was probably right.

Norman Quillan was a little man, slightly built, with thinning grey hair and a small moustache that gave him the look of a worried rodent. He looked a little nervous as he invited them to sit but many people did when the police came to call.

The flat was small but pleasingly decorated in shades of subtle green and the first thing Joe noticed was that there were no family photographs around the place. Emily sat down opposite the old man, smiling to put him at his ease. There were times when her down-to-earth bluntness worked wonders with the elderly.

'Now then, Mr Quillan,' she began. 'You'll remember those two lasses who went missing in Dead Man's Woods twelve years back?'

'You don't forget something like that in a hurry,' he muttered, avoiding Emily's eyes.

'Can you tell us what you told the officers at the time?'

'It's a long time ago. Haven't you got it on record or something?'

'Maybe there's something you've remembered since then,' said Emily.

'Well I haven't. I didn't see owt then and I don't remember owt more now.'

'Let me make a nice cup of tea,' said Emily, standing up. She looked at Joe as if to say 'you try'. Sometimes the one-to-one approach worked better.

Joe gave the old man a friendly smile. 'We called at your old house . . . met your nephew's wife, Jackie.'

The old man gave a dismissive grunt. 'That little tart,' he said with a surprising amount of venom.

'You don't like her?' Joe held his breath and awaited the answer.

'I don't like either of them. They conned me over that house. Only gave me half of what it was worth. Bloody stupid I was. But my wife had just passed away and I wasn't thinking straight.'

Joe gave him a sympathetic smile. The business of the house might have been in Norman Quillan's imagination or perhaps number fifteen needed a lot of renovation. Or maybe Rory Quillan was a sharp operator who did the dirty on his recently widowed uncle. He was keeping an open mind.

'Let's go back twelve years to the time when these two girls disappeared. Can you tell me what happened?'

'Nowt happened as far as I was concerned. We were away in Scarborough.'

'That's not far for a holiday.'

'It always suited me and the missus. I've never gone in for all this travelling. And what's wrong with Scarborough anyroad? Nowt.'

Joe nodded. 'You're right there, Mr Quillan. There's nothing wrong with Scarborough.'

Quillan met his eyes and gave a tiny smile of agreement.

'So how long were you away for? You're right about it being somewhere in the files but it'll save us a lot of time if you can remember.'

'I went on the Wednesday and stayed exactly a week. The Sea Breezes Guest House. Very nice.'

'Bet they did good breakfasts,' said Emily, entering the room with a tray of steaming mugs. She handed them round before sitting in the armchair next to Joe, wriggling her ample backside to make herself comfortable.

'They did that,' said Quillan, licking his lips at the memory of the generous Yorkshire breakfasts – full English and then some more.

'So your house was empty on the Saturday night?'

Norman Quillan hesitated. 'It were meant to be empty. Aye.'

'You were away so why shouldn't it be empty?'

'No reason.'

But Joe saw a flicker of uncertainty in the old man's bloodshot grey eyes.

'Do you remember the students at number thirteen at the time?' Emily asked. 'You were their landlord so you must have seen a lot of them.'

'They'd come round to pay their rent and tell me about anything that were wrong in the house but I can't say I knew any of them. None of them seemed to stay very long. Certainly no more than a year – some a lot less.'

'Why was that?'

He looked away. 'How should I know?'

'You must have had an inkling.'

'They only talked to me when they had a leaking tap or the fridge weren't working. I were their landlord, not their friend. They had their own concerns.'

'Did any of them mention if there was anything wrong with the house?'

'Aye, I've just told you. Always on about broken furniture and hot water and that. Did nothing but moan, some of 'em. Got too much in the end, all the fussing and griping. Some even tried to make out the place was haunted. I ask you . . . anything to get a reduction on the rent. But I wasn't falling for it.'

'Do you remember a girl called Jasmine who lived there twelve years ago?' asked Emily as she put down her half full mug of tea.

Quillan made a great show of thinking. 'Can't say I do. But, like I said, there were a lot of them.'

'She was tall and blonde,' said Emily. 'Probably the sort of girl you'd remember.'

'A lot of the girls were like that. Little whores, some of 'em.'

Joe caught Emily's eye. Had Quillan tried it on with some of his female tenants? It was hardly the sort of thing they'd get him to admit. But he'd have a try.

'I know the sort of thing,' he said. 'Bet some of them liked to flirt with you . . . persuade you to let them off the rent.' He leaned forward with a knowing smile. Man to man.

'Oh aye. Teasers I called them. Not that I ever . . .'

'From what I've heard about Jasmine, I bet she was one of them.'

'I don't remember no Jasmine.'

'That might not have been her real name. Do you remember any girl fitting that description living there around the time the two girls disappeared.'

As Quillan shook his head, avoiding their eyes, Joe knew that he had something to hide.

It was four o'clock when Joe dropped Emily off at police headquarters where she'd parked her car.

He was sure Quillan had been hiding something but not everything people hide from the police is necessarily sinister. However he was sure that Quillan had known the mysterious Jasmine. But was it some distant shameful memory that had led him to deny it? Or something else?

One person he hadn't met yet was Quillan's nephew, Rory. The man had, allegedly, duped his own uncle so he might be worth having a word with. But a lack of family feeling didn't necessarily mean he had anything to do with the two missing girls or Petulia Ferribie's disappearance. If, indeed, she had disappeared and not gone off somewhere of her own accord.

He left the pool car at the police station and walked back to his flat. A spell of early spring sunshine had brought people out in force and as he passed the Museum Gardens he could see families and young couples making the most of the fair but chilly weather.

He walked past the library and turned left past a row of elegant Georgian houses, now transformed into offices by the City Council. He saw the theatre on his right and made a mental note to get tickets for the latest production. But he'd have to see whether Pet Ferribie turned up before he made any firm arrangements. If the worst happened there'd be no time for theatres or much else for that matter.

The insistent ringing of his mobile phone interrupted his thoughts. He stopped walking and fished the thing from his jacket pocket.

'Is that DI Plantagenet?' said a male voice on the other end of the line. 'It's Andy Cassidy. We spoke earlier.'

'How can I help you, Mr Cassidy?'

Joe looked at his watch, hoping that whatever Cassidy had to tell him didn't require urgent action. He was to be at the

King's Head by the river at seven to keep his appointment with the mysterious K, and before that he had things to do – all the routine things that he'd had to put off when the Super decided to ruin his weekend.

'I've got some information.'

Joe waited for him to continue.

'Pet's tutor is a man called Ian Zepper. I think you should have a word with him.'

'You think he might know where she is?'

Cassidy hesitated. 'You should just have a word with him, that's all.'

Joe was left listening to the dialling tone. He stared at the phone for a few moments before dropping it in his pocket and walking on.

As he reached his flat grey clouds had begun to gather. Soon the darkness would come.

'So what did you have for lunch?'

Emily's husband, Jeff, was standing in the kitchen doorway. She looked at him and felt a little guilty.

'I just grabbed a sandwich,' she said. For some reason she couldn't quite fathom, she was reluctant to admit that she'd enjoyed a large Sunday roast in a pleasant pub in the company of Joe Plantagenet. Perhaps she wanted a bit of sympathy. Or perhaps she wanted Jeff to feel that his wrecked family Sunday had been worth it because of the sacrifices she was making to keep the streets of Eborby safe for law abiding citizens. Any hint that she had actually indulged herself in the process might have caused awkward questions to be asked.

Jeff stepped forward and kissed her cheek. 'You must be starving. We had pasta for lunch and there's still some left in the fridge.'

Emily forced herself to smile, but his noble attempts at being the supportive husband to a high-flying wife were just making her feel like the lowest form of rat. 'I'll help myself later. Everything OK?'

'Yeah. No problem.'

'How did Sarah get on at Sunday School?'

'Loved it. If we don't watch out she'll be signing up to become a nun.'

Emily began to laugh. 'No self-respecting convent would have her.'

She squeezed Jeff's arm. He had been the best looking lad in their hall of residence when they'd met at Leeds University. Time and the stresses of life had taken their toll, but he was still an attractive man. Looking in the mirror each morning, Emily always reckoned she'd come off far worse in the Anno Domini stakes.

'What about you? You've been called in all weekend so I presume it's something serious. But there haven't been any murders in the local paper.'

'Two teenage girls went missing twelve years ago and there's just been a new development.'

'What sort of new development?'

Emily hesitated. The mention of an MP would be bound to arouse Jeff's interest and, until they had investigated further, discretion might be wise. 'Nothing definite yet,' she said. 'We're still working on it.'

'Is there a chance the girls are still alive?'

'To be honest, love, I haven't a clue.' A wave of tiredness suddenly overwhelmed her and she stifled a wide yawn. 'I'm just going to have five minutes to myself. Be an angel and bring us a cup of tea.'

Jeff hurried off to put the kettle on. The kids were watching TV in the playroom but it was almost time for their stomachs to be refuelled so she knew her precious interval of peace would be short lived.

She made her way into the living room, kicked off her work shoes and sat down heavily on the sofa, pulling the footstool towards her and wriggling her body until she was sitting in complete comfort. She reached for the remote control and flicked on the tail end of the news.

TV companies traditionally reserve their cheerful or quirky stories for the end and today was no exception. For some reason the twentieth anniversary of the Eborby Music Festival had earned a place today and Emily leaned forward, interested to see something local for a change. The footage was of Saturday morning's parade along Stone Street. The City Waits were there at the head of the procession, dressed in medieval costumes, playing for an enthusiastic audience who were following them along the street, half walking, half dancing to the infectious beat of the tabor.

Then the camera panned through the crowd and came to rest on one face. A beautiful face. A willowy blonde girl with a slightly other-worldly aura tripping along at the edge of the crowd.

Emily's heart began to beat fast and she hardly noticed Jeff enter the room and place a mug of tea on the coffee table in front of her. She reached for the remote control and paused the picture, thankful that Jeff's love of new technology allowed her to do so.

'What's up?' asked Jeff. 'You look like you've seen a ghost.'

'She's supposed to be missing,' she said pointing at the screen.'

Before Jeff could answer, she reached for the phone on the side table. Joe would want to know that Petulia Ferribie had been caught on camera following the City Waits on Saturday morning.

Joe had switched his mobile off. Somehow he felt like being out of touch with the world, isolated from work and the demands of his distant family. He had put in the time over the weekend and now he was off duty and there was nothing so important that it couldn't wait till first thing on Monday.

Cassidy's call had intrigued him and, if Pet Ferribie didn't turn up before morning, he would follow it up. Although he couldn't help wondering what Cassidy's motive was for bringing that particular name to his attention. He hadn't mentioned it during their visit so it was clearly something he'd given some thought to since.

However, he still had a mystery of his own to solve. The identity of K. Ever since he'd received the letter he'd felt uneasy. For some reason, maybe the initial, maybe the similarity of the writing, it had reminded him of Kaitlin. And whenever he thought of Kaitlin he experienced the empty pain of loss, not as acute as it once was but there all the same.

He left his flat at six thirty, reasoning that if he arrived early and positioned himself in a corner of the pub to watch the comings and goings unobserved, he would hold the advantage.

He knew the Kings Head served Sam Smiths, which was one blessing. He had heated a bowl of tinned soup for himself as soon as he'd arrived home because even though he'd eaten a substantial lunch with Emily, he didn't want to drink on an empty stomach. Especially as he didn't know who or what he would encounter during the course of the evening.

It began to drizzle as he walked through the narrow streets to the river, sending the tourists scurrying inside the many pubs and restaurants that lined the way. Soon Joe had left the tight medieval streets for the wider thoroughfares lined with chain stores and bright shop windows. As he headed for the river the castle suddenly came into view, a single round keep on a steep mound. The rest of the fortress built by the Norman invaders to subdue the North of England had been demolished long ago to be replaced in the eighteenth century by a rather elegant prison which now housed a museum of everyday life.

Before reaching the castle, he turned down a small street to his right and saw the river at the end, grey and churning in the fading light. Another right turn brought him to the Kings Head perched on the river bank. In the summer all the outside tables would have been full but the chill air had driven even the hardiest drinkers indoors. The pub was filled with a blend of tourists, students and locals, united in their search for a quiet drink. Joe bought a pint of Sam Smiths bitter and found himself a seat in the far corner with an excellent view of the door. Each time someone came in, he watched the newcomer intently, trawling his memory for any hint of familiarity.

The pub was filling up fast and a group of standing drinkers blocked his view of the entrance and as seven fifteen came and went Joe wondered whether he should pay another visit to the bar. He had drunk as slowly as humanly possible when you're sitting there with nobody to talk to and now he only had an inch of beer left in his glass.

Then he looked up and saw her weaving her way through the drinkers, her eyes scanning the crowd for one familiar face. He shrank back into his seat, trying to look inconspicuous and he could feel his heart pounding like a hammer in his chest.

When she saw him her eyes widened. Her brown hair was shorter than it had been when he'd last seen her and her expensive belted raincoat flattered her slim, almost bony, body.

There was no escape now. She was marching towards him, pushing her way past a couple of men in deep conversation, almost spilling their beer and earning herself a 'steady on, love' and a dirty look. But she was unaware of her social faux pas. Her attention was focused on Joe. And she looked angry.

He drained his glass and stood up, uncertain how to greet her. In the end he managed to utter the only words that came into his head. 'It's been a long time.'

For a few seconds she said nothing. She just stared at him with bitter loathing. Then she spoke. One word spoken in a low hiss.

'Murderer.'

SEVEN

The King's Head had never struck Joe as a place for dramatic confrontations and somehow it seemed inappropriate in the midst of people whose sole desire is a quiet pint and a friendly chat. Other pubs he'd visited in the course of his work might have fitted the bill better.

He took her arm and shepherded her outside. All the way, he could feel her resisting, ready to throw off his guiding hand at any moment. But when he'd first joined the police Joe had been taught how to deal with unwilling suspects so he succeeded in tightening his grip and marching her to the door.

They were outside now amongst the empty chairs and tables set out overlooking the river. The chairs were damp and the tables were covered with little pools of water but Joe pulled out a chair and sat down – a wet backside seemed the least of his problems at that moment. Kirsten looked at the neighbouring chair with distaste before pulling a tissue from her handbag and wiping it carefully.

'To what do I owe the honour of this visit,' Joe began, trying to keep the sarcasm from his voice. Kirsten was Kaitlin's younger sister, spoiled and indulged. She had gone travelling in Europe shortly after the wedding and hadn't even bothered turning up for her sister's funeral. Kaitlin had heard rumours that she'd become involved with some Italian aristocrat but

Kirsten had never bothered to keep her sister up to date with her movements. At the time of Kaitlin's death she hadn't heard from Kirsten for over six months, not since she'd made it so obvious that she regarded her wedding to Joe as tawdry, suburban and a big mistake. A former trainee priest from a large Liverpool family with an Irish mother and a down-to-earth Yorkshire father was far beneath her. And the fact that Joe had joined the police made it even worse.

The sisters' parents had died when they were in their teens so Kaitlin and Kirsten were alone in the world. Alone and fairly wealthy. At the wedding Kirsten had accused Joe of being after Kaitlin's money. It wasn't true, of course, and when he had inherited her money on her death he'd been too grief-stricken to touch it so he'd given most of it away to charity. There were times he thought he should have kept hold of it in case times became hard, that his first impulse not to benefit from Kaitlin's death had been a little hasty. But he supposed it had done some good to someone.

'I've been finding out about my sister's death. I know what was said at the inquest.'

'You've taken your bloody time. You ignored Kaitlin after we got married and you didn't even bother coming to her funeral. What is it you want?'

'Justice.' She almost spat the word.

'I tried to contact you when she died but nobody knew where to find you.'

'I was travelling. Then I settled in the States for a while.'

'I take it you've only just found out that Kaitlin's dead?'

'I found out three months ago actually. It's taken me all this time to find out exactly what happened and get my head round it. Then I had to find you.'

'How did you do that?'

'Through my cousin Jenny.'

Joe nodded. He and Jenny exchanged cards and a letter at Christmas. Jenny was a nice woman, unlike the Kirsten he remembered.

'I told her not to tell you I was here. I said I wanted to surprise you.'

'You've certainly done that. How did you know about the King's Head?'

'I came to a party in Eborby once – a friend of a friend

from the university who had a flat overlooking the river. We came for a drink here the day after. I remembered it.'

'And you never thought to try to contact your sister before that?'

'I've been abroad leading a busy life. I thought I had a lifetime to get in touch with Kaitlin again. How was I to know she'd been murdered?'

Joe looked round. A group of students were passing their table, making for the pub. One of them looked at Joe curiously. 'Keep your voice down,' he hissed.

'You admitted at the inquest that you'd had a row. You said you'd argued and she stormed off. And the hotel receptionist saw you going after her.'

'Of course I went after her. I was worried.'

'He said you'd had a lot to drink.'

'I challenged that at the inquest. We'd had some wine with a meal but . . .'

'You were drunk. You went after her. You met her on the cliff path then you pushed her. And I'm going to prove it.'

Joe heart sank as he looked into his sister-in-law's eyes, cold and determined. Kaitlin had always said that Kirsten was used to getting whatever she wanted. The spoiled little sister.

'You can't prove it, Kirsten, because it didn't happen like that.'

'What were you arguing about?'

Joe hesitated. Why should he tell her? He owed her nothing. On the other hand, why not? It would show he had nothing to hide. 'We were arguing about you, if you must know. She'd not heard from you since you stormed out of the wedding and she was worried. She wanted to go and look for you. She was the elder sister and she had this misguided idea that she was somehow responsible for you but I told her she had to let go . . . that you hurt people and let them down. She was tearing herself apart with worry. I couldn't let her carry on like that. That's all I've got to say.' He stood up. 'Goodbye, Kirsten.'

He began to walk away. Kirsten's arrival had shocked him and he knew she could make trouble for him. And he didn't have time for trouble right now.

He half walked, half ran back to his flat, past the bright shop windows and the busy eating places.

When he got home he saw there was a message for him on his answering machine. Then he realized his mobile was still switched off. He'd been out of touch with the world for the past couple of hours. He listened to Emily Thwaite's message about the TV sighting of Pet Ferribie and he felt a frisson of excitement, glad of anything that would banish Kirsten's bitter, accusing face from his head.

As Monday morning dawned it looked as though the promise of a Yorkshire spring was over for the moment. The clouds had ganged together to form as mass of dirty grey and, although it wasn't raining yet, it looked as if those who ventured out without an umbrella or hood were on borrowed time.

Things were quiet at Bearsley Leisure Centre after the early morning rush of swimming enthusiasts trying to get a few lengths in before they set off for work. And Den Harvey took advantage of the lull to sneak out for a quiet cigarette. He knew that smoking was bad for his health but he was sick and tired of everyone he worked with at the leisure centre going on at him about it. He was sick of all those No Smoking signs and sick of feeling persecuted. And now his doctor was having a go at him about his diet and his weight as well.

But when he got home that evening Den would sneak up to his room and take his revenge on all of them, slaughtering them on his computer screen, seeing them disintegrate at the touch of a button. They might try and control his working life and his body but they couldn't control his mind.

Den stood amongst the bins at the back of the leisure centre, breathing in the aroma of rotting rubbish blended with the beloved scent of a newly lit cigarette. He tugged his tracksuit bottoms up and looked around. The back of the centre was the place other people avoided; the neglected backside of the ugly building. But it was Den's domain. His territory. He felt safe here.

When he heard his name being called, he froze, the hand holding the cigarette half way up to his lips. He took a step back into the shelter of the tall industrial bins and stood there perfectly still, hoping the boss wouldn't find him.

But today his luck was out. The boss had spotted him and he was walking over, clipboard in hand. And he didn't look pleased.

'A bulb's gone in the men's changing room. See to it, will you,' the boss said. He was a little man who reminded Den of a terrier he'd had as a child.

Den let the cigarette drop and stamped on it viciously, imagining it was the man's skull, and watched as the boss walked over to the bushes which fringed the concrete car park, thick gorse with scraps of litter hanging from its dusty foliage like votive offerings. Den saw him raise a tentative hand to push the branches aside and stare down at something on the ground.

The boss swore and staggered back a little, his hand clamped across his mouth, and Den shambled over to his side to see what the fuss was about.

On the ground, half hidden by the bushes, was a young woman, lying on her back as if asleep. Her fair hair was spread out around her head like a halo and her arms were neatly folded across her chest. She was beautiful, or rather she had been because now there was something wrong with her mouth. Her discoloured lips were parted to reveal a red mess of drying blood where her tongue should have been. She stared upwards with horrified eyes as though she was looking into the depths of hell.

'Call the police,' the boss said quietly.

Den hesitated for a few moments before rushing off to reception.

EIGHT

J oe wasn't sure what was making him feel so bad; whether it was the change in the weather or the memory of his meeting with Kirsten the night before. She had his address so he'd half expected her to turn up at the flat. She hadn't, but he knew that it would only be a matter of time before he saw her again.

When he arrived at Police Headquarters he made straight for Emily's office, raising his hand in greeting to his colleagues as he went. DS Sunny Porter was looking glum as usual; Sunny by name but definitely not by nature.

'How did it go last night?' Emily asked as he walked through her office door.

'Not well.'

'Sorry about that. Look, Joe, sit yourself down.'

He obeyed. Something had happened.

'A body's been found at the leisure centre. Young woman. Blonde. No ID. The Crime Scene team are down there now. Once we know what we're dealing with, I can get things organized. Tell everyone the state of play, will you, Joe? I'm off to tell the Super.'

'Is it Petulia Ferribie?'

Emily stopped in the doorway and turned to face him. 'Like I said, no ID on the body but she fits the description.'

'Only I had a call yesterday evening from Andy Cassidy.'

Emily's eyes lit up with sudden interest. 'Oh aye? What did he want?'

'He said we should have a word with Petulia's tutor at the university – an Ian Zepper.'

'Well, if it's her, we'll be doing that anyway. Come on.'

When Emily hurried away Joe stood for a few moments gathering his thoughts before marching out into the main office, shouting above the hum of Monday morning conversation – the sharing of weekend memories – to make himself heard.

As he outlined the situation he left out the name of Barrington Jenks, mindful of the Super's emphasis on discretion. Then he broke the news about the body at the leisure centre and told them to prepare for a full scale enquiry. It was best to start with a worst case scenario: if it turned out to be accident, suicide or natural causes, they'd think all their birthdays had come at once.

He met Emily in reception and they walked out to the car park. At least if the morning turned out to be eventful he'd have no time to dwell on Kirsten.

Their destination was a short drive away through the thick morning traffic. When they arrived the leisure centre entrance was festooned with crime scene tape and a crowd of curious onlookers had gathered outside the sealed off area, craning their necks to see the action. As Joe emerged from the car he looked up at the sky. The rain had stopped but probably not for long.

They were directed to the rear of the modern box-like

building where a row of huge waste bins stood by a back door. Opposite, on a patch of scrubland, a white tent had been erected to protect the body and any available evidence from the elements.

After they'd donned protective overalls they walked slowly towards the tent where the photographer's flash bulbs lit the shadows like forks of lightning.

Inside the tent Dr Sally Sharpe squatted by the body on the ground going about her gruesome business. As soon as she saw Emily she gave her a friendly smile. Then she spotted Joe and the smile became shyer.

'So what have we got, Sally?' Emily asked. She kept her professional distance and avoided looking at the body.

'Young woman. Late teens, early twenties. Natural blonde. Five foot five.'

'How long has she been there?'

'I'd say she's been dead roughly thirty-six hours. That means some time on Saturday night. Sorry I can't be more accurate.'

'That fits with what Matt heard on the phone,' said Joe quietly. 'He might have heard her being killed.'

Emily nodded. 'Possibly. Has the body been moved?'

'I'd put money on it.' She gave Joe a nervous smile. 'But I can't say for definite yet.'

'Cause of death?'

'She's been stabbed twice in the heart. But there's no sign of a weapon.' Sally hesitated. 'And whoever killed her cut her tongue out.'

Emily swore softly. The news of the mutilation had come as a shock.

As Sally stepped back so they could get a proper look Joe took his wallet from his pocket and extracted the photograph of the four residents of number thirteen Torland Place. He looked at the body sprawled on the ground, half concealed by dusty shrubs with scraps of litter hanging from their twisted branches. Then he looked at the photograph again and handed it to Emily.

'It's her alright. It's Petulia Ferribie.'

Emily sighed. 'At least we've got an ID. What about the next of kin?'

'We don't know much about the next of kin except that

there's a stepmother and her father's abroad. The university should have more information. We should go and see the housemates . . . break the news.'

Emily turned to Sally. 'The tongue – would you say it was removed after death?'

Sally nodded. 'Yes. That's one thing I'm pretty sure of. I can do the post-mortem this afternoon. That OK?'

'Fine,' said Emily absent-mindedly. Joe knew she was thinking of all the procedures that had to be set in motion. The incident room. The interviews. Informing the next of kin. And subjecting her housemates to more questions – not quite so gently this time. Someone must know why she died. And the best place to start was at home.

'Who found her?' Joe asked.

'The leisure centre manager,' Sally answered. 'He came out to look for one of the maintenance men who was supposed to be on duty but he was round the back having a crafty fag. He spotted the body and dialled nine nine nine.'

Emily caught Joe's eye. The person who finds the body is usually the first port of call. And, presumably, this one would be on the premises waiting for them like a good citizen.

They left Sally and the Forensic team to it and made their way to the building where the staff were gathered in the foyer. A couple of the young women were sobbing, others looked stunned. A young man in a tracksuit with the self-consciously athletic look of a sports instructor had a comforting arm around the shoulders of a pretty black girl who looked more bored than upset.

The man behind the reception desk was small and wiry with a shaved head and a vaguely military look. He was wearing a red polo shirt but he had a natural air of authority that some required a business suit to achieve. As soon as he saw Emily and Joe enter through the automatic doors, ID at the ready, he came out from behind his desk to greet them, hand outstretched.

'Peter Darman, Manager. Bad business. We're all shocked; that goes without saying.'

'Of course,' said Joe. 'Is there somewhere private we can . . . ?'

'We'll need to speak to all the staff,' said Emily as Darman led them behind the front desk into a small office bearing the legend 'Manager' on the door. 'Someone might have seen or heard something suspicious. And I presume you have CCTV here?'

Peter Darman's well scrubbed cheeks turned a delicate shade of red. 'Well . . . er . . . actually it hasn't been working for the past few weeks. I've put a request in to the Council for it to be fixed but these things take time.'

'Your maintenance staff couldn't deal with it then?' said Joe.

'No. It's a specialist job, or so they say at the council offices. Please sit down.'

Joe and Emily made themselves comfortable.

'Is there anywhere I can conduct interviews?' Emily asked sweetly.

'Of course, Chief Inspector. You can use this office if you like.'

This was what Joe knew she was hoping for. She nodded a gracious acknowledgement of the manager's selfless generosity with his personal space and got down to business.

Darman didn't need much encouragement to launch into a detailed account of how he discovered the body. He spoke as though he had gone over the story time and time again in his head, which he probably had. Joe always liked a thorough witness.

Soon it was Darman's turn to give up his seat behind the desk to Emily and call in his staff one by one.

The story was the same each time. It had been an ordinary Monday morning and nobody had seen or heard anything unusual. The clichés were trotted out again and again. Nobody could believe that such a thing could happen and the general consensus of opinion was that it was either 'terrible', 'shocking' or 'awful'.

The sixth member of staff to be interviewed was the man who had been with Peter Darman when the body was found. Den Harvey, in contrast to his boss, was somewhat overweight. His well-worn tracksuit bottoms had a tendency to slip down over his bulging middle and he kept hauling them up for decency's sake. He had a round, unhealthy-looking face and Joe caught a strong whiff of sweat as the man sat down reluctantly in front of them.

As Harvey gave them the account of the discovery in his

own words, Joe noted that it varied a little from Peter Darman's. Harvey reckoned she was probably a student at the university. You could tell them a mile off, he said. And he seemed to know that she'd been stabbed. When Emily asked him how he knew, he merely shrugged and said it was simple. He took a special interest in murder, he said almost proudly. He liked reading true crime books and, if you knew what you were looking for, these things were obvious.

Joe was about to ask more questions but Emily gave his knee a warning nudge under the desk. They watched the man leave in silence. But as soon as he was out of the room Emily spoke.

'I'd like to find out more about our Mr Harvey.'

'So he's on our list?' Joe said with a conspiratorial smile.

'Oh I think that goes without saying, Joe, don't you?'

Matt was alone in the house. But as he tried to concentrate on his work, he kept hearing sounds, muffled thuds and shuffles as if someone was downstairs. But he knew the others were out. At first he tried to ignore it. But eventually he put his music on. The house was getting to him. And however many times he tried to tell himself that it was all in his head, he still felt like an unwelcome visitor in the place. It wasn't something he could put into words but he knew there was something there that didn't want him . . . or any of the others for that matter. It watched from the shadows, hostile and full of resentment. It wished them ill. He'd always prided himself on being level headed – a man of science. But since he'd found out about the history of the house, the place frightened him.

He sat at his desk for a while staring at the notes in front of him, his eyes hardly focusing. Then he remembered that a couple of days ago he had seen an article in the local paper about a clergyman who worked at the cathedral. The journalist had portrayed this George Merryweather as a pleasant, down-to-earth man, even though his role was the Diocesan exorcist – or, Deliverance Minister as he preferred to be called. Matt had torn the piece from the paper and kept it, not quite knowing why. Perhaps it was the thought that Obediah Shrowton or his victims hadn't quite gone away. He wasn't sure but he kept hold of that newspaper cutting like a talisman. If things got really bad in the house, George Merryweather seemed the type who wouldn't laugh at his fears.

He spread his notes out on the desk in front of him and turned up the volume on his iPod. Then he heard something behind the thumping rhythm of the music. The doorbell. Someone was at the door.

He switched the music off and made his way downstairs. The sight of DI Plantagenet and DCI Thwaite standing on the doorstep with solemn faces told him something was wrong. When they'd come before they'd been friendly and smiling. But now they looked like the bearers of bad news. He stood aside to let them in.

'Let's go and sit down, shall we,' Joe said gently.

Matt allowed himself to be shepherded into the living room where he sat on the sagging sofa.

'We've found a body,' Joe said softly. 'And I'm afraid we think it's Petulia. We'll need to talk to you and everyone else in the house. And we'll need to contact her next of kin.'

'I'm sorry,' Emily said. 'It must be a shock.'

Matt felt numb, as though his body didn't quite belong to him. He'd been worried about Pet but somehow he hadn't expected this brutal finality.

'Her family . . . do you know where they live?'

'No. I only know her dad's in Dubai and she didn't get on with her stepmother.' He took a deep breath. 'How . . . how did she die?'

'We think she was murdered.'

Matt could hear his heart thumping as if it was trying to escape the cage of his chest. 'Where was she found?'

'Behind Bearsley Leisure Centre. Do you know of any reason why she should be there?'

Matt shook his head vigorously. Pet had never been one for sweaty gyms or early morning swims and he said as much to Joe and Emily.

'Is anybody else in?' Joe asked.

Before Matt could answer he heard the sound of the front door opening and they all looked round as Jason entered the room, wearing his combat jacket, buttoned up against the cold of the morning.

'This is starting to feel like police harassment.'

Matt turned round. 'Shut up, Jason. Pet's dead.'

Jason froze. 'You're joking,' he said after a few long seconds.

'It's hardly the sort of thing I'd joke about,' Matt said. 'They found her body this morning. At the leisure centre.'

Jason opened his mouth to say something then shut it again. He looked shocked but not particularly upset.

'They need to ask us some questions . . . and they've got to trace her family.'

'She didn't get on with them.'

'So I've heard,' said Emily. 'But they still need to be told.'

Jason bowed his head, his first gesture of sorrow. 'How did she die?'

'She was murdered . . . stabbed,' said Emily bluntly.

'I expect it was a mugging gone wrong.' He looked round. 'I'm bloody starving. Hope there's some bread left.'

Matt felt anger rise like bile in his throat and he almost forgot the presence of the two detectives. All he saw was Jason, mocking and uncaring, smearing Pet's memory.

He flung himself at his housemate, fists clenched, and tried to aim a punch at his face. But before he could make contact he felt a pair of strong arms pulling him away. DI Plantagenet had him in a restraining hold, muttering calming words in his ear. After a few moments Matt shrugged him off. 'OK, OK, I'll leave it.'

He looked at Joe and saw sympathy in his eyes, as though he understood. Then he felt the tears coming.

Barrington Jenks climbed into the first class carriage of the London train, thankfully separated from the crowd of less privileged humanity who were being herded into the overflowing second class carriages.

The attendant smiled to greet him. 'Good morning, sir.'

He gave the man a gracious nod in return before making for his seat. Once he was settled, he took out his official briefcase, preparing to make a pretence of working. He laid the documents out on the table before him but he didn't see the words on the paper. He had other things on his mind.

His wife was expecting him at their London flat for lunch then he intended to put in an appearance at the House. What he didn't know was that his well-planned day was about to be disrupted.

When his mobile phone rang he looked at the calling number and answered swiftly, aware that his hand had begun to shake.

'Yes?'

'I've booked a room at the Turpin. Be there in an hour.'

'I'm on my way to London. I can't just . . .'

'Suit yourself.' There was a pause. 'But the police might be interested in . . .'

'OK. I'll be there.'

The train wasn't due to set off for ten minutes and he had to make a decision. After a few moments' consideration, he gathered his papers together, spilling some on to the carriage floor. He knelt to retrieve them, hardly aware, in his agitated state, that the position was undignified, hardly worthy of a Member of Parliament and an Under Secretary of State in the Department of Justice. At last, when the papers had been rounded up and corralled into his briefcase, he looked up and saw that a woman in a grey business suit was watching him with detached interest. He gave her an apologetic smile and hurried off the train.

He had little choice. Jasmine had summoned him. And disobedience wasn't really an option.

Emily had organized a detailed search of Petulia's room and contacted the university for details of her next of kin: a father in Dubai and a stepmother in Dorset who would have to be told the bad news. When she'd enquired about Pet's tutor, Ian Zepper, she'd been told that he was at a meeting in Sheffield that morning but he'd be back after lunch.

As the father wouldn't be easy to reach, Joe arranged for the Dorset police to inform the stepmother and then sort out a car to bring her up to Yorkshire. He couldn't help recalling how two police officers, one a young rookie the other a sergeant who had seen it all before, had come to the hotel to break the news that Kaitlin's body had been found at the foot of some nearby cliffs. He knew how it felt to be on the receiving end of something like that and the memory made him feel slightly sick, especially when he thought of Kirsten trying to rake the whole thing up again.

But he couldn't dwell on his sister-in-law's thoughtlessness. He needed to discover everything he could about Pet Ferribie.

He couldn't forget the fact that Andy Cassidy had made the

effort to call him with Ian Zepper's name. He needed to know more about Pet's relationships and perhaps another go at her housemates would pay off.

Matt had already given his statement and somehow Joe thought he seemed the straightforward, reliable type who may have been a little in love with Pet. And if this was the case he seemed to have accepted her lack of reciprocal affection philosophically.

Matt reckoned that Pet might have had a bit of a crush – a delightfully old-fashioned term, in Joe's opinion – on her tutor, Ian Zepper. She'd been planning to move into a flat in Zepper's house the following year so maybe they were close – but she'd never said much about their relationship.

Matt had called Caro at the university and she'd returned as soon as her lecture was over. She was downstairs now, still apparently cool and businesslike after uttering the obligatory expressions of shock. Only her clenched hands and nervous eyes betrayed that she felt Pet's death more than she cared to let on.

Jason had retreated to his room like a sulky child after his spat with Matt and hadn't come down again. When Joe went up there he could hear music drifting from the room. Thomas Tallis Mass for Four Voices. It seemed Jason shared his musical tastes. He knocked and when there was no answer, he turned the handle but he found the door was locked.

'It's DI Plantagenet. Can I have a word?'

'I've nothing to say. No comment.'

Joe took a deep breath. 'I can break this door down and then you can answer some questions down at Police Headquarters if you'd prefer.' He stood waiting for the threat to have the desired effect.

Eventually the door opened and Jason Petrie stood there in front of him. 'I would have thought all this would be a bit beneath you with a name like yours,' he said with a smirk.

Joe, who had heard it all before, didn't dignify the remark with a reply.

'Like the music,' Joe said as he entered the room. It was tidier than most student rooms he'd seen. And the audio equipment was top of the range.

'It's Thomas Tallis. Sixteenth century.'

'I know.'

Jason raised his eyebrows and looked at Joe as though he suspected he was lying. 'I studied music for a year in Manchester. Then I got sick of it and decided to switch to English, which I've since dropped . . . hence my visit to the dole office first thing this morning.'

'If you studied music, you and Pet must have had a lot in common?'

'I wouldn't say that,' he said quickly. 'I like to live danger-ously. How did Pet put it? I like kissing the demons.'

'Kissing the demons. Was that something she made up?'

'No idea. But it was something she accused me of doing. When I asked her what it meant, she said it was flirting with dangerous situations . . . or people.'

'And did she kiss the demons?'

'I really couldn't say. Mind you, I always thought that she had secrets that she didn't share with us mere mortals.'

'What secrets would they be?'

'Haven't a clue.'

'Was Matt close to her?'

'He never stood a chance. Born to be mild, that one. And besides, I reckon she liked her men much older . . . and with more money.'

'Did she ever mention her tutor, Ian Zepper?'

Jason grinned. 'I heard from a friend of a friend that they'd been seen huddled together sharing secrets and sweet noth-ings. Very furtive. I've heard that he plays in an early music group.'

Joe thought for a few moments. 'She was last seen on Saturday on her way to the Early Music Festival. Could she have been meeting him there, do you think?'

Jason gave an inscrutable smile and Joe sensed that he was enjoying himself, tantalizing the police, letting out tiny drips of information. 'You'll have to ask him yourself.'

'We will. Is there anyone else you can think of who knew her well – friends or lovers?'

Jason shook his head. Then he looked straight at Joe, his expression serious. 'She was very beautiful.'

'I've seen her.'

'Yes, but she was dead. That's different.'

There was something cold in the way Jason said the words, almost as if he knew that her lovely face had been desecrated, and Joe felt a shiver travel up his spine. 'Did you have a relationship with her?'

'That depends what you mean by a relationship.'

Joe leaned forward, man to man. 'Did you sleep with her?'

'Unfortunately I wasn't her type. She didn't sleep with students.'

'Do you know of any students who took exception to that?'

Jason shook his head. 'I expect a lot of men – or maybe even women – were disappointed but I'm not aware of any who took it badly. Even our little Matt accepted his rejection.'

'Was Pet with anyone at the party last Friday?'

'No. She was just drifting round looking bored and lovely.'

'Was there anyone at the party you didn't recognize?'

'There were people from Caro's and Matt's departments but . . . Hang on, there was someone who didn't seem to be with anyone. Not that I could describe him – or it might even have been a her. All got up as the Grim Reaper; skeleton mask, black cloak; even carried a scythe.'

'Go on.'

'I never saw him take his mask off, not even to have a drink. And he was standing on the landing . . . watching, if you know what I mean. It seemed a bit odd at the time but . . . Well, we'd all had a few drinks and . . . Like I said, I only caught a glimpse – and I never saw his face.'

'Are there any photos of the party?'

'I don't know but I can ask around.'

Joe stood up and thanked Jason. After an inauspicious start, he'd turned out to be quite helpful. Now all he had to do was to see if any of the other housemates had spotted the Grim Reaper. And if any of them knew his identity.

The Turpin Hotel stood just outside the city walls on the south side of the river. It was modern and in need of refurbishment. But it was cheap, anonymous and used by penny pinching tourists and adulterous couples alike.

The automatic door swished open as Jenks walked in and he bowed his head as he hurried forward into the foyer. The young receptionist wore a cheap navy suit, too much make-up and a bored expression and she hardly looked at Jenks as he approached, which suited him fine.

'Room for Torland. I believe my wife's already here.'

The young woman typed fast into a computer keyboard before handing Jenks a plastic swipe card. 'Room three twenty-five. Third floor. Lift's over to your right. Have a nice day.'

Not wanting to draw attention to himself, Jenks resisted the temptation to make a sarcastic riposte. He picked up his brief-case, covering it carefully with his coat to obscure the official lettering, and as he made for the lift he found himself looking round for watching eyes like an inexperienced shop lifter.

He was relieved when nobody shared the lift with him. His biggest fear was being recognized – the possibility that few people are familiar with the face of their local MP never occurred to him – and he dreaded the prospect of making polite grunts to a fellow traveller. When the lift door opened a corridor lined with anonymous doors stretched in front of him and he walked until he arrived at room three twenty-five.

He hesitated for a second then he swiped his plastic key and when he saw the tiny light turn from red to green, he pushed the door open.

She was sitting on the bed and Barrington Jenks's first thought was that time had been kind to her.

'Hello, Jasmine,' he said quietly.

Then she raised the knife to her painted lips and smiled.

Cassidy worked from home, which had its advantages. And its disadvantages. It cut commuting to a minimum. But on the other hand you could never really escape the office. Or the police.

They had come calling that morning to break the news about Pet. He had made noises of shock and regret, adding the words 'not that I knew her well, of course,' to allay any suspicion on the part of the two Detective Constables, one a lad in his twenties with a crew cut, the other a young Asian woman.

They had asked questions, taken a brief statement, asked where he was at eleven thirty on Saturday night, thanked him and left. And they had seemed to accept his story that he'd spent Saturday night with an estate agent friend who'd called round with some papers for him to look at.

He picked up his mobile phone again. Each time he'd dialled the number he needed, it had gone straight to voice mail. He clenched his fist and brought it down on the desk, unable to control his frustration.

'What is the matter, Andy? Is there something I can get you? Coffee?'

He dropped the phone on to the desk as though it was red hot and swivelled round in his chair. 'Piss off, Anna.'

The young woman in the doorway looked at him, a hurt expression on her face.

'I'm sorry.' He held out his arms. 'Come here.'

She walked towards him slowly and when she came within reach he pulled her towards him with a violence that made her gasp. Then, as she slumped on to his knee, he kissed her, his hands exploring her slim body and encountering no resistance.

He whispered something in her ear and she pulled away. 'But that is a lie.'

'Not really. It's the truth. I just need you to back me up. If it's a lie, it's only a tiny white one. And the police probably won't ask you anyway, but if they do . . .'

She nodded. 'Very well.'

He put his hands under her armpits and hoisted her upright. 'Off you go now. I've got work to do.'

He watched with a glow of satisfaction as she left the room reluctantly. And once she was out of earshot he picked up his mobile and dialled the number again.

This time it was answered.

'Ethan. Look, the police might be in touch with you. If anyone asks, when you called round here on Saturday night with those papers, we had a drink and you stayed till midnight. OK?'

When he heard the answer he smiled. It was all fixed. Sorted. And maybe now Ian Zepper would get what he deserved.

NINE

Caro had no more lectures that day but that didn't mean she didn't have work to do. She had always been the conscientious sort, keeping up with her reading and essays so that she didn't get left behind. The truth was that she'd never felt particularly confident about her abilities. While other girls at her private school had floated effortlessly along on a sea of good grades with minimum effort, Caro had had to strive for every A and B she gained.

Since she'd moved into number thirteen her marks had started to slip and she knew that if she didn't do something about it, it would all end in tears and ignominy. There had been times when she'd thought that the house itself was making her restless and unable to concentrate. She liked to be in control – and that was something she was finding increasingly difficult in Torland Place.

She looked down at the mobile phone she'd been turning over and over in her hand and suddenly recalled that she'd seen Matt taking pictures with it at the party on Friday night. He'd found it on the mantelpiece and he'd been snapping away when she'd seen him and snatched it back, making it quite clear that he had no right to interfere with her private property. His riposte was that she shouldn't have left it there and he probably had a point but she'd put it down during the preparations and forgotten about it. The police had asked for pictures but she'd forgotten all about the incident till now.

She began to flick through the pictures, viewing the images of drunken revelry with increasing disapproval. Until she came to a picture of Pet pouting at the camera. Teasing. She stared for a while at the image of the dead girl. Strange, she thought, how life can be so swiftly snuffed out.

It seemed hard to believe that there was nothing of Pet left but a lifeless, rotting corpse. When she'd been alone in her room last night, she'd been sure she'd smelled her dead housemate's distinctive perfume and heard a rustling over by the door. Then she thought of the seance and shuddered. She should never have allowed it. She knew that now.

She continued to scroll through the pictures until she saw one that caught her attention. One of the detectives had told her that Jason had seen somebody dressed as the Grim Reaper at the party and she'd thought it was Jason's idea of a joke. But here he was, a figure draped in black with a half-hidden skeleton face, leaning over the banisters at the top of the stairs, watching. She suddenly went cold. Here was Death standing in the shadows, seeking out someone to devour – and that someone had been Pet.

She put in a call to the number DCI Thwaite had left before examining the picture more closely. Surely Death was just a person in fancy dress, someone with a macabre sense of humour. But there was something behind the anonymous figure, a nebulous, vaguely human shape, faint and misty. But it was probably something that had got on to the lens, a spot of liquid maybe. There was always some rational explanation.

Petulia's stepmother was being driven up to Eborby to identify the body. Sally Sharpe was booked to do the post-mortem at four thirty so, if Joe and Emily were to interview Mrs Ferribie beforehand, time was tight and there was still a lot they didn't know about Pet Ferribie's life.

'Ma'am.'

Joe and Emily looked up and saw DC Jamilla Dal standing at the door of Emily's office.

'We've looked through the CCTV footage of the Early Music Festival on Stone Street. The victim's there one minute and then there's nothing after that. She must have slipped away down a side street or alley.' She took a deep breath. This wasn't all. 'And we've got an ID on the musician she was watching.'

Joe tilted his head to one side. 'Let me guess, is it Ian Zepper?'

Jamilla's eyes widened in surprise. 'How did you know?'

'His name's already come up.' He looked at his watch. 'He was out this morning but he should be back at the university by now.'

'Do you want me to ring the university and find out?'

Emily shook her head vigorously. 'No. I prefer the element of surprise.' She glanced at her watch. 'If we're quick we can get over there before Petulia's stepmum arrives.'

Joe didn't say much as they drove out to the university campus, built in the 1960s just outside the far-flung suburbs on the south side of the city. He drove on autopilot, the problem of Kirsten still nagging at the back of his mind, although he was trying his best to forget her and her poisonous words.

He parked the car in an area marked staff only and they made straight for the administration block, walking beside the large lake around which the University of Eborby had been built. It was said that there were more geese and ducks there than students and, from the squawking and quacking as they passed, Joe could quite believe it.

When they reached the concrete admin block they were greeted by a plump middle-aged woman who seemed to take a visit from the police in her stride. She expressed no curiosity when they asked whether Ian Zepper was on the premises, but told them that Dr Zepper had just finished teaching and should be found in his office in the music department. Joe thanked her and followed her directions, Emily walking silently by his side.

The music department was housed in another concrete block, no concession having been made by the 1960s' planners for artistic sensibilities. A student carrying a violin case directed them to Dr Zepper's office on the ground floor and Joe's knock was greeted by a weary 'Come in if you must.'

Joe pushed open the door and stepped inside, warrant card at the ready. He was conscious of Emily behind him and he knew she'd be taking in the scene and making her usual snap judgements . . . which usually turned out to be right.

He recognized Zepper immediately from the TV footage Emily had showed him earlier, although now he was dressed in an open-necked striped shirt and corduroy trousers rather than medieval costume. He had a mouth that naturally turned up at the corners and Joe sensed that he possessed that most elusive of qualities, charisma.

He stood up and shook hands, a concerned frown on his face. 'What can I do for you? If it's about that speeding fine, I assure you the cheque's in the post.' His lips twitched upwards in a wary smile. 'But I expect they all say that.'

'It's not about speeding, Dr Zepper. You were playing with the Eborby Waits on Saturday morning, I believe?'

'That's right. One of the Waits is away and I stood in for him at the festival. Early music is a particular interest of mine. The original Waits, of course, were employed by the city – they were given livery and four pounds a year to play music during the winter months and act as watchmen and announce the time around the streets.' He hesitated, aware that he was talking too much. 'Look, what's this about?'

'Do you know a girl called Petulia Ferribie?'

'She's one of my students. Why?'

'I'm afraid she's dead, Dr Zepper.' Joe watched the man's reaction carefully.

Ian Zepper looked genuinely shocked. 'Dead? How? When? Was it an accident or . . . ?'

'Her body was found first thing this morning behind Bearsley Leisure Centre.' He paused. 'She'd been murdered.'

Zepper slumped back into his chair, stunned. Then he looked up at Joe accusingly, as though he suspected he was playing some cruel joke. 'Are you sure it's Pet? Has anybody identified her?'

'We've identified her from a photograph and her step-mother's travelling up from Dorset to do a formal ID.'

'You've got it wrong. It can't be her.'

'Why do you say that?' Emily asked.

Zepper didn't answer, he stood up and stared out of the window which gave a view of the lake, as though seeking inspiration.

'Petulia was last seen on Saturday morning in the crowd watching the concert given by the Waits. She appears on news footage of the event watching your performance very intently. Then she disappears, probably down some alley or side street.'

Zepper put his head in his hands. Then, after a few moments he looked up. 'There's an old story that a beautiful woman in white used to emerge from one of the city churchyards and follow the Waits – always at a respectful distance – then she'd suddenly disappear. It was said she was a ghost but . . .' He suddenly looked a little embarrassed. 'I'm sorry . . . but there was something a little other-worldly about Pet. Sorry, I'm rambling, aren't I, but it's come as a shock.' He straightened his back and took a deep, calming breath. 'Look, I'd like to help you but I really don't know how I can.'

'I take it you saw Pet at the concert?'

'I noticed her in the audience at one point but I didn't have a chance to acknowledge her.'

'Where did you go when the concert was over?'

'We changed back into our normal clothes at the Early Music Centre then we all went for lunch and a few pints at the Swan on Ditchgate. I was with my fellow musicians till around three o'clock. Look, like I said I saw her in the audience then I never saw her again. And I certainly had nothing to do with her death.'

'We never said you did, Dr Zepper. We're just speaking to everyone who knew her.'

'Of course. I'm sorry. Look if I can help in any way . . .'

'Were you at a party at Pet's house in Torland Place on Friday night by any chance?'

'No. I'm not in the habit of going to student parties.'

'Do you know a man called Andy Cassidy?' Joe asked.

There was no mistaking it, Zepper had turned pale. But he soon regained his composure.

'I knew him when he was younger. I used to teach his sister the piano.'

'Why would he want to implicate you in Pet's disappearance?'

Zepper remained silent for a few seconds. Then he shook his head, avoiding Joe's gaze. 'I've really no idea.'

Joe didn't believe him but he let it rest . . . for now.

'Who were Pet's special friends? Anybody she used to hang round with. Anyone you can think of who might be able to help us.'

'You'd have to ask the students she lived with.'

'I believe she was planning to move into your house next year.'

'I have a self-contained flat that I let to students. She was going to share with another girl from the department.'

'Was she close to this girl?'

'I don't think so. It was just an arrangement of convenience as far as I know.'

'We'll need to speak to everyone who knew her in the department.'

Zepper gave a resigned nod. 'I'm sure nobody here would be able to help you. Surely it was a mugging or . . . ? Was she . . . you know . . . sexually assaulted or . . . ?'

'We're not sure yet, sir,' said Joe quickly. There had certainly been no sign of sexual violence but they would have to wait for the post-mortem to learn more.

Joe had waited till the end to ask the next question. 'Were you close to Pet?'

'There was nothing improper about our relationship, if that's what you're getting at. She was an unusual girl; very sensitive.

And she would have made a very fine musician. Her death's a tragedy, Inspector, but I know nothing that might be relevant to your investigation. I'm sorry, I can't help you.'

The vehemence of his words almost convinced Joe that he was telling the truth. Almost, but not quite.

'Where were you at eleven thirty on Saturday night?'

'I was at home. And before you ask, I have no witnesses. I did some work and had an early night.'

They took their leave with a warning that they might be in touch. In Joe's experience it was always best to leave them a little on their guard.

'What do you think?' Joe asked as he climbed into the driver's seat.

'I think he knows more than he's letting on. Do you agree?'

Before Joe could answer, his mobile phone began to ring. When the call ended he turned to Emily. 'Mrs Ferribie will be here in half an hour.'

Emily did up her seat belt. Facing the relatives of a murder victim was something she always dreaded.

Shame is a powerful emotion and it was one that Barrington Jenks felt strongly as he boarded the later train to London.

When he'd first met Jasmine in that bar he'd been an up and coming estate agent in Eborby. He'd been ambitious and single minded but he'd always found time for a spot of dalliance in his spare time before politics took over his life completely. Then, after that first encounter they'd lost touch – until she'd contacted him again when he'd been elected for parliament eight years ago. Until he'd put his head above the parapet and become a public figure.

After that she kept in touch, a voicemail here, a message at his constituency office there. She'd never asked to meet but the hint had always been there. At times it frightened him. But sometimes living dangerously makes you feel alive.

Jasmine had been surprising in that bland, worn hotel room . . . surprising and dangerous. It had been a thrilling reminder of his past. A past that would be the end of his political career if anyone were to find out. Financial scandal was one thing in the world of Westminster and sex was another. But what he and Jasmine had done all those years ago would surely ruin him. There would be no redemption after something so terrible.

Jenks settled himself down in the first class compartment, well away from anybody who might conceivably vote for him, and opened his briefcase. It was time to get down to business.

Like her stepdaughter, Jane Ferribie wore her silky blonde hair long and straight. She was dressed in well fitting jeans and a white shirt that Emily later said must have cost a fortune. From behind she would have passed for a teenager and, even face on, she had the unlined look of a woman in her mid thirties who attended the gym each day. Maintaining looks like that tends to demand a lot of single-minded effort. But Joe's training for the priesthood, although interrupted, had taught him never to make judgements. Instead he wondered why she felt she had to go to so much trouble to hold back the years.

As she talked to Emily, he soon learned the answer. Jane was Pet's father's second wife and a year ago she'd abandoned him to live with a much younger man. Her husband had been due to move to Dubai with his work and, as she hadn't wanted to live in the Middle East, the decision had been easy. She'd left Paul and moved in with Carl, and Pet had shown her disgust by never speaking to her again. Keeping up with Carl was hard work, of course. And she hadn't told him about Pet's murder . . . he didn't like illness and death.

Emily caught Joe's eye. Jane might be on borrowed time as far as Carl was concerned and probably deserved their sympathy, with or without a step daughter in the mortuary.

'I'm so sorry for your loss, Mrs Ferribie,' Joe said after a long silence.

'Thank you,' she said with a weak smile. 'I can't tell you anything about her life here, you know.' Her tone was almost defensive. 'We were never what you'd call close. I only married her dad when she was fifteen and after I left him she never spoke to me again.'

'What about Pet's biological mother?'

There was a pause before Jane answered. 'When Pet was eleven she disappeared – walked out of the house one day and never came back.'

'It would have been natural for Pet to want to find her,' said Joe. 'Do you know if she ever tried?'

'I don't know. I don't think so.'

Joe couldn't help feeling a little sympathy for this woman thrust into a family with a dark hole at its centre – a mother who went out one day and never returned, leaving a damaged child who was bound to give her successor a hard time. Perhaps she couldn't be blamed for seeking comfort in the arms of Carl or any other available man. Who was he to judge?

'We need to contact your husband,' said Emily, handing Jane a sheet of paper.

Jane took it and scribbled an address. 'That's the only address I've got for him,' she said, handing it back to Emily.

'Tell us about Pet,' said Joe. He'd been leaning on the edge of Emily's desk but now he pulled up the spare chair and made himself comfortable.

Jane looked at him. 'I tried really hard at first but she kept knocking me back, making sarcastic remarks, deliberately excluding me. She made me feel as though I wasn't welcome . . . which I wasn't, I suppose. She used to call me the Wicked Stepmother.'

'Was that to her friends?'

'She never had many friends – or if she did she never brought them home. She called me that to her father. And he never told her off about it,' she added as though this had caused years of simmering resentment. 'She just spent hours practising her violin and piano. Hour after hour of scales and half finished tunes. Used to drive me mad.'

'I can imagine,' said Joe. 'So she never confided in you at all?'

'You're joking. She was a little bitch if you must know.'

'So you don't know if there was anyone she was afraid of?' Joe knew the question was futile. Pet had kept her distance from the 'Wicked Stepmother' and she was probably the last person who would learn her innermost secrets.

Jane shook her head. 'And before you ask, I don't think her father would know any more than I do. Like I said, we weren't what you'd call a close family.'

Joe realized this was a considerable understatement. He was starting to get a picture of Pet Ferribie now and it wasn't a happy one. She'd kept her distance from her family and her housemates. She'd been beautiful but she'd had no close friends.

'Then she tried it on with Carl,' Jane said unexpectedly.

'How do you mean?' Emily asked.

'She started ringing him, asking to meet.'

'And did he?'

'He met her for a drink once. He said it was best to put her straight.' She hesitated. 'She said she'd go to bed with him if he'd finish with me.'

'What was his reaction?' Joe asked with genuine interest. The Ferribies' family life seemed to contain all the scandal and emotional excitement of a TV soap opera.

'He told her to get lost. She was trying to get at me and Carl wasn't falling for it,' she said confidently.

Emily glanced at Joe then she stood up. 'Are you ready to identify her?'

Jane stood up and brushed her hair away from her face. 'Yeah. OK. Let's get it over with, shall we.'

They drove to the hospital in silence and Joe watched as the sheet was drawn back to reveal Pet's pale, beautiful face. The mouth was closed now, the horror of the severed tongue carefully concealed. He watched Jane, anticipating cool indifference.

But he saw tears in her eyes which was the last thing he expected.

Den Harvey left work early after telling Mr Darman that he wasn't feeling well. Discovering that girl's body had played havoc with his nerves. And his nerves were never good at the best of times.

As he walked through the male changing rooms the echoing voices of the swimmers drifted through on the chlorine-scented air and suddenly he felt a little faint. It was too hot in there, hot and damp like a tropical jungle. He had to get out. He had to get home.

When he reached the staff room he put his key in the battered metal locker in the corner. As the door creaked open he looked at the photographs he had stuck inside. Some of the women at the Leisure Centre would have objected . . . if they knew. But he was careful not to let anybody into his private world where women were naked and compliant and they didn't put up a fight or answer back. A world quite divorced from the reality of his life.

He knew there was nobody watching him so he put out a hand and lovingly brushed the glossy paper thighs of the girl who was lying against his locker door, spreadeagled there in two dimensions for his delight. Then he pulled out his rucksack, slung it over his shoulder and turned the key in the door, knowing that his paper girl would be waiting for him in the morning.

He left the leisure centre by the back door because he wanted to avoid any awkward questions from Tracey on reception . . . and also because he wanted to see what was going on. The police were still there, of course. He knew from all the true crime books he read that they always took their time at a crime scene. He knew all about the search for tiny scraps of evidence and the painstaking sifting of clues. And he knew what they would do to the girl's body on the post-mortem slab. He had read about it so often.

And once he'd even experienced the reality of death in all its inglorious horror. And it had changed him forever.

It wasn't far to the red brick terraced house he shared with his mother in Banff Street and when he opened the front door he heard her voice from the room she always called the front parlour. 'Is that you?'

Silly question. He answered 'yes' automatically and made his way upstairs, his footsteps muffled on the richly pattered carpet.

Once inside his room, he leaned against the door for a few seconds, gathering his thoughts. Then he turned the key in the lock and sat down at the computer desk in the corner, resting his bare feet on the floor.

When the computer screen flickered into life, Den began to type. Three words.

Kissing the Demons.

TEN

It was the second time in an hour that they'd visited the mortuary. The first time they had brought Jane Ferribie to identify her step daughter. Then they had taken her back to her hotel on Boothgate before returning to witness the post-mortem from behind a newly installed glass screen. Emily took up her position, arms folded, and Joe stood beside her while Sally Sharpe began work.

Sally kept up a commentary into the microphone suspended above the table.

'There seem to be traces of adhesive on the wrists, face and ankles so it looks like she was restrained with some sort of tape, possibly for some time before she was actually killed. The angle of the knife wounds indicate she was stabbed with a slight downward thrust,' said Sally without emotion as she penetrated the wound in the dead girl's chest with a sharp instrument. 'Which means that her killer was probably taller than her and right handed.'

'Can't you be more specific, Sal?' Emily spoke into the microphone in front of her.

'I can only tell you what I find. Conjecture costs extra.'

Joe noticed Sally glance in his direction as she picked up the saw that would slice the top off Petulia Ferribie's skull. The pathologist was an attractive woman with a mischievous sense of humour and sometimes he wondered why he didn't just ask her out for a meal. But since that CID Christmas party when she'd had too much to drink and made it plain she fancied him, he suspected that her embarrassment had erected a barrier between them. Perhaps he would attempt to break down that barrier one day. But with Pet lying there with her internal organs open to view, it seemed inappropriate to think about it.

'There's no sign of sexual assault,' Sally said. 'In fact she was a virgin. I didn't think you got many of them to the pound at Eborby University.'

Joe raised his eyebrows and looked at Emily.

'That's a turn up for the books,' she said. 'So we're not looking for a lover or a rapist?'

'Doesn't look like it,' said Sally. 'Was she robbed?'

'No handbag was found with her. But her purse was in her pocket, as were her keys. There was a five pound note in her purse and a bit of loose change. And the body was moved,' Emily said. 'I've yet to come across a mugger who goes to that much trouble. Anything else we should know, Sal?'

'The toxicology tests will take a while to come back but I'm afraid I can't add anything to what I've already told you.'

Joe saw Emily sigh. The dead girl's clothes would be sent to the lab where they would be examined for any minute clues to where she was killed. But for the moment they had little to go on.

They left the mortuary and made for the car park.

'Where to now?' Joe said as he unlocked the car door.

'I'm off home,' said Emily. 'But I'll be available if there are any developments.'

Joe drove them back to headquarters and dropped Emily off in the car park before walking up to the incident room.

When he entered the office Sunny greeted him with a raised hand and Joe knew from his expression that he'd found something new.

'I've been doing some digging on the people we've interviewed so far and one of them's done time for murder,' Sunny said, handing Joe a sheet of paper. 'I reckon we've got ourselves a prime suspect.'

'He's got an alibi.'

'It has been known for people to tell us porkies from time to time.' Sunny had always had a cynical approach to human nature.

Joe looked at his watch then he studied the details Sunny had given him. 'We'll send someone round to pick him up. I'll give the boss a ring.'

Sunny walked away with a smug look on his face as Joe made the necessary calls. However, half an hour later the patrol car sent round to pick up Pet's landlord, Andy Cassidy, called in to report that he was away in Leeds for the night and wouldn't be back till the following morning.

Matt hated his room. It always felt cold and clammy and he hadn't slept well since he'd moved in. Now that Pet had gone he supposed he could take over her room. Then he had a sudden pang of conscience that he'd considered taking advantage of her death.

He tried to focus on his work but he couldn't concentrate because the whispering had begun as it often did once darkness fell. At first he'd thought it was the wind in the trees but now it seemed to come from within the house, like hushed voices in a distant room, talking so quietly that he could never quite make out the words. He sat still and listened, wondering whether he was going mad.

The others claimed that they hadn't heard it but he knew from the look in their eyes that they had. He was sure that's why Jason had suggested the seance, so he could find out what they were dealing with. But, of course, Jason had denied it. According to him, he'd sensed nothing strange in the house. The seance had been 'a laugh'. No more.

But Matt felt that it was time to find out for sure. Caro would disapprove and Jason would mock but he needed to settle the question once and for all.

He opened the top drawer of his battered desk and took out the newspaper cutting. The Reverend George Merryweather's email address was on it and, after a short period of thought, Matt switched on his computer and began to type.

He didn't know whether he believed in that sort of thing, but surely it couldn't do any harm.

Joe arrived back at his flat just after nine thirty and the first thing he did was check the answer phone for messages before switching on every light in the place to dispel the darkness. It had been a frustrating day, packed with promising leads that had seemed to come to nothing.

Then they'd hit the jackpot when they'd discovered that, at the age of sixteen, Pet's landlord, Andy Cassidy had murdered his own sister and had been committed to a secure hospital for five years. His sister, Grace, had been a year younger than him and a talented pianist. He had stabbed her with a kitchen knife and had hacked off three of her fingers before his horrified mother had discovered him kneeling by her body, sobbing.

According to psychiatric reports he'd been pathologically jealous of his sister for most of his life, envying her musical talent and habitually seeking attention in the most destructive of ways. However, he'd been adamant that he'd done no wrong, claiming that he'd found his sister like that and been too shocked to get help. Nobody had believed him.

After Grace's death he'd blossomed academically and he'd gained good GCSEs in the secure hospital, something his doctors had taken as a sign of his recovery. On his release he'd gone to college to do his A Levels and had won a place at Eborby University studying psychology of all things. His psychiatrists had pronounced him cured. He'd been one of their success stories.

The files also mentioned that Ian Zepper had been Grace Cassidy's piano teacher and Joe thought this might explain the animosity Cassidy clearly felt towards him. And if that level of resentment still existed, it might mean that the psychiatrist's verdict had been over-optimistic.

The fact that Cassidy had murdered his own sister so brutally put him right at the top of their suspect list. It was just a question of breaking his alibi and getting the evidence.

Cassidy's alibi had been provided by a man called Ethan McNeil, an estate agent he did business with from time to time; a man he described as an old acquaintance. Uniform had called at McNeil's address in the suburb of Bacombe and his wife had confirmed he'd indeed been out at Cassidy's and hadn't got home till after midnight. But he and Emily still planned to pay him a visit at work first thing the next day. They'd have more chance of getting at the truth if they caught him unprepared.

Joe switched on the TV. It was a detective drama that bore scant resemblance to real life but he left it on for that very reason. He needed something to take his mind off the day . . . and off the possibility that Kirsten might contact him any moment with more accusations. He felt unable to relax knowing she was there in Eborby, working against him in the shadows, spreading poison.

He opened a can of beans and put two slices of bread in the toaster. Student food; comfort food. He had just finished eating when the phone rang and he used the remote control to kill the volume of the TV before picking up the receiver. Fearing that it would be Kirsten, he felt his hand shaking a little as he said a wary hello. But when he heard the cheerful voice on the other end of the line, he smiled to himself in sheer relief.

'I hope I'm not interrupting anything important,' the voice said.

'I never mind being interrupted by you, George. How are you?'

'Remarkably well. I presume you're dealing with the murder of that poor girl at the leisure centre?'

'Yes.'

'Actually . . .' George paused and Joe knew something important was coming. 'I've just been speaking to one of her housemates. A young man called Matt Bawtry.'

'I've met him.'

'He's worried.'

'And he contacted you rather than the police?'

'That's the point, Joe. His worries are rather more my territory than yours. He thinks there's a malevolent presence in the house.'

Joe remembered how he'd felt when he entered thirteen Torland Place. There had definitely been some indefinable quality about the atmosphere – hostility perhaps – but he'd put it down to the fraught relationship between the occupants. But perhaps it stemmed from something else. Something deeper.

'I don't know what Matt told you but the house does have a rather gruesome history. In the nineteenth century a man called Obediah Shrowton butchered his family and a couple of servants there. He's invited me round tomorrow. I'll say a few prayers . . . the usual. I don't suppose you'll have time to . . .'

'Probably not, George. Sorry.' He was about to say they had a suspect to bring in but assuming Cassidy's guilt at this early stage was probably tempting fate.

'Matt suspects that the poor girl's death's got something to do with the house.'

Joe was about to say: 'That's nonsense.' But he stopped himself. They didn't have a clue why Pet died. A connection with the house was as likely as anything else. 'He never mentioned all this to us.'

'Perhaps he thought you wouldn't take him seriously. Sometimes people tell me things they wouldn't say to a policeman,' said George without any hint of smugness. 'So if I learn anything – anything that's not personal or confidential, of course – I'll let you know.'

'Thanks, George,' said Joe before promising that he'd arrange to see him soon. Perhaps George would be the person to talk to about the problem of Kirsten. Or maybe that was something best kept to himself.

He opened a bottle of Old Peculier and settled down in front of the TV.

One thing was absolutely certain. Pet hadn't been killed by any ghost resident in thirteen Torland Place. Her murderer was flesh and blood.

*   *   *

On Tuesday morning Emily arrived in the incident room like a human whirlwind, assigning tasks and rushing through the morning briefing with no-nonsense efficiency. Caro at Torland Place would have envied her, Joe thought.

The pictures of the Torland Place party that Caro had provided were pinned up on the noticeboard. Nobody at the house had been able to identify the person dressed as the Grim Reaper. It was a mystery. One that Emily wanted to solve.

When she had finished speaking, she grabbed hold of Joe's arm and steered him into her office.

'You're on top form today,' he said.

'I want this sorted. We need to see Cassidy,' she hesitated. 'Her housemates hinted that he was sniffing after Pet. What if she turned him down and he reacted like he did when he killed his sister? It's the same MO, Joe. Stabbed twice in the heart. It's too much of a coincidence, don't you think.'

'He cut off his sister's fingers.'

'Pet's tongue was cut out. Grace Cassidy's crime was being a good pianist. He might have punished Pet in a different way. Perhaps she's given away some secret or said something he didn't like.'

'I take it he's not back home yet?'

'I've got a patrol car waiting outside his house. I don't want him warned off by that Anna. She looks the devoted type.'

'So are we going to blow his alibi to bits?'

She looked at her watch. 'Uniform couldn't get hold of Ethan McNeil last night but we know where he works and he should be arriving at his office about now. I want to go and spoil his day before he has a chance to tuck into his first cappuccino.'

The office of McNeil and Dutton, Estate Agents, was a short walk away, just the other side of Wendover bridge and opposite the Museum Gardens. And when they arrived the place was locked but they could see a light behind the closed vertical blinds so Emily hammered on the door.

After a minute or so the door opened a few wary inches and when they announced themselves the door swung open to reveal a tall young woman in a short straight navy skirt and matching jacket. She was in her thirties, Joe guessed, with a round face, small eyes and thin lips; the sort Joe's mother would have described as 'no oil painting'. And there was a hint of aggression in her manner, like a lioness prepared to defend her young.

'We're here to see Mr McNeil,' said Emily.

The woman drew herself up to her full height. 'I'll ask if he can see you . . .'

'He'll see us,' said Emily, taking a step forward. 'Through there, is he? We'll find our own way.'

The woman barred the way. 'I don't think he'd like . . .'

But Emily marched round her and the woman stood staring at her with barely disguised hostility, angry at this intrusion into her boss's working day. The picture of the devoted employee.

Emily didn't bother knocking on Ethan McNeil's office door. Instead she let herself in, warrant card at the ready. Her intention of getting there before he had his first cappuccino was thwarted – the coffee cup beside a framed photograph of a smiling woman and baby was already half empty and a copy of the *Daily Express* lay open on his desk.

'What is it, Carla? I'm busy.' Then he looked up, his pock-marked face clouded with anger, and when he saw it wasn't Carla who'd disturbed him he rose from his seat. 'Who the hell are you?'

Emily made the introductions and McNeil sunk back into his executive leather swivel chair, suddenly meek, the model of cooperation.

'We've been talking to Andrew Cassidy and he says he was with you on Saturday night till midnight.'

'Er . . . that's right. I took some papers round for him to have a look at. Why? Andy's not in any trouble, is he?'

Joe watched the man's expression. His eyes flickered from side to side as though he were searching for an escape route.

'Do estate agents usually deal with legal papers?' said Joe innocently. 'Isn't that usually dealt with by solicitors?'

'They were council reports . . . about planning permission on a property he's considering buying.'

'I see. You're absolutely sure you were with him all night? Was there any time he might have slipped out for half an hour, say? Or perhaps you weren't sure of the time you left.'

'I must admit I wasn't paying much attention to the time but I'm sure I left around midnight.' He hesitated. 'Or it could have been a little bit earlier, I suppose – say quarter to. I can't really be sure.'

'That's dedication to the job,' said Emily. 'You wouldn't find me working that late on a Saturday night unless I had no option . . . unless I had something like the death of a young student to investigate.'

McNeil gave her a smooth smile. 'It's different when it's your own company, Chief Inspector. You work whenever you have to and it was the only time Andy could fit the meeting in. He's a busy man.'

Joe looked at Emily. He could tell that, like him, she didn't much like the man but that didn't necessarily mean he was lying.

'Did you know Petulia Ferribie? She was one of Mr Cassidy's tenants at thirteen Torland Place.'

'No.'

'Do you and Andy Cassidy see much of each other?' Joe thought the question was worth asking.

'We have a drink from time to time. Mainly business.'

'How long have you known him?'

'Quite a few years actually.' Joe sensed that the subject was uncomfortable and he thought he knew the reason why.

'So you know about the time he spent in prison?'

McNeil looked away. 'Andy was ill. What he did was terrible but they put him in hospital, not prison.'

'Did you know his sister, Grace?'

It was a few seconds before McNeil answered. 'I'd met her but I didn't know her well.'

'I'm surprised you wanted to keep in touch with him.'

'I didn't particularly. But our paths crossed through work and . . . I wouldn't describe our relationship as close.' McNeil hesitated. 'Andy and I don't share the same interests, Inspector.'

'Go on.' Joe caught Emily's eye. He wanted McNeil to talk, to tell him everything he knew about Cassidy.

'Sometimes Andy makes me feel a little uncomfortable. His attitude to women and . . .' He shook his head. 'Like I said, I don't want to get him into trouble.'

'Please. We need to know everything.'

'It's just that he's a bit of a ladies' man – likes to go out to bars and clubs and parties. I'm happily married with a lovely baby daughter and . . . Well, I'm just not into that sort of thing any more.'

'What sort of thing?' Joe looked at Emily who was listening intently.

'Well, a couple of months ago he asked if I'd like to go to a strip club with him and a few friends. I made an excuse.'

'What about his girlfriend? Anna, is it?'

'I think she's just one in a long line.'

'Do you know the names of any of his other women?'

McNeil shrugged apologetically. 'Sorry. Like I said, I'm happily married and I don't take much interest in what he gets up to.'

'We'll send someone along to take a statement,' she said. 'And I'd be grateful if you had another think about the time you left Cassidy's on Saturday night. Perhaps you heard the news on the car radio or . . .'

'I'm pretty sure it was around midnight but . . .' Somehow he didn't sound very convincing.

As they took their leave, Joe gave a reassuring nod to the woman who had now resumed her place at the front desk.

'I think it's time we found out more about Mr Andrew Cassidy,' said Emily, shutting the office door behind her and stepping out on to the street.

ELEVEN

When they arrived at Cassidy's house Anna seemed nervous and Joe was careful to keep his dealings with her gentle. He said it was nothing to worry about and asked when she expected Cassidy home.

'I don't know. He never said.'

'Where's he gone?'

'Leeds. He has properties there,' she said. She sounded defensive and he wondered why.

'Were you here on Saturday night?'

'I went out to visit a friend but I came back later . . . about half past eleven.'

'Was Mr McNeil here when you got home?'

She hesitated, unsure of herself. 'I think so. But I did not

see him. They were in the room with the door shut. Business.
I went to bed early.'

'So Mr Cassidy was definitely here?'

She nodded warily.

'Your English is really good,' he said with an encouraging
smile. 'How did you meet Mr Cassidy?'

'I apply for a job as his cleaner. He advertise in the
newsagent's window.'

'And you became . . . involved?'

She thought for a moment and in the end she decided on a
nod.

In view of what they'd learned about Cassidy's past, there
were questions they had to ask. 'Would you say he has a
temper? Has he ever been violent towards you?'

She looked up sharply. 'No. What kind of a man do you
think he is?'

In the face of this spirited defence, Joe backed down. It was
clear that Anna wasn't going to dish any dirt on her lover.
And perhaps even her story about him being there at eleven
thirty on Saturday night couldn't really be trusted. Cassidy
had an alibi for Pet's murder alright – from a man who might
well be stretching the truth out of a misplaced sense of loyalty
and from a young woman who had a lot to lose. He looked
around the tastefully opulent room. Everything comes at a
price.

Emily's phone began to ring and she answered it. Her only
words were 'Right' and 'Thanks'. She ended the call and gave
him a nod of triumph. Cassidy had arrived home.

Emily put a hand on Anna's arm when they heard the front
door open. But even if she called out a warning, there were
a couple of DCs outside in an unmarked car who'd do the
necessary.

When the door to the drawing room opened, Cassidy hovered
on the threshold. 'What can I do for you this time?' He
addressed Joe, ignoring Emily.

Joe informed him that they were taking him in for questioning in connection with the murder of Petulia Ferribie and
recited the familiar words of the caution. And as Cassidy
was led out protesting his innocence, Joe saw that Anna was
crying.

*   *   *

Not everybody is delighted to see an exorcist sitting sipping tea in their kitchen, not even when he is known by the less dramatic title of Deliverance Minister, which Matt thought sounded like a cross between a midwife, a postman and a politician.

George Merryweather had arrived at thirteen Torland Place at midday and, fortunately, Matt had managed to get home just in time. He hardly wanted to leave the clergyman to the mercy of Caro or Jason who were sceptical at best, hostile at worst.

Matt had expected to see a cadaverous figure in a cloak rather than a round, middle aged, good-natured man in casual slacks and an open-necked shirt. He felt a little disappointed, as though the church were short-changing him. But on the other hand, he was rather relieved that the clergyman seemed so easy to talk to.

He had told George about the seance, the history of the house, the police enquiries about Jasmine and Pet's murder, and he was surprised when George said he'd already looked up Obediah Shrowton on the Internet. Somehow he hadn't associated exorcists with computer technology but then he remembered that he'd contacted him by email. Even those who deal with that most ancient of mysteries, the human soul, have to keep up to date these days.

'So you think there's a hostile presence in this house?' George asked gently.

Matt thought it sounded rather ridiculous when someone put it into words but he nodded.

'I'll begin by saying a prayer. It often does the trick, you know.'

Matt hadn't been in a church in years, not since his days in the cub scouts. But he sat there with his head bowed while George spoke softly to a God Matt hadn't really given a second thought to since childhood. He was surprised that, somehow, the words seemed comforting. And he was glad that Caro and Jason weren't there to sneer, as he knew they would.

When George finished Matt sensed that the atmosphere was a little lighter. Or maybe he was imagining it.

George was just finishing his mug of tea when the door opened.

'Who's this?' Caro stood there, arms folded, glaring at George.

George stood up and put out his hand. 'George Merryweather. Matt here asked me to pop round.'

'So who are you?' Jason stood behind Caro, looking as though he was ready to back her up and eject the interloper if necessary.

'I work at the cathedral.' George turned to Matt. 'You have my number. Get in touch any time, won't you. Don't bother to see me out.' He gave the two newcomers a friendly smile and left the room.

Once they'd heard the front door close Caro spoke. 'Who the hell was that?'

'Just someone I read about in the local paper. I thought he might be able to help.'

'With what?'

'This house. With Obediah Shrowton.' Suddenly Matt suspected that he'd gone over the top and felt his face redden with embarrassment.

'Who is he? Some weirdo psychic?'

Matt fished the newspaper cutting out of the pocket of his jeans and handed it to Caro. She read it then handed it to Jason who scanned it then gave a derisive snort.

'Deliverance Ministry. You don't believe all that crap do you?'

Matt glared at him. 'You seemed happy to believe in it when you were organizing that bloody seance.'

Jason shrugged, unable to think of an answer.

'Anyway, I think it's already working,' said Matt, gaining in courage. 'I think the place seems less . . . .'

'Less what?' said Jason, his face forming a sneer.

'Less . . . threatening.' He paused. 'Anyway, where were you when Pet died?'

Jason spun round and left the room, slamming the door behind him.

Each time Joe's phone rang, he feared it was Kirsten. She was lurking at the back of his mind, unpredictable and dangerous. If she chose to, she could make a lot of trouble. And he reckoned she was crazy enough to do it.

Cassidy was downstairs waiting to be interviewed. Joe had

been in favour of doing it right away but Emily had disagreed. She wanted to keep him in a state of nervous suspense to soften him up. It wasn't the first time he and Emily had disagreed on tactics, and he imagined it wouldn't be the last.

Joe needed some fresh air so he left police headquarters and walked towards the city centre. As he walked he could see the cathedral towers protruding above the rooftops reminding him that it was time he spoke to George to find out how he'd got on at Torland Place. There was something in that house that wasn't right. But could it have anything to do with Pet Ferribie's death? In the circumstances, every small possibility was worth following up.

When he reached the cathedral he entered by the main door and he was greeted by a row of counters issuing tickets to tourists. He watched for a while. All his instincts told him it was wrong to charge admission to what was, principally, a place of worship. On the other hand, the upkeep of the vast architectural treasure ate up millions of pounds each year so he supposed there was little option. But he hadn't just come to look so he sidled up to one of the staff and said he was there to see Canon Merryweather. He was admitted with a polite nod and he made his way into the nave.

He had been inside the cathedral so many times but its beauty never failed to astound him. He paused for a while and sat down, bowing his head, unsure what he was praying for: the bringing of Pet's killer to justice; a resolution to the twelve-year-old case of the two missing girls; or that Kirsten would get out of his life and stay out. He tried to concentrate. But it was useless.

He made for the north aisle, heading for the oasis of chaos that George Merryweather optimistically referred to as his office.

He pushed open the door and saw that George was still wearing his old anorak.

'Come in, come in. I've just got back from Torland Place.'

'How did you get on?'

George's smile vanished. 'I'm not sure.'

Joe cleared a pile of books off a chair and made himself as comfortable as possible.

'Matt seems a nice lad. More sensitive than his housemates, I'd say.'

'You met all of them?'

'Briefly. They seemed rather hostile to the idea of spiritual help. Not that I can blame them. The violent death of a friend must have come as a dreadful shock.'

'According to them, the dead girl wasn't really a friend. Apparently they all got on well in the hall of residence but when they moved into Torland Place, things changed.'

'I certainly sensed hostility in that house and I don't think it was just the sceptical housemates. Matt's right: there's something deeply unpleasant there.'

'You know about its history?'

'You mean Obediah Shrowton? Matt told me about the seance.'

'There's another case connected with that house.'

George leaned forward. 'Really?'

Joe told him about the two missing girls who'd vanished from the wood behind the house but he was careful not to mention Barrington Jenks, even though he knew George was the soul of discretion. When he had finished George sat in silence for a while, thinking.

'I remember those girls disappearing,' George said after a few moments. 'But I didn't realize that there was any connection with that particular house. It's strange how a location can become the hub of a series of unfortunate events,' he added quietly.

'You think that house is at the centre of all this?'

George smiled. 'I always keep an open mind.' He looked Joe in the eye. 'Is something else bothering you, Joe?'

Joe stood up and walked over to the far side of the room where he stood staring at a copy of Holman Hunt's 'Light of the World', the picture that graced a thousand vestries and vicarages throughout the land.

Then he turned to face George who was wearing an expression of patient expectation. 'Kaitlin's sister's contacted me.'

'Is that bad?'

'She's accusing me of Kaitlin's murder.'

George sat for a few seconds, still and silent. 'Where did she get this idea from?'

'She's been nosing around and she thinks she's come up with evidence.' He paused. When he'd first come to Eborby George had helped him through his grief – the combined grief caused by Kaitlin's death and the tragic shooting of his colleague, Kevin, some time later, an incident in which Joe himself had been seriously injured. Joe had shared his feelings and George had provided a sympathetic ear.

But there were some things he hadn't told George. Things that he'd been too ashamed to admit to. Things that, somehow, Kirsten had managed to discover.

'It's all nonsense, of course,' said George.

'Of course,' Joe replied quickly.

'Then tell her.'

'I have but she can still make life uncomfortable for me.'

'You must remember that she's lost a sister so she'll be looking round for someone to blame.'

'It was a long time ago.'

'The pain doesn't go away. You should know that.'

'She and Kaitlin never got on. She disappeared abroad just after our wedding and never bothered to keep in touch so I had no way of contacting her when . . . She's only recently found out that Kaitlin's dead.'

'That explains why she's behaving like this. She feels guilty that she didn't treat her sister better while she was alive. Be patient with her, Joe. That's all you can do.'

Joe stood there, wondering whether to share the truth with George. He was one of the few people he trusted absolutely but something made him hold back. He drained his mug and looked at his watch. It was time to get back to the incident room.

TWELVE

Cassidy sat facing Emily and Joe, his solicitor by his side. The solicitor was a young man who had the eager look of a novice to the game. There were times when Emily really missed Fred Hacker, the duty solicitor at her old station in Leeds. Fred had always believed in giving the police a fighting chance.

Emily gave the suspect a cool smile. 'I believe you knew the dead girl, Petulia Ferribie.'

'She was a tenant of mine.'

'You're no stranger to murder, are you, Mr Cassidy?'

Cassidy stared at her, opened his mouth to say something, then thought better of it.

'Did you think we wouldn't find out? Everything's on computer these days. We can bring up a name at the touch of a button and that marvellous little machine gives us chapter and verse on everything that person's done wrong. We know all about you, Mr Cassidy. We know what you did to your sister. We know about the secure hospital. I suppose when you've killed once it's easier the second time round. Was it easy to kill Pet? What have you done with the murder weapon, by the way? You might as well tell us because we've just sent a team round to search your house. If you tell us what you used and where it is now it'll save a lot of time.'

Emily looked sideways at the young solicitor, challenging him to argue. He made a feeble plea for his client not to say anything incriminating but, apart from that, it seemed that he'd run out of ideas.

She opened the file in front of her, going for the kill.

'At the age of sixteen you stabbed your younger sister, Grace, with a kitchen knife. You also cut off three of her fingers. She was a brilliant young pianist, by all accounts and you were jealous of her. I suppose it got too much for you, your sister getting all the adulation and attention.' She paused. 'It was the same with me and my sister,' she said. 'She was the blue-eyed girl, my parents sent her to a posh school while I had to make do with the local comp. It gets to you after a while, doesn't it? Festers like an infected wound.' She put her face close to his. 'Until you just can't stand it any longer. She was going to be my cousin's bridesmaid and I deliberately spilled ink on her dress.' She looked at Joe. 'You know, it's the first time I've ever told anyone.'

'I don't see what that's got to do with . . .'

'There were times when I felt that I could cheerfully kill my sister back then, Mr Cassidy. I didn't, of course or else I wouldn't be sitting here now heading a murder enquiry. But I know how it feels. I know what made you do it.'

Cassidy stood up, sending his chair flying backwards. The solicitor, alarmed, put a hand on his arm and hissed at him to sit down. But his advice was ignored.

'You don't know how it feels to be accused of something you didn't do. You don't know what it's like to be locked up for years with doctors bleating in your ear all the time, telling you they know what you're feeling. And when you tell them straight that you didn't do it, they shake their heads and smile and say you're in denial. Then you feel like punching their stupid, smug faces. What part of "I didn't kill her" don't you understand?'

Emily glanced at Joe. Somehow she hadn't expected such a violent reaction from Cassidy. The doctors might have been right about him erasing his horrific act from his memory. But, on the other hand, if he was innocent and nobody believed him, his adolescence must have been a living hell.

'But you acknowledged that you'd done it,' she said. 'You confessed.'

'Only because that was the only way to get them off my back. All the time the person who really killed my sister has been out there somewhere.' He paused. 'Have you spoken to Ian Zepper?'

'Are you suggesting that he had something to do with Grace's death? He had an alibi.'

'Provided by his wife. Wives have been known to lie for their husbands.'

'His wife's a well-respected medieval historian, I believe.'

'Everybody lies, Chief Inspector. You should know that by now. Even well-respected medieval historians. I've heard they've split up since then so maybe now she'll tell a different story.'

Emily stood up. 'We'll need to talk to you again, Mr Cassidy.'

The tape was switched off and the suspect led away to the cells to contemplate their next meeting.

'Maybe we should have another word with Zepper,' said Joe.

'Maybe. But whatever Cassidy says, his alibi was checked at the time and it stood up.'

Joe's mobile phone began to ring. As he answered it, Emily watched his expression carefully but she found it hard to tell whether the news was good or bad. He ended the call and looked at her.

'That was Sunny. Nothing incriminating's been found at Cassidy's house. But the tech people are going through his computer files as we speak.'

'He didn't kill her with a bleeding computer, Joe.'

Joe didn't answer and Emily regretted her sharpness. She was under pressure and the thought of some computer expert muddying the waters by turning up any fraudulent business dealings made her heart sink.

'Heard any more about Jenks?' she asked wearily. 'I just know the Super's going to summon me into his office some time soon to ask me if there's been any progress.'

'Surely he realizes that it's been pushed down our list of priorities.'

'If some miracle happens and I'm ever promoted to Super, don't let me get like that. If I ever start licking the arses of bigwigs and politicians, take me out and shoot me, will you.'

'Will do, ma'am. And there's been nothing more on Jenks. I've sent that video of the two girls off to the lab to be enhanced but . . .'

'What about Jasmine?'

He sighed. 'I was going to contact the university and ask them to go through their records but . . .'

'As it's linked to number thirteen we'd better get it done.'

'If we don't find her, it puts Barrington Jenks MP right at the scene when those girls disappeared.'

'Did you believe his story?'

'I don't know.'

They'd arrived at the incident room. It was buzzing with activity, which was just how Emily liked it.

'Anything to report?' she called out as she walked in, causing several officers to flock round her.

'Ma'am,' said Jamilla. 'The tech people have just been on. They've been going through Cassidy's computer and there's one file with a password they're still trying to get into.'

'Let me know when they do.'

Joe made for his desk and found the enhanced still from the video of the two missing girls had come back.

Emily watched while he opened the envelope. There in the bushes was a face. It was half concealed by foliage but it looked like a man and the arm pushing back the branch appeared to be tattooed – or perhaps it was the sunlight reflecting the mottled pattern of the leaves. He handed it straight to Emily and she stared at it for a while before touching

Joe's hand. 'The video was taken in Jade's garden. Her parents might know who this is.'

Joe nodded but she knew what he was thinking. Bothering the missing girls' parents again was the last thing either of them felt like doing.

Joe looked at his watch. It was six o'clock already. Emily was still in her office half buried in overtime request forms and witness statements. He rose from his seat and walked over to her office door and when he pushed it open she looked up.

'Come in, Joe. Sit down. I had hoped to get home for a couple of hours but . . .' She indicated the heap of files on her desk. 'What do you make of Cassidy?'

'He's a convicted killer. And his estate agent friend seemed a bit hazy about the time he left on the night of Pet's murder so his alibi could be shaky. And there's also the possibility that he has predatory sexual tastes.'

'We've found absolutely no evidence of that so far. But it's early days. What about the boys Pet lived with? Do you see either of them as a murderer? Similar motive, maybe . . . Thought they were on a promise . . .'

'Matt strikes me as being a nice lad. As for Jason . . . well, I'm not sure. He says he was out busking at the time of her death but, as yet, no witnesses . . . none that have come forward anyway. The removal of the tongue suggests to me that someone's silenced her. Or someone thinks she's betrayed them by something she's said. But I could be wrong,' he added with a smile. 'I have been before.'

'Haven't we all.' Emily glanced at the clock on her wall. 'I'd better phone Jeff and tell him I'll be a bit late again. Fancy getting something to eat before we start the evening shift?' Her eyes met Joe's. 'Sod the diet. You can't conduct a murder investigation on an empty stomach.'

Emily claimed to be fighting a constant war against flab but she always seemed to welcome any excuse to raise the white flag and surrender. She swept out of the office ahead of him and as they were leaving the building, Joe's heart lurched as he saw a familiar figure walking towards them.

Kirsten was bearing down on Joe like a ship in full sail, her pale trench coat open and flapping behind her in the breeze. And he knew that he had to take evasive action.

'Who's this?' said Emily, her eyes shining at the prospect of scandal. 'Looks like the vengeful mistress. What have you been up to?'

'I'll explain later,' he said. Kirsten was getting closer and there was no escape.

'I need to talk to you in private.' Kirsten said. Her hair was wild and she spoke with the conviction of an avenging angel.

Emily took herself off to sit on a vacant bench a few yards away, handbag on knee, straining to listen.

'What do you want, Kirsten?'

'I'm off to Devon. I'm going to get conclusive evidence.'

'You'll be wasting your time.'

She wasn't listening. 'And when I get it I'm going to give it to the relevant authorities.'

'Good. They'll find nothing and maybe then you'll leave me alone.'

She put her face close to his. He could smell her cloying perfume and feel her warm breath on his cheek. 'Oh I'll never do that, Joe. Even if you manage to fix it with the local police down there, I'll keep on until my sister gets justice.'

She swung round, almost hitting him with her shoulder bag, before rushing away. Emily had stood up and watched as Kirsten disappeared behind a neighbouring building.

'Come on, Joe, you've got to tell me. Who the hell was that?'

'My sister-in-law.'

'Something tells me she doesn't like you much.'

'You're not wrong there. I need a drink.'

They walked the quarter of a mile to the Star in silence. The pub was experiencing the quiet lull between the tourist invasion and the evening rush so they were able to claim a cosy seat in the corner of the lounge bar. Joe went to the bar and bought a pint of Black Sheep for himself and a red wine for Emily. He sat down and Emily took a long sip, smacking her lips with satisfaction. 'So, tell Aunty Emily your troubles.'

For a few moments Joe sat in silence, wondering where to begin. Then he launched on a brief summary of Kirsten's allegations.

'It's taken her long enough to get round to it.'

'I think that's the problem. She feels bad about neglecting her sister and she's taking it out on me.'

He picked up one of the cardboard menus that were propped up in the centre of the table. 'What are you having?'

'Lasagne. What about you?'

Joe scanned the menu. After his encounter with Kirsten his appetite had left him. 'I'll just have an omelette.'

'Don't let this business get to you.' She paused. 'Unless you're guilty, that is. Sorry, only joking. Do you want me to have a word with her? I'll put her right.'

Joe shook his head. He just wanted to change the subject and forget it.

He was relieved when the conversation moved on to the case and, as they ate, Emily used him as a sounding board to get things straight in her mind.

He couldn't get Barrington Jenks' connection with thirteen Torland Place out of his head somehow. And then there was George's interest in the place. A mass murderer had lived there, a man who had killed his family and servants. Something in Obediah Shrowton must have snapped to make him commit such an atrocious act and suddenly he wanted to find out more, although he doubted whether he'd have time with his current work commitments. Maybe when they found out what had become of Jade and Nerys, and Pet's killer was brought to justice.

They walked back to the police station through the narrow medieval streets with their overhanging upper storeys. At least, as far as Joe could tell, Kirsten hadn't decided to follow them.

After checking that nothing new had come in, Joe saw Jamilla sitting at her desk, tapping away at her computer. He walked over to her and perched on the corner of her desk. But she had nothing exciting to report. She'd taken the picture of the figure in the bushes to Jade Portright's parents but they had no idea who it was. The visit had been a waste of time and, according to Jamilla, had only served to raise the parents' hopes.

Joe made for Emily's office. The beer was making him feel a little drowsy. Perhaps he should have followed Emily's advice and eaten something more substantial than an omelette.

'You look how I feel,' said Emily with a sigh as he sat down.

But before she could say any more, Sunny burst in and,

from the expression on his face, Joe could tell that he was the bearer of interesting news.

'I've checked out those names like you asked, ma'am. Den Harvey, the handyman at the leisure centre, was questioned about the death of a woman eleven years ago. She was his girlfriend and she was stabbed in an alley near his house. His mother provided his alibi and nothing could be proved against him.' He paused. 'And there's something else. The victim's eyes were gouged out.'

Joe let the news sink in for a few seconds before speaking. 'We'd better bring him in then.'

Death felt at home in the darkened streets of Eborby, hood raised against the legions of watching CCTV cameras. Things had been so much easier for that man who'd killed five people so brutally in Valediction Street all those years ago.

He wanted the anonymity of darkness so he avoided the main thoroughfares filled with drinkers and tourists, favouring the narrow snickleways that ran between the older buildings and meandered between ancient streets. Some were framed by archways, others were just narrow passageways, part of the great rabbit warren that had been Eborby city centre since the middle ages. They bore names like Cheat's Yard, Slaughterman's Passage and Mad Maggie's Way. If Death hadn't been so preoccupied he would have found them interesting.

He passed the cathedral and hurried under the archway of Monks Bar. He knew where he was heading. He knew the Enemy.

When he reached his destination, he saw that the Enemy had left the blinds up, giving him a good view inside. He would have preferred to target the woman, but he hadn't been able to trace her address among all the Thwaites in the local phone directory. Plantagenet, however, had been an easy name to track down. And besides, there was bound to be a woman in his life. Or a close female friend or neighbour whose fate would cause him pain. It was just a question of watching and waiting.

Death kept his hidden vigil for a while until the Enemy appeared at the window and lowered the blinds.

Show over. For now.

THIRTEEN

When the team assembled at seven thirty the next morning, Emily briefed them about the murder of Den Harvey's girlfriend. Eighteen-year-old Sharon Bell's eyes had been stabbed repeatedly so that her face was left a bloody mask of horror. Den had been questioned, but his mother provided him with a watertight alibi which the investigating team had been unable to break.

At the time of Sharon's murder Den had been helping his mother prepare a room in a local church hall for a hot pot supper. Then mother and son had gone home to watch a TV programme; a detective series which was one of Mrs Harvey's favourites. When he'd been interviewed he'd been able to recite the whole plot, including the identity of the murderer. And, as the pair hadn't possessed a working video at the time, this was taken as proof that he was telling the truth.

'Why didn't the mum stay for the hot pot supper?' one of the DCs asked. It was something Joe had been wondering himself.

'She was caretaker of the church hall and she wasn't invited. But one of the event organizers – a Mrs Groves – locked up and dropped the keys off at the Harveys' house on her way home. She confirmed that both mother and son were in when she called. In fact Den answered the door. This was at ten.'

'So he was telling the truth.'

'Possibly. But there are distinct similarities between Sharon's death and Pet's. Both were stabbed twice in the chest before their faces were mutilated.' She looked round. 'I want some of you to go through the Sharon Bell files to see if there are any familiar names in there – anything that connects her with Pet Ferribie. At the moment the only link we've got is Den Harvey. I take it he's being brought in?'

'A patrol car's gone to pick him up, ma'am,' said Sunny.

'Good. I want to know when he arrives.'

Sunny held up a sheet of paper. There was more. 'That password protected file on Cassidy's computer – it was just accounts. Do you want someone to go through them . . . the fraud squad?'

'No, Sunny. We're too busy to do the tax man's dirty work for him. Leave it.'

She began to march towards her office just as one of the DCs burst in to announce Den Harvey's arrival.

She turned to Joe. 'I think we'll handle this one ourselves, eh. You ready?'

Den Harvey had been put in interview room number three, a windowless room painted a depressing shade of grey and lit by a pair of fluorescent strip lights. The table was bolted to the floor and what was at first glance a thin black dado rail half way up the wall was in reality a panic strip rather than a design statement. On the advice of his mother Harvey had requested the presence of the duty solicitor, a middle aged, overweight man who wore an expression of exasperated boredom on his flushed face. Joe knew it was nothing personal because he always looked like that.

'We'd like to talk to you about Sharon Bell,' said Joe after they'd introduced themselves for the benefit of the tape recorder humming at the far end of the table. 'You remember Sharon?'

Den glanced at the solicitor who was turning a pen over and over in his fingers. ''Course I remember her. She was my girlfriend.'

'She was murdered,' said Emily, looking him in the eye.

Den bowed his head. Joe could hear his breathing, fast and slightly wheezy. He fumbled in his pocket and pulled out a blue inhaler, held it to his lips and the thing gave a muted hiss. Emily watched and waited until his breathing eased. Then she spoke again.

'You were questioned at the time.'

Den looked up. 'I wouldn't have harmed a hair on her head.'

'I've heard that she was two timing you.'

Den shook his head vigorously and a small flurry of dandruff landed on the table's shiny black surface. 'That's a lie. She said she needed time to sort out her feelings, that's all.'

Joe leaned towards him, his fingers arched. 'How did you feel about that, Den?'

'I wasn't happy. But . . . Well, it was up to her, wasn't it?'

'Some people would get very upset about something like that. Upset enough to kill.'

'Not me.'

Joe spoke quietly. 'Sometimes something happens that overwhelms us . . . makes us lose control.'

'There's no way I'd have done anything like that. I was never one of those lads who'd carry a knife round to feel big. Ask anyone who knows me. Ask my mum.'

Emily asked the next question. 'Where did you meet Pet Ferribie?'

'I never met her.'

'Did she come to the leisure centre?'

'I don't know. I'm on the maintenance side so I don't see the punters.'

'When you found her body did you recognize her?'

'No way. Anyway, it was Peter who found her, not me.'

'But you were out there.'

'I'd only gone out for a smoke. I didn't see her. I had nothing to do with it.'

'What's worrying us, Den, is that there are some similarities between Pet's death and Sharon's. You see our problem, don't you? You knew Sharon and you're there when Pet's body is found. You're the connection between the two murders. Where were you at eleven thirty on Saturday night?'

'I was home. I was with my mum.'

Den put his head in his hands and when he looked up there were tears forming in his eyes. 'I didn't do anything,' he said. 'I'm innocent.'

'We'll need to search your house,' said Emily. 'We can get a warrant but it'll be easier all round if you give us your permission.'

'Go ahead. You won't find anything.'

Emily stood up, announcing that the interview was at a close.

'Can I go?' Den asked. He looked at the solicitor who was busy polishing his glasses on a grubby handkerchief.

'Not just yet,' said Emily. 'We'll need to talk to you again.'

As they stood up to leave, Joe found himself feeling a little sorry for the man.

Joe felt restless. He was still waiting for technical support to report on the location of Pet's mobile phone at the time Matt had called her and heard what were, he'd concluded with hindsight, her dying agonies. Pet's body had been dumped at the leisure centre but they needed to know where she'd died.

Emily had been summoned by the Super who had wanted an update on the Barrington Jenks connection. There was nothing much to report and Jenks would now be up in Westminster doing what the taxpayers paid him to do. He would return at the weekend to take his constituency surgery but until then he would be living in his sheltered parliamentary bubble.

The previous day Joe had contacted the university to ask them whether a student called Jasmine was registered at the appropriate time but either Jenks's Jasmine had lied about being a student or Jasmine wasn't her real name. Or there was always the possibility that Jenks hadn't told them the truth.

The phone on his desk rang. Scientific Support had traced Pet's mobile at the time of Matt's final call to her last Saturday night to the city centre. The Queen's Square and Fleshambles area. Not far from the place where she was last seen following the Waits during the music festival. He ended the call and sat for a while, wondering where somebody could imprison and murder somebody without exciting comment in such a busy, bustling district.

He wanted to speak to Matt again about the call. But before he did, there was something he had to check.

Jamilla was at her desk in the corner of the incident room going through witness statements, making notes. She looked as though she'd be glad of a distraction.

'Jamilla. Have you still got Pet Ferribie's address book?'

Jamilla leaned over and took a plastic bag containing a small book with a floral cover from a tray at the back of her desk. 'I've contacted everyone in there,' she said, handing the bag to Joe. 'It's remarkably empty for a girl of that age. There are a few old school friends. A cousin in Devizes. Her father's address in Dubai. But . . . Oh, I don't know. It just seems a bit odd.'

He looked at Jamilla for a few moments. From past experience he had learned to trust her judgement. 'When's the father coming?'

'Tomorrow. First flight he could get apparently.'

'Is Andy Cassidy's name in that book?'

'Yes. But no address. Just his number.'

'What about Ian Zepper?'

She opened the address book and handed it to Joe. On the page allocated to the letter Z, not usually the most populous of pages, were three numbers: one marked home, one marked uni and one marked mob, presumably for mobile. Zepper's home address in Pickby was also there. He flicked through the book until he found Cassidy. As Jamilla had already pointed out, there was no address, just a mobile number.

There was no entry for Den Harvey and the rest of the names in the book meant nothing to Joe, apart from the one under D for Dad. Pet's mum, so he'd been told, had disappeared when she was young, and had never attempted to contact her daughter again. Her stepmother, Jane Ferribie's mobile number was there but no address.

When he reached the back of the book something caught his eye. It was written in bold capital letters on the inside of the back cover. 'Paolo GP'. He stared at it for a while before handing the book back to Jamilla.

'Any idea who Paolo is? No address or phone number, just GP by the name.'

'A doctor perhaps?'

'Check if there's a GP called Paolo in the area, will you? Or maybe her father will be able to throw some light on it when he gets here. When I go to Torland Place I'll see if her housemates can tell me anything about it.'

Before he left the office, he asked one of the younger DCs to go through any available CCTV footage of the Fleshambles area at the relevant time. Pet's body had been moved. And if they were really lucky, the whole thing might have been caught on camera. But he wasn't getting his hopes up.

Caro hadn't been sleeping well. She tried to tell herself that it was Pet's murder that was making her jumpy but she knew that the real cause was that stupid seance and its aftermath.

Each night she lay awake in the darkness listening to the sounds. They seemed to be coming from somewhere above her, maybe in the sealed off loft they'd never been able to access. It didn't sound like birds; the sort of birds that nested in lofts didn't drag things around.

She had never been the imaginative type but recent events had changed all that. Everything seemed to have changed since Obediah Shrowton entered their lives.

When she heard the door bell ring she made her way downstairs. There was a shadow behind the stained glass of the front door and somehow she knew it was the police. But after Pet's murder, it was hardly surprising that they wouldn't leave them alone.

She opened the door. It was DI Plantagenet and he was smiling apologetically. 'I know you must be getting fed up with us but I'm afraid I need to speak to you again.'

Caro stepped aside to let him in. And then she turned and saw Matt standing in the living room doorway.

'I wanted to thank you for those photographs of the party,' Joe said.

'No problem.' Caro replied.

'We're still trying to identify that person dressed as the Grim Reaper.

'We've asked around but nobody knows who it was.' Caro hesitated. She'd kept her suspicions to herself for far too long for fear of making a fool of herself. 'I thought it might be Pet's tutor, Ian Zepper.'

'What made you think that?'

'Well she had a bit of thing for him and she was going to live in a flat in his house next year. The Grim Reaper – I don't know what else to call him – seemed to be watching her and I just thought she might have invited him, that's all.'

'Why didn't you say you thought it was him?' Matt spoke for the first time.

'Because I'm not sure. I didn't want to accuse someone who might be innocent.

'Dr Zepper says he wasn't at the party.'

'Then it wasn't him,' said Caro.

'There's something I'd like to ask you both. Have you ever heard Pet mention the name Paolo?'

Matt and Caro shook their heads.

'He might be a doctor – a GP?'

'We go to the university medical centre and I'm pretty sure there's no Paolo there.'

'Matt, I know we've gone over this before but have you remembered any more about that last phone call you made to Pet's number?'

Matt frowned. 'I've told you . . . it sounded like 'please . . . no.' Then there was a sort of . . .' He wrinkled his face in concentration, trying to find the right words. Then he made a noise, a cross between a gasp and a yelp. 'Look, it was over so quickly. I've gone over and over it in my head but that's all I remember.'

'Did you hear anything in the background?'

'Like what?'

'A voice, music, traffic. Anything.'

Matt shook his head. 'No, like I said the call only lasted a few seconds.'

Caro suddenly felt a wave of irritation. 'Look, why do you keep asking us all these questions? You should be out looking for whoever she met last Saturday. That's when she disappeared.'

'Following the Waits like that woman in the story,' Matt said softly.

'What's this?' Joe asked.

'It's just an old ghost story. A beautiful woman used to follow the Waits when they played in Queen's Square. When they moved off towards Stone Street she just vanished.'

'Eborby's got ghosts coming out of every orifice,' Caro said, annoyed with Matt for muddying the waters. 'Crap for the tourists.' She looked round for support but she couldn't read Matt's expression. He looked as if he was in a world of his own. A world where Pet might vanish and then reappear.

Once the DI had left, Matt went upstairs and Caro returned to her own room to settle down to work. A hefty dose of economic theory would dispel the demons that seemed to have moved into number thirteen since the day Pet disappeared. Or perhaps they had been there long before that, listening behind the battered skirting boards, hiding in crevices, stirring up trouble, disturbing the peace.

However, as soon as she'd sat down at her desk and opened her file, the door to her bedroom burst open and when she looked up she saw Jason standing there, breathless, as though he'd run up the stairs.

'I've just seen him.'

'Who?'

'Zepper. I asked him straight. Was it you dressed as the Grim Reaper?'

Caro stood up. This was something she needed to hear. 'And?'

'He denied it. Have the police checked his alibi?'

'Probably. Just leave it to them now.' She took a paper from her file, hoping Jason would take the hint that the conversation was at an end. But, on the other hand she couldn't ignore the fact that the Grim Reaper had been there, scythe and all. It had to be someone . . . and probably someone they knew. Caro had asked around everyone who'd been there but nobody had been able to throw any light on the mystery.

If she didn't change the subject, she knew Jason would go on and on about it, worrying at the subject like a dog with a bone. And she was getting heartily sick of thinking about Pet's murder. Pet had irritated her in life and she was continuing to do so in death.

Jason turned to go. But Caro had a question.

'Have you ever heard weird noises from the loft . . . as though someone's up there?'

'I thought it was pigeons.'

'It's not birds.'

'Well we can't get up there to have a look cause the entrance is sealed up.'

'Which is odd, don't you think? I mean the water tanks must be up there and . . .'

Jason's eyes lit up as though he'd suddenly been struck by a brilliant idea. 'Why don't we have another seance? We can try and get in touch with Pet. She can tell us who killed her.'

'That's sick. Now piss off and leave me alone. I've got work to do.'

'Mind old Obediah doesn't get you in the night,' Jason said with a chuckle as he stalked off down the landing, leaving Caro's door wide open.

The black cloth lay in the bottom of the incinerator, licked here and there by orange tongues of flame. Soon the cloth would be reduced to a pile of grey but the mask and the scythe were more problematic. Plastic melts and leaves a sticky mess that, once cool, solidifies into a mutilated residue. But the remains could be buried in a place where nobody would think to look, all evidence destroyed.

Death gave the fire a hard prod with an old wooden stake. It was almost time to kill again. But he had no need of a uniform to complete the task.

FOURTEEN

There had been a time when Joe had enjoyed solitude. When he'd just left university a life of spiritual contemplation had seemed so attractive. The peace, the connection with the eternal, the chance to consider the great questions of life. But love and age had altered everything and since he and Maddy had decided on an amicable parting, the thought of returning to his silent flat each night depressed him a little.

He thought of Emily with her chaotic home life. She moaned about it sometimes, saying that juggling her priorities left her exhausted. But as he entered his narrow hallway, he would have done anything to exchange places with her.

He heard the phone ring and he froze for a few seconds before picking up the receiver.

It was her. But some instinct had told him that already.

He took a deep breath. 'Kirsten. What can I do for you this time?'

'I'm in Devon.'

'And?'

'I'm going to ask the police down here to reopen the case.'

'You need evidence to do that.'

'I'll get it. I hear that you've been living with another woman. You never mentioned her.'

'That's because it's none of your business.' He suddenly realized that he sounded too defensive – as though he had something to hide.

'You haven't killed her as well, have you?'

'We decided to go our separate ways and she's in London now. And I've never killed anyone.'

'That's a lie.'

'What do you want? I'm busy.'

'I think I've found a witness.'

'A witness to what?'

'Wouldn't you like to know? I'll be in touch.'

He stood there listening to the dialling tone and wondering

whether, if Kirsten had been standing there in front of him, he'd be tempted to commit murder. Are we all capable of the ultimate act of violence, given the right provocation? He'd known the answer once in his seminary days. Original sin. But now he lived in a world of doubts and he sometimes longed for the old certainties.

He needed to get Kirsten out of his head so once he'd eaten he took out his laptop. Before her call something had been nagging at the back of his mind and when he typed in the name Obediah Shrowton he was surprised by the number of sites dedicated to famous killers. The poor old policemen who brought them to justice didn't seem to be afforded any similar immortality, which struck him as rather unfair.

There were pages dedicated to Obediah and his dreadful deed but Joe clicked straight on to an account of the trial. He needed the facts without sensational additions.

Obediah Shrowton had been a devout and upright man and in that courtroom he had sworn on the Bible that he was innocent of all the charges laid against him. He never wavered from his story that he'd arrived home to find a dreadful scene of carnage and that he'd collapsed with shock after trying to revive the blood-covered victims, hoping one or more of them might still be alive.

But the thing that caught his attention particularly was Shrowton's assertion that before the murders he'd been receiving threats which he hadn't taken seriously. He also named the culprit in court: a young butcher called Jacob Caddy who had harassed his wife after she'd rejected his advances. Caddy, however, had been given an alibi by his mother and the police found no evidence against him. But then any potential witnesses to his alleged harassment had been hacked to death at number thirteen Valediction Street.

Joe closed the lid of the computer. Maybe it was wrong to leap to the obvious conclusions.

Cassidy had left the house without a word, leaving Anna seething with resentment as she always did when he treated her like a servant. When they had begun sleeping together she had assumed that her status in the house would rocket. But little had changed; she still worked and cooked while he made use of her.

She peeled another potato for that night's meal, comforting herself with various scenarios of revenge. She could steal his credit cards and take the train to Leeds where she could hit Harvey Nichols before he'd even know she'd gone.

Or, alternatively, she could make a bit of trouble for him. She'd seen him with the murdered girl, Pet. He had taken her into the drawing room, closing the door so that she couldn't overhear what they were saying or doing. She knew that he hadn't mentioned the girl's visit to the police, just as he hadn't told them about that man who sometimes called – the scruffy one who worked at the leisure centre where the girl's body had been found. There was a lot she could tell the police about Cassidy. But first she needed to check something out.

She abandoned the potatoes and helped herself to a glass of wine from the open bottle on the worktop. If Andy was arrested and put in prison, would she have this lovely house all to herself? She would have to use all her cunning but she was sure that she could manage it. After all, she'd be doing him a favour . . . looking after his property while he served a life sentence.

She put the glass down and picked up the phone. This would be easy.

Matt had never considered himself to be a violent man and he had never felt the temptation to hit anybody before. But when Jason had said that he wanted to get in touch with Pet to ask her who'd killed her, he'd lost control and landed a rather feeble punch on Jason's jaw. Jason had wanted to make her death into a silly parlour game. In Matt's opinion he should have showed more respect.

Jason had merely smiled that maddening, superior smile of his before accusing Matt of being scared of what Pet might say. Maybe he was the killer and he didn't want the truth to come out. Matt hadn't dignified this with a reply. But the fury he felt had surprised him. Perhaps he was capable of murder after all. He'd certainly felt like killing Jason that evening and the realization disturbed him. Then Jason had gone out with his guitar, saying he was going to do a bit of late night busking. Maybe he knew he'd pushed things too far.

Now it was almost eleven and Matt sat in bed; but he knew he wouldn't sleep because it was bound to begin again at any moment. The footsteps, the dragging, the hint of voices which could be the wind in the chimney. It would be there above his head. He held his breath and waited.

There it was. Tap tap tap. Then a dragging sound. Then silence again.

Matt hugged the duvet around him and suddenly felt a desperate need to talk to someone who wouldn't judge him . . . who wouldn't call him stupid. He found the card George Merryweather had left and picked up his mobile phone off the bedside table. He knew it was late but he needed help.

'George,' he said when he heard a voice on the other end. 'It's Matt Bawtry from Torland Place.'

'You sound worried,' said George. 'I'm listening. Take your time.'

'There are noises . . . above my room. In the attic.'

'Have you had a look up there?'

'It's sealed off.'

'I'm sure there'll be some simple explanation but if it's worrying you I'll call in again if you like.'

Matt could feel his heart beating fast. 'Can you come now?'

George hesitated. 'Can it wait till tomorrow? I'll call first thing. Then perhaps we can take more . . . more drastic measures to sort out your little problem. And I assure you that even if there is a restless presence, it's unlikely to do you or your friends any harm.'

That was it. He'd have to wait there in that room overlooking the woods until the morning with God knows what going on above him. He lay down in the bed, keeping his bedside light on, and shut out the world by pulling the duvet over his head.

But the silence seemed worse than the noises.

When Anna reached the cathedral she tried Andy's mobile number but there was no reply so she put her phone back in her bag.

She felt a little nervous now as she walked through the darkened, winding streets. Eborby seemed to have a strange atmosphere at night, as though there was something there beyond what she could see; as though the air was filled with all those busy ghosts from the city's past, going about their business like their mortal counterparts.

There was a chill in the air and she pulled her coat tightly around her as she passed an open pub door, catching a whiff of stale beer and fried food mingled with the stronger smell of tobacco smoke from the huddle of smokers gathered outside the front door, puffing away with intense concentration.

She reached the end of Pottergate and found herself in Queen's Square. A busker, a slender boy with a beautiful face and dark curls, was singing beneath the trees in the centre of the square while passing tourists, mellowed by wine, threw coins into his guitar case. Anna watched him for a while before hurrying past. He was good but she was too concerned with her own problems to be generous.

The narrow mouth of the Fleshambles was directly in front of her. The top storeys of the buildings there almost met above the street and as she walked past the wide windowsills where the city's butchers had once displayed their bloody wares, the street felt like a tunnel. There were still tourists about, lapping up the quaintness, but none of them noticed Anna slipping down a narrow snickleway between two shops. She could see the market square at the end of the passage but instead of walking on she turned right and stopped. Although everywhere was in darkness she knew this was it.

She pushed the door and it swung open silently to reveal a flight of narrow stairs. She climbed them slowly and when she reached the top she heard the front door behind her open and bang shut.

And when she turned round she gave the newcomer a tentative smile.

FIFTEEN

Thursday morning was dull with an icy chill in the air, which wasn't unusual March weather in that part of North Yorkshire. As Joe had been unable to sleep, he'd arrived in the office at six thirty, reasoning that he might as well make use of the early hour to go through reported sightings of Pet Ferribie between the time of her disappearance and her death. Not that he believed any of them. He was as sure as he could be that she'd been abducted shortly after she was last caught on CCTV and kept somewhere until her killer was ready to dispose of her.

Den Harvey had been released late the previous day after a spate of fruitless questioning and Joe now seized the chance to familiarize himself further with the murder of Sharon Bell. Because of the similarities to Pet's murder, he was as sure as he could be that the same killer was responsible. And there was always the possibility that there had been more than two victims.

By the time Emily arrived at work he had discovered one nugget of gold buried in the mountain of paperwork. The team investigating the murder of Sharon Bell had interviewed a friend of Den Harvey's – one Andrew Cassidy. As Joe entered Emily's office to break the news of this unexpected connection, he noticed that she looked tired, as though she'd dragged herself out of bed with considerable effort.

'We'd better have another word with Cassidy,' she said. 'He knew both dead girls, Pet and Sharon. And his sister, Grace Cassidy, was stabbed like the others.'

'But her hand was mutilated instead of her face.'

'If it had been her face we might have made a connection sooner.'

'Pet was found at Harvey's place of work so he's not off the hook yet. Cassidy might have introduced him to her.'

'OK. We'll talk to Harvey then we'll give Cassidy another grilling.'

They walked down the corridor side by side and Joe noticed Emily give the stairs to the upper floors a quick, fearful glance as she passed.

He knew what was on her mind. 'Has the Super mentioned Barrington Jenks recently?'

'No. Jenks is in London for the week.'

'So when are we going to break the news to him that this Jasmine doesn't exist?'

'She might exist, Joe. She might not have told him her real name. She might have chosen something more exotic to create the right impression.'

'I think old Quillan, the ex-landlord, recognized the name.'

Emily gave him a knowing look. 'Perhaps our Jasmine paid her rent in kind.'

'Mmm. There's something odd about the Jasmine story and

we need to get to the bottom of it. I want to have another word with the families of Nerys and Jade.'

Emily rolled her eyes. 'Must we, Joe? It'll only get their hopes up.'

'We don't know for sure that those girls are dead. No bodies have ever been found.'

Emily didn't answer and Joe knew that years of experience had taught her to be pessimistic. But he still preferred to cling to a scrap of hope, however tiny.

They drove to Bearsley and Joe parked the car outside Den Harvey's terraced house. The pavement was filled with overflowing wheelie bins and as they emerged from the car Joe could hear the low growl of a bin lorry somewhere in the distance, the next street perhaps.

They'd already checked that Den was on a late shift so, with any luck, they'd find him – and his mother – at home.

Den himself answered the door and it was hard to read his expression as he stepped aside to let them in. It might have been bored resignation but Joe didn't think it looked like guilt.

Den led them into the front parlour; a room untouched by time. There was no TV here; this was a room kept for best and for visitors. When Den had been interviewed about Sharon Bell's murder this was no doubt where the initial questioning had taken place. Now history was repeating itself as it often seemed to.

Den closed the door behind him and invited them to sit. 'I can't tell you any more than I did yesterday,' he said, sounding a little defensive.

'We've been looking at the Sharon Bell case and we've come across something we'd like to ask you about,' Joe began.

Den looked wary. 'What's that?'

At that moment the door burst open and an elderly woman stepped into the room. She was tall and the old-fashioned crossover apron she wore emphasized her barrel-like figure. It was a long time since Joe had seen an apron like that and on Mrs Harvey it looked as formidable as armour.

'Why can't you leave him alone?' she said. 'You had him at that police station for hours yesterday. I've already said he was here with me. Are you calling me a liar?' She put her hands on her hips, a mother defending her young.

'No, of course not, Mrs Harvey,' said Emily sweetly. 'We just think Dennis might be able to help us, that's all. He's not under arrest.' The word 'yet' hung in the air unsaid.

Mrs Harvey sat down beside her son who looked rather embarrassed. But it was her house and unless they took Den down to the station again for questioning, there was nothing much they could do to get rid of her.

On the other hand, Joe thought, she might be useful. Mothers often remembered the most surprising things about their sons' friends.

'Do you know a man called Andrew Cassidy?'

Joe saw Den glance at his mother, as though seeking permission to reply. In the end it was Mrs Harvey who got in first.

'Andy. You remember Andy, Dennis. He got put away for killing his sister. And I'd thought he was such a nice boy. Always very polite. His family lived in a big house in Bacombe. And he went to St William's School.' She looked at Emily as though she expected her to be impressed. 'I were right pleased when our Dennis started to go round with him. He weren't like some of the lads round here.'

Joe smiled to himself. This woman was a snob and, to her, the big house in Bacombe and the place at a private school seemed to trump the inescapable fact that the boy had murdered his own sister and spent time in a secure hospital.

'How did you come to know Andy?' Emily addressed the question directly to the son.

'It were at that camp, weren't it, Dennis?'

'Is that right, Den?' said Emily. 'Which camp was this?'

'It was held once a year in the summer holidays,' said Mrs Harvey answered. 'Yorkshire Schools and Youth camp. YSY. Isn't that right, Dennis? I didn't want you to go but your teacher said it would do you good.'

Den nodded meekly.

'So you met Andy at this camp?' said Emily.

This time Den got in first. 'Aye. We were in the same dormitory. We found out we were both from Eborby so we stayed in touch when we got home.'

'And you saw each other often?'

'There was a time when Andrew was always round here, wasn't there, Dennis?' the mother butted in proudly. 'And you went to see him. You stayed over sometimes.'

'Was that around the time his sister was murdered?'

Mrs Harvey's expression changed. She opened her mouth to speak but no sound came out.

'Yeah. Mum wouldn't let me go round there after that,' said Den matter-of-factly.

'You knew his sister?'

'Yeah. She was very good at the piano and she let me have a go once.'

'Did you ever meet her piano teacher – Ian Zepper his name was?'

Den nodded earnestly. 'Aye.' He hesitated. 'When he was there, she was different . . . all flirty with him, like. They used to be locked away in that room for hours on end.'

'You think there was something going on?'

Den shrugged. 'I don't know. Might have been.'

'Have you seen Andy since he was released?'

Den wavered for a few moments. 'Once or twice.' He glanced at his mother.

'Do you mind if we talk to Dennis alone, Mrs Harvey?' said Emily in a tone that brooked no argument.

Mrs Harvey stayed put for a few seconds but eventually she hauled herself out of her armchair with some difficulty, telling Den that she'd only be in the next room if he needed her. Joe watched her shuffle slowly from the room, each painful movement exaggerated for their benefit.

Once his mother had gone Den seemed to relax and Joe found himself feeling a little sorry for him. But he wouldn't let pity influence his judgement.

'We've not had a look at your computer yet, have we, Den?' Joe said.

'You can't. Not without a search warrant.' He sounded nervous, as though there was something on that computer he didn't want them to see.

'We can get one but it'll be much easier if you just let our technical people have a look at it. They'll take good care of it.'

Den's face turned an unpleasant shade of red. 'I need it.'

'We won't keep it long,' Joe said by way of reassurance as Emily made a quick call to Scientific Support. 'Where was Andy when Sharon was killed?'

'He'd just got out of prison . . . or hospital or whatever they called it.'

Joe had been wondering whether Sharon had died while Cassidy was behind bars but now it looked as though he was still in the frame.

'Did you kill Sharon, Den?'

The man's face twisted with anguish. 'Of course not. I loved her. She was fantastic.' There was a long pause. Then 'I haven't always been like this. I used to want to be a teacher . . . go to uni. But after she died I just went to pieces.'

'I thought you'd had a row on the night she died.'

'That wasn't serious. I wouldn't have harmed a hair on her head. Anyway, I was with Mum when it happened. I wish to God I'd gone to the pictures with Sharon like she asked but Mum wanted me to help with . . . That's what we rowed about, if you must know. Me being so bloody weak.'

'Any chance Sharon went to the pictures with someone else?'

'No. She wasn't two-timing me . . . that was a lie.'

'Andy Cassidy was the landlord of the girl whose body was found at the leisure centre. If you and he were friends you might have met her.'

Den shook his head vigorously. 'I never met her.'

'You seem very sure.'

'I am. I never saw her till . . .'

'Did Andy ever mention her?'

Den took a deep breath. 'He might have done.'

'What did he say?'

'Just that he was helping her with something. And before you ask I don't know what it was.'

'When did you last see him?'

'A few days ago.'

'Where did you see him?'

'At his house. I went there.'

'When?'

He thought for a moment. 'Monday night.'

'After you'd found Petulia's body?'

He nodded. 'Yeah. I needed to talk to him but she said he was busy.'

'She? Do you mean Anna, the Polish girl he lives with?'

'She wasn't very nice to me. She told me he was busy but when he came to see who was at the door he asked me in,' he said with a hint of triumph.

'And what did you want to see him about?'

'That's private.'

'Nothing's private to us,' said Emily sharply.

'It's got nothing to do with the police.'

'You're not doing yourself any favours being obstructive like this.'

'I'm not being obstructive. Some things are private, that's all.'

Joe decided on a new approach. 'Have you seen Grace Cassidy's piano teacher, Ian Zepper, since she died?'

'No.'

Emily touched Joe's arm and he followed her out into the hall. Mrs Harvey was doing something noisy in the kitchen and she had the door open, watching them intently. Emily whispered to Joe that Scientific Support said they'd be over right away and she didn't want to leave Den alone with his computer so that he had a chance to delete anything relevant. When they returned to the front parlour and sat down Den was looking increasingly nervous. There was definitely something he was holding back.

'Perhaps it would be best if you came back to the police station with us to answer some more questions,' said Emily.

'Why? I've already told you that I don't know nothing about that girl's murder. I haven't done nothing.'

'You were a suspect in Sharon's murder and now you're connected with another girl murdered in a similar way.'

'I haven't done anything wrong.'

'Get out of this house.'

Mrs Harvey was standing by the door, arms folded. 'He had nothing to do with Sharon's murder . . . or this latest one. You asked him where he was on Saturday night . . . well he was here with me. And I'll swear to that in any court in the land. Now get out.'

At that moment the doorbell rang and Joe could see the relief in Emily's eyes. The cavalry in the shape of Scientific Support had arrived.

'We'll need to take your computer away, Den. We'll let you have it back as soon as we can.'

Den Harvey looked distraught. But he knew better than to argue.

*   *   *

When Joe returned to the office there was a message waiting on his desk. Please ring Steve Portright. It took Joe a few seconds to place the name before he realized that Steve Portright was Jade's father.

He looked at his watch. Cassidy hadn't been answering his phone and it would be a while before Scientific Support came up with anything on Den Harvey's computer so he made the call.

Portright sounded agitated and said he needed to talk urgently. Joe told him he'd be round as soon as he could.

When he told Emily where he was off to, she asked if he wanted company but he reckoned that Portright would be more forthcoming if they talked man to man.

'I just hope Jamilla's visit hasn't raised their hopes,' Emily said as he turned to leave.

He drove out to the Portrights' address in a neat cul-de-sac of small red-brick, semi-detached houses about half a mile from where their daughter was last seen. The houses had been built for workers in the nearby chocolate factory by their benevolent employer but the chocolate factory was now owned by a multinational company and many of the houses had been sold on the open market.

He knew from the files that Steve Portright and his wife both worked in the factory. But today they were home. And this made Joe suspect that something had happened.

Mrs Portright – Sue – answered the door and invited him in. She was a small, thin woman with short, bottle blonde hair. Her face was heavily lined and she smelled of tobacco. She had the look of someone who lived on her nerves.

She led Joe into a small living room where there wasn't a thing out of place; not a spot of fluff on the pale carpet or a cushion dented by human form. Joe wondered how anybody could live like that.

'Your husband said he had something important to tell us.'

The door opened and the man who stood there was below average height with the pugnacious look of a fighting dog. His head was shaved and he wore a T-shirt that showed off a pair of tattooed arms. Joe couldn't see much resemblance between Jade and either of her parents. But he'd never had a chance to see her in the flesh; film and photograph can deceive.

Joe shook hands with the man and sat down. 'You said you had something important to tell us.'

'I've seen her. I've seen our Jade.'

'Seen her? Where?'

'In town. Coming out of Boots on Coopergate at eleven thirty this morning. I've taken a bit of time off work and I got the bus into town to pick up a fishing rod I'd ordered and I just saw her coming out of the shop. Then when I called out to her she disappeared.'

'Do you think she heard you?' Joe didn't think for one moment that Portright had really spotted his daughter. It was probably a case of wishful thinking.

'She sort of half looked round and . . . she heard me alright.'

'And you were sure it was her, weren't you, love?' It was Mrs Portright who spoke. She sounded as though she was trying to convince herself that her husband's story was true.

Joe sat in silence for a few moments. This couple wanted to believe in their own personal miracle but it was up to him to play devil's advocate.

'How come you're so certain that it was her? If she is . . . if she is still alive then she'll have changed a lot in twelve years.'

Steve Portright leaned forward and jabbed an accusing finger at Joe. 'I'd recognize my own daughter anywhere.'

'Perhaps it was someone who looked like her. Look, I'm sorry to seem so negative but we have to be sure before we take any action.'

'She looked round and I saw her eyes. One was slightly lighter than the other – only slightly, most people wouldn't notice. It must be in your files.'

'So you got quite near to her?'

'About twelve feet away.'

'If it was Jade, why didn't she acknowledge you?'

Steve Portright shifted awkwardly in his seat. 'We had a row before she . . . Maybe she feels awkward about it. Look, we only want a chance to make things right.'

'Remind me what the row was about.' Joe had read it in the file but he wanted to hear it from the parents' lips.

'She wanted to go to this club in town and stay out late and . . . just the usual teenage stuff.'

Joe nodded. To the teenage mind that might have been worth a token protest, maybe even staying away for a couple of nights. But twelve years of making your parents think you're dead? Somehow he couldn't quite see it.

Joe stood up. 'I'll get someone to go through any CCTV footage we can find of the Coopergate area at that time. We might need you to point out the woman you think is your daughter.'

'It was my daughter. We'll find her. I know we will.'

Joe glanced at Mrs Portright who was sucking on a freshly lit cigarette. She didn't look as confident as her husband.

In fact Joe thought she looked a little frightened.

When Andy Cassidy had returned from Leeds the previous night before it had been late. Normally Anna would have been there waiting for him but the house had been in total darkness and there was no sign of her.

He'd checked her wardrobe but he could see nothing missing apart from her handbag and the coat she usually wore. Then, feeling exhausted, he'd undressed and climbed into bed.

When he awoke the next day and realized that she still hadn't come home, he wondered whether he should report her missing. But involving the police would only draw attention to himself. And that was the last thing he wanted.

He spent the morning in a meeting at the Council offices near the library, his mind still on Anna, and at two o'clock he called in to his house, only to find that everything was just as he'd left it that morning.

He saw the light blinking on his answering machine and he rushed to listen to the messages. But his heart sank when he heard it was Inspector Plantagenet. He wanted another word.

Cassidy sat for a while, contemplating the best course of action. He had to get the police off his back somehow.

As he was just about to go into the kitchen and make himself a drink, the doorbell rang and he stood there, statue still, torn between pretending he wasn't in and facing whatever the police had in store for him. Eventually he walked slowly out into the hall and when he peeped through the spy hole in the front door, he saw Joe Plantagenet standing on his doorstep beside the plump blonde DCI.

'We'd like to talk to you about Den Harvey,' Joe said as they stepped inside.

Cassidy led them through to the drawing room and invited them to sit.

'You know Den Harvey?'

'I know him.'

'You met at a school camp when you were teenagers.'

'That's right. YSY. The aim was to bring different social classes together from schools all over Yorkshire. I was at St William's and Den was at the local comp. We got on pretty well for a while so I suppose we were one of YSY's successes.' He looked the Inspector in the eye, the model of cooperation.

'And you stayed friends after you were convicted of killing your sister.'

'We lost touch for a while. But recently we've met up a few times.'

'Den was there when Pet Ferribie's body was found,' said Emily. 'Now I've never really believed in coincidences like that.'

'Eborby's not a huge city, Chief Inspector.'

Emily leaned forward until Cassidy could almost feel her warm breath on his cheek. 'He seems an unlikely friend for someone like you to cultivate.'

'Den's brighter than he looks. And he hasn't always been such a slob. He was OK before he let himself go and put on all that weight, although he was always a bit of a mummy's boy. If Sharon hadn't died I reckon it would have been a different story: he'd have cut the apron strings and flown the nest. Instead he turned into a sad loser. I feel sorry for him, if you must know. He's had a raw deal.'

'You knew Sharon?'

'She was a nice kid. Bit wary of me though.'

'Hardly surprising.'

'I was innocent so she had no reason to be worried.'

'What's your relationship with Den now?'

'Like I said, we meet up sometimes.'

'So what do you have in common?' she paused. 'Adventurous sexual tastes? You admitted yourself that you're a bit of a ladies' man.'

Cassidy could feel his face burning and hoped it wouldn't be noticed. 'My tastes are pretty tame really.'

'Did you ask Pet to join in with any adventurous activities?'

Cassidy shook his head vigorously, annoyed at the implication of the question. 'No way. What do you think I am?'

'That's what we're trying to find out,' said Joe. 'I can't help feeling there's something we're missing.'

Cassidy gave him a guarded smile, sensing they were moving on to dangerous ground.

'Have you any photographs of that YSY camp you were at?' the DCI asked sweetly.

Cassidy thought for a moment. Then he remembered the box of keepsakes he'd brought from his childhood home; the box he'd put in the back of a cupboard and never opened because he knew it contained pictures of his sister. He hauled himself out of his seat, suddenly feeling like an old man. The weight of memory was a heavy burden.

He left the room and returned five minutes later with a photograph – a group picture in faded colour of adolescent boys, casually posed in front of what looked like a log cabin. There were some boys in the background too but they obviously weren't meant to be included in the picture. He handed it to the DCI.

'This is some of the Eborby contingent. That's Den there.'

He saw the two officers peer at the picture as though they hoped it contained the answer to all their problems. But eventually they gave up.

'Do you mind if we borrow this picture?'

Cassidy nodded.

'Where's Anna?' Joe asked.

'I'm not sure. She didn't say where she was going.'

This seemed to satisfy them. But as they were making for the door Joe turned to face him. 'We've spoken to Ian Zepper.'

Cassidy felt his heart begin to thump against his chest.

'I understand that his relationship with Grace was close.'

'That's one way of putting it.'

'You think it was . . . inappropriate?'

Cassidy walked over to the window and stared out for a few moments, considering his reply. 'She was only fifteen and she was infatuated with him. And yes, I think they were having sex.'

'Did your parents suspect?'

'My dad was on his own . . . too busy to bother much. And Zepper talked the talk – how Grace was so talented and he wanted to develop that talent and all that crap. He and Grace had a row about a piece of music she wanted to play for an exam. He had a temper.' He paused. 'And whoever killed her hacked off her fingers.' He saw the two police officers look at each other. 'Zepper said it was just a difference of opinion about a piece of music. He said it didn't really matter that much and the police believed him.'

'Did you?'

'I'd like to prove he was lying. I'd like to clear my name.'

'Thank you, Mr Cassidy. You've been very helpful.'

They were words Andy Cassidy had never expected to hear from a police officer and he couldn't help smiling to himself as he shut the door.

When Joe returned to the incident room there was a message from George Merryweather waiting on his desk. Could Joe ring him back? Joe dialled George's number and the phone was picked up after three rings.

'Joe, I'm glad it's you. I'm worried about something . . . and it involves a murder victim.'

Joe sat back in his seat, picked up a pen and began to doodle on a blank sheet of paper in front of him. 'Go on.'

'Have you eaten?'

Joe looked at his watch. It was two o'clock already and he'd had nothing since breakfast. 'I'll see you at the National Trust café in fifteen minutes.'

He thought he'd better let Emily know where he was going and as he entered her office she put phone down with a sigh.

'Pet's dad's arrived from Dubai. He'll be here about four.'

'I'm going to have a word with George Merryweather. He says he has some information for me.'

She smirked. 'The Exorcist. Has he got a message from the other side?'

Joe rolled his eyes. He'd heard it all before. 'He's been talking to Pet's housemates. Maybe they told him things they wouldn't tell the police. I won't be long.'

'You'd better not be.' She paused. 'Do you think Jade is alive?'

'Do you?'

'The poor bloke's probably clutching at straws.'

Joe raised his eyebrows. 'I know it sounds awful to say this but I didn't like Steve Portright.'

Emily gave him a conspiratorial smile. 'Tell you the truth, Joe, neither did I. But none of the parents were suspected at the time. Off you go then,' she said with a wink.

Joe hurried out of the building and walked quickly through the streets to the cathedral, weaving in and out of ambling tourists. He reached Vicars Green and saw the National Trust café on the corner where the Green meets Gallowgate. George was waiting for him as promised at a corner table and they ordered sandwiches and a pot of tea to keep body and soul together.

They lowered their voices, which was probably unnecessary as the young woman on the table next to them was preoccupied with keeping her two young children entertained and under control. Joe found himself watching her. He would have liked children himself but life hadn't worked out that way. He caught the young woman's eye and smiled but she shot him a suspicious look.

'Now then, George, what did you want to tell me?'

'I had a phone call from Matt Bawtry last night. He was in a bit of a state. He's been hearing odd noises. And he had a fight with Jason last night because he wanted to hold a seance to contact the murdered girl.'

'I'm surprised Caro didn't put a stop to it.'

'In spite of appearances I think it's Jason who controls that house.'

Joe didn't reply. The social dynamics of thirteen Torland Place wasn't something he'd really given much thought to.

'According to Matt he arranged the fancy dress party they had.'

'And he was one of the last people to see Pet alive.'

'I called round to see Matt this morning. Jason was there and he gave me a bit of a hard time. Asked me how I could believe such nonsense and all that. I told him that there's an earthly and often mundane cause for nine out of ten of supposed psychic phenomena but there are always things that can't be explained. I invited him to share his opinion of what had been going on.'

'And what did he say?'

'Nothing. And I don't think he was comfortable with that.'

'With the place possibly being haunted?'

'With there being something beyond his control.'

'What did Matt have to say?'

'He's frightened, Joe. He thinks that whatever's in that house is responsible for Pet's death. He's convinced there's some kind of curse on the place.' He took a sip of tea. 'I'm going there tomorrow.'

'To do an exorcism?'

'To pray. In the meantime a theology student I know is finding out all he can about the Obediah Shrowton case using primary sources that might tell us something the Internet can't.'

Joe took the last bite of his sandwich. 'You should have my job,' he said, looking at his watch. 'I'll have to go, George. Let me know how it goes tomorrow, won't you?'

'Heard from Kirsten?'

Joe shook his head. 'She's gone down in Devon. Let's hope she decides to stay there.' He stood up to leave.

'Take care, Joe,' George said as a parting shot after they'd said their farewells. He sounded concerned and Joe wondered why.

He got back to the incident room at ten past three and made straight for Emily's office. As he passed Jamilla's desk he saw that she was studying her computer screen intently and making notes. Intrigued, he stopped and spoke to her.

'Found anything interesting?'

Jamilla hesitated for a few moments before answering. 'A young woman was found stabbed in London seven years ago.' She hesitated. 'The killer had tried to hack off her nose. I'm waiting for the Met to get back to me with the details.'

Joe's brain was racing. 'Think it could be our man?'

'There do seem to be similarities. Her name was Roni Jasper, aged twenty-one and she was found in an alleyway not far from the House of Commons.'

He told Jamilla to keep up the good work and hurried to Emily's lair.

'Has Jamilla told you about the murder in London?'

'Yes. But don't get too excited, Joe. It might be nothing to do with our case.'

He sat down on the visitor's chair. Emily was right; they really shouldn't be making connections that might not exist.

'It's coming up to half three,' she said. 'Why don't we both go and meet Mr Ferribie off his train and we can take him to the pub for a chat. Let's face it, he'll be miserable enough without making him suffer the interview room.'

Emily was right. The police station was no place for a grieving relative. Especially one with the cast iron alibi of being over a thousand miles away at the relevant time.

They both put on their coats before leaving the office; rain was forecast and the clouds looked ominous. But Joe sensed that Emily was glad to get out of the incident room into the fresh air.

They walked slowly and it wasn't long before they reached the rather grand entrance to Eborby station. The place was bustling as usual but it didn't take them long to cross the ornate bridge over the tracks and reach the draughty platform where the London train was due to arrive.

After waiting expectantly for five minutes they saw the train in the distance, approaching at a stately pace. Soon the sleek engine glided past with a shrieking of brakes and the carriages drew to a halt in front of them. They stood back and watched the passengers disembark, searching the sea of faces for lone men of a certain age.

Suddenly Joe felt Emily grab his sleeve and haul him backwards. 'There's Jenks,' she hissed.

'Four-day week,' said Joe in a loud whisper. 'Can't be bad. Do we have a word or . . .'

'No. But we could pay him a call sometime – ruin his weekend.'

'The Super won't be pleased.'

'The Super can take a running jump off the city walls. Jenks is in something up to his neck . . . if only we knew what that something was.' She released her grip on his sleeve. 'Any sign of Mr Ferribie?'

'That could be him.' Joe pointed at a tall man in his late forties with a small wheelie case. He was tanned with grey, well cut hair and he wore chinos and an open necked shirt that seemed unsuitable for the chilly northern spring.

Emily stepped forward. 'Mr Ferribie?' The man nodded warily and Emily thrust out her hand. 'I'm DCI Emily Thwaite and this is DI Joe Plantagenet. We could go back to the police station and have some disgusting tea from the machine or there's a good pub nearby . . .'

'The pub would be fine.' He sounded grateful. 'It's a bit colder here than where I've been.' He opened up the case and took out a cagoule which wouldn't keep out the Yorkshire breeze, but it would keep him dry if the heavens decided to open.

Joe took charge of the wheelie case as they made their way out of the station and crossed the busy road. Ferribie looked rather lost and Joe felt sorry for him. A pint of Black Sheep would do him the world of good.

Once in the pub Emily found a free table and Joe went to the bar. When he returned he found the pair deep in conversation.

'I was just saying to Paul here that we're doing our best to find out who killed Pet,' Emily said as he put the drinks down.

Paul Ferribie nodded. He looked as though the reality had started to dawn on him. Back in Dubai it had probably seemed like a bad dream.

'Paul tells me that Pet chose Eborby University because her mother was last heard of here.'

Joe caught Emily's eye. This was something new. 'Have you met Pet's housemates?'

Paul shook his head. 'I haven't seen my daughter for over a year. Maybe if I'd stayed in England to look after her . . .'

'Don't blame yourself,' said Emily.

But Joe knew her words were futile. The man would be blaming himself until his dying day.

'I left her with her stepmother. I thought everything was OK between them until Jane took it into her head to go off with some . . . Pet was upset about it, what with her mum vanishing like that and . . . I should have come back and tried to sort things out but we were busy with a new contract. I offered to pay for her to come out to stay with me but she had her university work and her music and . . .'

Joe put a reassuring hand on his arm. 'If you don't feel like talking now . . .'

Paul drained his pint. Joe got him another. After taking a couple of sips from the new glass, he took a deep, shuddering breath.

'What do you need to know? If there's anything I can do to help . . .'

'Tell us about your first wife,' said Emily gently.

'Her name was Helen and she looked just like Pet . . . a

beautiful, fragile blonde. She was what they used to call a free spirit.'

'Go on.'

'She started taking art classes. She had no talent but I never said anything. You don't like to trample on people's dreams, do you? She began to hang around with artists – or rather people who liked to call themselves artists.'

'She had affairs?'

'I never asked. Looking back, I can see that she only stayed with me for the financial security. I don't think she'd have enjoyed starving in a garret whatever she might have said.'

'Was this after Pet was born?'

'Oh yes. Pet must have been about eleven. I suppose all this art business started as a way of filling the time once Pet was at school.'

'What happened when she left?'

'She came from Eborby originally and she said she fancied going back. I thought it would just be for a few weeks but then she wrote to me to say that she'd met someone else – a chef. She said she was staying and not to bother looking for her.' He bowed his head. 'I wondered how she could do that to Pet. But some people are just selfish; they say they want to find themselves and sod everyone else.'

'You never tried to look for her?'

'After about ten months I came up here. I didn't have an address but I checked if she was on the electoral register and I even made enquiries at the police station but nobody had heard of her. Then I traced a man she'd shacked up with for a while. He was a chef like she said. Paolo Jones his name was.'

Joe caught Emily's eye. It looked as if the mystery of Paolo had been solved.

'He told me she'd stayed with him for a few weeks but then she'd gone looking for a place of her own. He swore he didn't know where she was and I believed him. As a last resort I went to the police and they asked me if I wanted to report her missing but she'd gone of her own free will and what's to say she hadn't moved on somewhere else?'

'You say Pet was hoping to find her. Do you know if she made any progress?'

'She called me to say she'd met someone who'd offered to

help. She said he owned property around here and he had useful contacts.'

'Did she tell you his name?'

'Sorry.'

But Joe thought that Cassidy fitted the bill perfectly and it would explain their secretive meeting. However, if that was the case, why hadn't Cassidy been open with them?

'Do you mind if we talk some more tomorrow? I'd like to get to the hotel and have a lie down before . . .'

Joe nodded. He'd almost forgotten that Ferribie was due to identify his daughter's body later that afternoon. 'If there's anything you need . . .' he said.

'Only my daughter back,' Pet's father replied as he drained his glass.

Nurses never liked to cross the railway bridge next to the General Hospital alone after dark. Many years ago a girl had been attacked there and the area's reputation for danger had lingered long after the event like an unpleasant odour.

The only source of light was a tall street lamp overhead which cast a sickly yellow glow on the scene. But it was a short cut and the perils of the night were pretty low on Mrs Ackroyd's list of priorities that Thursday evening. She had other things on her mind as she began to climb the litter-strewn concrete steps up to the bridge, such as how she was going to cope when her elderly mother came out of hospital.

As she placed her sensible shoe on the bridge she looked around, suddenly aware of the loneliness of the place. It was then that she noticed something pale, lying half hidden by the bushes. And when she realized that it was a bare and beautifully shaped human arm – a female arm extended out as if its owner was deep in carefree sleep – she retraced her steps and pushed the bush aside a little, muttering a tentative 'hello'.

But the owner of the arm couldn't have heard because her ears had been severed leaving a bloody mess on each side of her head. And she was dead so she was in no position to say anything ever again as Mrs Ackroyd's scream rang through the evening air.

SIXTEEN

E mily had arrived home in time for dinner after taking Ferribie to view his daughter's body. She'd watched Jeff and the children at the kitchen table, listened to their banter and their childish whingeing and listened to Jeff talking about a colleague's coming wedding. But her mind was still there in that mortuary with Paul Ferribie.

She was sitting on the sofa, pretending to be engrossed in *Coronation Street*, when her mobile phone rang and she rushed out of the room to take the call. The body of another woman had been found near the hospital, next to a bridge over the railway line.

She walked back into the living room where Jeff had been sitting in his favourite armchair. But now he was standing up, looking at her with a mixture of expectation and disappointment.

'Sorry, love. Got to go out. They've found another body.'

She gave her husband's arm a squeeze and stood on tiptoe to kiss his cheek.

'What time will you be back?' he asked, although he should have known better.

Emily gave her usual reply of 'as soon as I can' and left the house. Another dead woman. Just what she needed on a cold Thursday night.

As she drove towards the hospital, she was suddenly struck by the thought that Den Harvey didn't live too far away from the scene. His mother had sworn he'd been with her on the night of Pet Ferribie's murder but, in Emily's opinion, an alibi from a doting mother is no alibi at all.

She drove along Boothgate, turning right into the road that ran parallel to the railway line, and when she saw people milling about in white crime scene suits under the harsh glow of arc lights she knew she had reached the right place. She parked the car and sat there for a while, summoning the will to face whatever was up there, before clambering out of the car. When she reached the steps of the railway footbridge, the scene manager handed her a white crime scene suit which she struggled into with as much dignity as she could muster.

She ventured on to the bridge and saw Joe standing in the light spilling from the arc lamps, blocking her way. He looked upset; not like some coppers she'd known who'd been hardened by years of dealing with death at the sharp end.

'What have we got?'

'It's Anna,' he answered after a few seconds.

'Andy Cassidy's Anna?'

Joe nodded. 'And the bastard's cut her ears off.'

He turned and led the way towards the action. Emily followed behind, steeling herself for what she was about to see.

'She was hidden in bushes but a passer by who'd just come from the hospital spotted an arm,' said Joe.

Emily took a deep breath. 'You sure it's Anna?'

'See for yourself.'

They had reached the white tent that had been erected over the body. It reminded Emily of a garden party gazebo but this was no jolly gathering. Inside the tent Sally Sharpe was kneeling by the body of the young woman she'd last seen at Cassidy's house. The corpse lay amongst dusty shrubbery which had been pushed back to enable the crime scene people to do their work. The officers went about their business quietly, as though they didn't wish to disturb the young woman who'd sunk into the sleep of death.

Emily looked at the dead woman's head and shuddered.

'Cause of death?'

Sally looked up. 'Two stab wounds to the heart. Same as the girl at the leisure centre. If I was a betting woman, I'd put money on it being the same killer.'

'And the mutilations?'

It was Joe who answered. 'I've been thinking. Pet's tongue was cut out. Sharon Bell's eyes were gouged out and Anna's ears were cut off. I know we're waiting for the Met to send the crime scene photos of that woman down in London but the report did mention damage to her nose. Do you see a pattern emerging?'

Sally stopped what she was doing. 'Sight, hearing, taste. The five senses.'

Emily saw her eyes meet Joe's. She looked rather pleased with herself.

'So we've just got touch to go.'

'I think we've had touch already,' Joe said quietly. 'Andy Cassidy's sister's fingers were cut off.'

Emily flipped open her mobile phone. 'I'm sending someone round to pick Cassidy up right away.'

The tiny notebook lay at the back of the desk drawer and Ian Zepper took it out and opened it carefully. He wasn't sure how Pet had found out that his relationship with Grace Cassidy hadn't been purely that of teacher and student but she had. And she'd used her knowledge to extract promises he hadn't really felt inclined to keep. Grace was fifteen but she'd been so full of life. A unique girl with a unique gift and the body of a woman. Strange how some unions can seem almost spiritual; a meeting of two souls. Abelard and Eloise. Master and pupil. Zepper had always been able to justify even his basest actions.

Andy had suspected but he'd had no proof. It had been their secret, kept from Grace's unsuspecting father; kept from Andy and his gawky adolescent friends. One of those friends – the one Grace said was always watching her, the one who gave her the creeps – had walked in on them once but nothing had been said. Pet knew all about it, of course, and now she was dead like Grace. Beautiful Grace, the golden girl who would never grow old.

He hadn't remembered Pet's notebook was still in his drawer until a couple of days after her death. It was the little pink notebook she habitually kept in her shoulder bag and she'd left it on his desk accidentally after a tutorial. He'd tell the police about it, of course, but first he needed to ensure that there was nothing in it that would reflect badly on him. He read it through closely, taking in every word.

And as he did, one sentence in particular caught his eye. 'Mum certainly liked kissing the demons,' she wrote. 'The trouble is the kiss of a demon can be fatal.'

It was raining that Friday morning and the weather reflected Joe's mood. He had spent most of the previous night questioning Cassidy who had seemed genuinely shocked at Anna's death. But in Joe's experience, some of the most sincere and elaborate displays of grief had come from the person responsible for the crime.

He didn't know why he'd connected the death of Cassidy's sister with the other killings. But once he'd hit on the five senses theory it had seemed to fit perfectly. However, he knew that he could be wrong.

Emily had ordered everyone to attend a briefing at eight o'clock sharp and he thought she looked tired. But that was hardly surprising; he felt pretty shattered himself.

He recalled that George was due to visit thirteen Torland Place that morning. But unless it turned out to have something to do with Pet's death, it was none of his concern now.

When he heard Emily's voice summoning the CID faithful he gathered with the rest of the team for her briefing.

'Cassidy claims he got home on Thursday night and found Anna had gone,' she began. 'He says he didn't bother reporting it because he thought she'd be back. We've had people searching through her things. They've found her passport. Her name's Anna Padowski and she's from Kraków. Her family are being notified.'

Joe cleared his throat. 'There are also a couple of people we need to talk to again. Den Harvey and Pet's tutor, Ian Zepper who, incidentally, also taught Cassidy's sister the piano. Cassidy was convicted of his sister's murder but now I think he's trying to implicate Zepper.'

He saw Emily give a nod of approval, just as a uniformed policewoman rushed in and handed her a note. She opened it and after a few seconds she looked up.

'On the night Anna disappeared she received a call from a pay as you go mobile which has been traced to the Fleshambles or Queen's Square area; the same location as Pet's phone when Matt Bawtry made that last call to her. Cassidy claims that he was in Leeds last night and the call definitely wasn't from his number.'

'There was nothing to stop him buying an anonymous pay as you go phone and using that to lure her to wherever she was killed. Same goes for any of our suspects.'

'A murder phone,' said Sunny from the audience. 'I've heard of that before. Takes some forethought and organization, mind.'

'We're looking for an organized killer,' said Joe quietly. 'I think he chooses his victims carefully. And he might even get them to trust him.' He frowned. 'We never did identify who was dressed as the Grim Reaper at the Torland Place party, did we?'

'So the Grim Reaper's our prime suspect,' Emily said, rolling her eyes to heaven. 'Very appropriate. Or alternatively he or she might have nothing to do with it. Anyone got anything else to share with us?'

One of the newer Detective Constables, a red-haired lad in his twenties, raised a tentative hand. 'A report's come in from Forensic, ma'am. Traces of red and blue fibres were found on Pet Ferribie's clothes. Blend of wool and nylon. The report says they come from good quality carpet, probably fairly new . . . hence the loose fibres.'

'So get on to all carpet firms in the area and see if they've laid a carpet fitting that description anywhere over the past few months.'

Joe saw the young man's face turn red before he hurried off to do Emily's bidding.

Emily continued. 'It seems the victims are bound with tape and kept somewhere until he kills them. We need to find out where. And the killer moves them somehow so I want all CCTV footage between the Queen's Square area and the spot where Anna was found gone through, as well as anything from near the leisure centre at the time Pet's body was dumped.'

There were some low groans from the audience.

Emily clapped her hands. 'Come on, get it done and there's a drink for whoever finds something.' She turned to Joe. 'How does the killer move the bodies about, eh?'

Joe frowned. 'Van? Car boot?'

'Possible. We've got the post-mortem later, don't forget.'

'How could I?'

Emily marched off but no sooner had she gone than Jamilla tapped him on the shoulder. 'Sir, Lee's been going through footage of Coopergate. He's found Steve Portright. He's walking towards Boots then he stops suddenly, as if he's spotted someone.'

'Can you pinpoint the person he's interested in?'

'Come and see for yourself,' she said.

It was an offer he couldn't refuse. He followed Jamilla to the AV room, confident that he'd be able to pick out Jade Portright in any crowd. After all, her face had been imprinted on his memory for almost a week now. But that had been her teenaged face, as yet unformed by time and experience; if Jade was still alive, she might have changed quite a bit during the intervening years.

In a while the AV room would become rather crowded with junior officers anxious to win themselves a pint from the DCI, all huddled around TV screens staring at CCTV footage of varying quality from the relevant hours. But at the moment those tapes were still being gathered together so he and Jamilla had the room to themselves.

Spotting Steve Portright was easy but scanning the street for someone who might or might not be his missing daughter proved more difficult. Eventually he fixed on one possibility. She was slim with straight fair hair and she was certainly the right age to be Jade, but he couldn't see her face as she had her back to the camera.

But the more he rewound the tape and watched the young woman, the more convinced Joe became that he'd seen her somewhere before . . . if only he could remember where it was.

Barrington Jenks had spent a restless night alone in his king size bed. For one dangerous moment he had feared that his wife would insist on returning to Eborby with him. But he had persuaded her to stay in London saying that he'd be involved in meetings with his constituency staff most of the weekend so life up in the north would be cold and tedious. She was a southerner by birth so she'd believed him.

He had lied about the meetings of course. He had a surgery for his constituents on Saturday afternoon but, apart from that, his time was his own. Which was good because he had things to see to that he wouldn't want his colleagues or constituents to know about.

As he drove from Colforth to the Bearsley district of Eborby, he was uncomfortably aware of all the cameras tracking his journey. CCTV, traffic cameras with number plate recognition software; as a politician he'd supported them all enthusiastically but now he was starting to regret it. It would be far too easy for the police to trace his movements if they were so inclined. However, he lacked the skills of a professional criminal who could secure anonymity by stealing a car or using false number plates so he would just have to trust in the police's inefficiency. According to some of his constituents, there was never a bobby about when you needed one.

When he reached Torland Place, he drove past the house slowly. For the first time his large black BMW seemed to be a liability rather than something to impress the lower orders. It was far too noticeable and he needed to be inconspicuous.

When he'd passed the house Jasmine had been looking out of the window as arranged. And now he parked a little way down the road and waited for her to join him, his heart beating fast.

He could see her in the rear view mirror, walking casually down the street. Nearer and nearer. When she drew level with the car he leaned over and opened the door. She got in.

'We must have hidden it well but we've found it,' she said breathlessly. 'We'll need help to move it. Tonight.'

'I don't want a mess in this car.'

'We've got bin bags. You can drive out to the country and we'll dispose of it there.'

He looked at Jasmine. She looked so much older now, and lined with worry. The sins of our youth sometimes come back to haunt us.

'I don't want to put it anywhere which might point to my involvement,' Jenks said weakly.

'You're involved whether you want to be or not.'

Jenks clutched the steering wheel to stop his hands from shaking. 'What . . . what state is it in?'

'You squeamish?' Jasmine's voice was mocking and Jenks suddenly felt like lashing out. 'You'll see for yourself tonight.'

'Can't we use your car? I . . .'

'It's tiny. No boot space. You've got plenty of room.' The car door opened. 'See you tonight. Midnight.'

Jenks sat there, his hands still fixed to the wheel. As Jasmine disappeared down the road he was surprised to see a chubby clergyman with a bald head walking towards her house.

The last thing he'd have expected Jasmine to do was to get religion.

SEVENTEEN

Anna had been fully clothed but now she was naked. Her clothes lay bagged up on a steel trolley at the end of the white tiled room, ready to be sent for forensic examination.

As Sally began work Joe glanced at Emily who stood beside him behind the glass screen, arms folded.

'I never like this bit,' she muttered.

'You and me both.'

Sally kept up a running commentary of what she was doing and every so often she looked up at Joe and smiled. He'd always found Sally to be good company, in spite of her gruesome profession. But somehow he just couldn't detach the professional Sally from the private woman in his mind. He knew it was ridiculous but it was something he couldn't help.

When Sally had finished and her assistant was clearing up, she took off her surgical gown and joined them in her office.

'It's almost identical to Petulia Ferribie. Similar knife wounds from the same angle. The only difference is that he's removed her ears this time instead of cutting out her tongue.'

'There was a similar murder down in London,' said Joe. 'A woman was found stabbed twice through the heart with damage to her nose. The DCI in charge of the case thinks the killer was disturbed before he could finish whatever it was he wanted to do. When the post-mortem report arrives, will you have a look at it for me . . . tell me if you think it's the same killer?'

Sally nodded. 'No problem.'

'Thanks,' Joe said. There used to be a time when Sally would drop casual hints about seeing Joe off duty and mention a film or a pub she fancied trying. But it seemed she'd given up. And Joe was rather surprised that he felt a stab of disappointment.

'I noticed something about Anna's clothes when she was

undressed,' Sally said as Joe and Emily reached the threshold of her office.

'What was that?'

'There were some fibres on her coat that looked like carpet fluff. There were similar fibres on Pet Ferribie's clothes.'

'They were carpet fibres. Blue and red.'

'So they're killed somewhere with a blue and red carpet.'

'Now all we've got to do is find it,' said Emily who'd been listening intently. She began to march off down the corridor that led out of the mortuary to the outside world of the living.

Joe thanked Sally and hurried after her.

The incident room was almost deserted when Joe and Emily returned. Some of the team were out making enquiries at the hospital and the houses in the area where Anna's body was found. Others were trying their luck with carpet firms and some were still in the AV room trying to earn that promised pint from the boss. But, as yet, it seemed they weren't having much luck.

Emily found a report on her desk from Scientific Support. They'd gone through Den Harvey's computer and found nothing of interest apart from a file called 'Kissing the Demons', full of downloaded Internet pornography. Nothing too disturbing and no kids, Emily was relieved to discover. But the title he'd chosen intrigued her. She'd heard the phrase before . . . at thirteen Torland Place if she remembered right.

'Has anybody managed to trace the chef Ferribie's missing wife was supposed to be shacked up with?'

'With a name like Paolo Jones he shouldn't be hard to find . . . if he's still in the area.'

Joe heard a tentative knock on the office door. When it opened, Jamilla was standing there and she looked as if she had news. 'The Met have emailed through details of that murder in London. It certainly looks similar.' She handed a file to Emily who sat down at her desk to read it.

Joe couldn't resist looking over her shoulder. She had reached the post-mortem report now and he could see the pictures of the naked body of Roni Jasper, aged twenty-one at the time of death. Roni was a drug user who worked as a prostitute. The Met had followed many lines of enquiry but had eventually drawn a blank. Case unsolved.

Joe studied the pictures with the dawning realization that the Met's cold case had just turned red hot. The two stab wounds to the chest looked identical to those on the bodies of Sharon, Pet and Anna. Coincidence was always a possibility but Joe was certain now that the three women were killed by the same man.

Emily was still scanning the pages of statements and reports for familiar names.

'I was hoping to find Cassidy's, Harvey's or Zepper's names amongst all this lot but there's no sign.'

'If she was a working girl there's a good chance she was killed by a punter. And they usually prefer to remain anonymous. We need to find out if any of our suspects were in London at the time of the murder.'

Emily looked up at Jamilla and smiled sweetly. 'Can I leave that to you, Jamilla? Use your charms and don't mention why you want to know where they were.'

'Right, ma'am.' Jamilla turned to go.

'We do know someone who would have been in London at the time,' said Joe. 'Someone who would have been in the Westminster area.'

After a couple of seconds Emily's lips turned upwards in a smile of realization. 'Our local MP. Of course. But he wasn't here to murder Anna last night.'

'Wasn't he? We saw him at the station, remember.'

Emily banged her forehead with the palm of her hand, annoyed with herself. 'I've had so much on my mind I almost forgot. But where was he when Sharon and Pet were killed?'

'That's something we'll have to find out.'

'Well we can't just do a routine check. Remember what the Super said about discretion.'

'Anyone would think the man's above the law.'

'We've got to keep the Powers that Be happy, but I think Jenks might be worth another visit. No need to tell the Super if it's just a routine chat, is there.'

Before Joe could reply, a young Detective Constable poked his head round the open door. 'Excuse me, ma'am, sir. I've traced that chef. Paolo Jones. He works at the Gunpowder Plot. Head chef no less.'

A smile spread across Joe's face. 'Gunpowder Plot. GP.'

He turned to Emily. 'I'll go and have a word. Any news on Anna Padowski's family yet?'

Emily sighed. 'It's being dealt with.' She looked at her watch. 'Lunch time. Not a good time to interview a chef.'

'All the better. He won't have time to cook up any clever answers.'

The Gunpowder Plot stood in the centre of the city, on one of the thin and winding medieval streets that radiated out from the cathedral. Its restaurant was rather expensive in Joe's opinion, but popular. By the time he walked through the door it was coming up to two o'clock but the place was still busy.

Joe was met at the door by a thin young woman in black who asked if he wanted a table. When he showed his warrant card she summoned over the manager. After a hushed conversation, he was led to the kitchen where he found the man he was looking for.

As he walked in Paolo Jones was berating some unfortunate young chef for ruining a sauce. The victim, overweight with ginger hair and freckles, hung his head miserably. He looked about twelve, Joe thought as he watched him hurry away to fetch fresh ingredients. And the omens weren't good for a blossoming career in the restaurant industry.

Paolo himself was around forty with dark brown eyes and jet black hair which showed slight smudges of grey around the temples. He was around five feet eight and wiry, as though he worked out at the gym. Joe had once heard it said that a fat cook was a good advert for his or her food; if this was the case, Paolo Jones certainly didn't fit the bill. As he introduced himself he noted that, unlike many people in the same situation, Jones didn't look in the least bit daunted; only mildly curious.

'What can I do for you, Inspector?'

'Sorry to trouble you at lunchtime.'

'No problem. The rush is over.'

'We're investigating the murder of Petulia Ferribie.' He didn't think it was worth mentioning the others just yet. 'I believe you knew her mother.'

He looked round. 'You'd better come into my office.'

'Can they manage without you?'

'The lad I was bollocking is on work experience. And he

doesn't seem to be enjoying the experience.' He smiled, showing a row of perfect teeth. 'And the feeling's mutual. Hang on a sec,' he said before calling to one of his colleagues to keep an eye on things. The reply was 'Yes, chef,' barked in a manner that was almost military.

Paolo Jones led him to a utilitarian office and invited him to sit.

'Did you ever meet Petulia?' he began.

'Yes. She was an odd girl. Very pretty but . . . there was something about her. Something not quite right.'

Joe inclined his head, hoping for more. And he wasn't disappointed.

'Her mother always used to say she was a fey child . . . hard to get close to. I never met her back then, of course . . . when I was with Helen. She got in touch with me a few weeks ago because she was trying to find out what happened to her mother.'

'You must have heard about her death on the news. Why didn't you come forward?'

Paolo made a sweeping gesture with his arm. 'I work bloody long hours and I just haven't had time. Besides, I haven't got anything useful to tell you. She came to see me and I told her I didn't know what happened to her mum. That's it.'

'You lived with her mother.'

'Me and Helen were shacked up together for a few weeks when she first came up to Eborby but once the initial bout of lust had worn off it became an arrangement of convenience.'

'How did you meet?'

'In a bar. She was older than me but she was a very attractive woman. She'd run away because she was sick of her boring husband and she came to Eborby because she'd lived here as a child. She didn't let on that she had a kid at first and when I found out she'd abandoned her daughter I must admit she went down in my estimation. It's one thing to get sick of a husband but to get sick of your own child . . . Not nice.'

'So she wasn't a nice woman?'

'I didn't say that. It's just that I didn't approve of what she'd done. Not that I'm a saint or anything. But a kid needs a mother, don't you think?'

'When exactly did you meet Pet?'

'About three weeks ago. She wanted me to tell her what had happened to her mother and I had to tell her I didn't know. After me and Helen had been together a few weeks we knew it wasn't working so she looked for somewhere else.'

'Where did she move to?'

'That's the strange thing. She moved all her stuff out . . . said she'd got this fantastic place and she'd invite me round once she got settled. We'd split up but we were still on friendly terms. Anyway, after that I never saw or heard from her again. It was as if she'd vanished off the face of the earth.'

'Didn't you think that was odd?'

'She was a free agent. I assumed she'd decided to leave Eborby. Or she might have had second thoughts about the boring husband and gone home. Now I know different.'

'Do the names Ian Zepper or Dennis Harvey mean anything to you?'

Paolo shook his head.

'Andy Cassidy?'

'Yeah. Pet mentioned him.'

'What did she say?'

Paolo frowned. 'She said he was her landlord and she was sure he knew something. I asked her if he had any connection with Helen but she didn't answer. Then she asked me if I had anything of her mum's and I remembered I had a suitcase full of some old junk – papers and all that – up in my loft. Helen didn't leave much behind but I remember shoving some stuff of hers into the case to give to her later. I'd forgotten all about it till Pet started talking about her.'

'Did you tell her about it?'

'Yeah.' He hesitated. 'She popped round to my place to have a look.'

'Did she take anything?'

The chef thought for a few moments. 'I don't think so. But she asked for a piece of paper to jot down some addresses.'

'What exactly did Helen leave?'

'Just a few old leaflets . . . about flats and houses and all that. I don't know why I didn't chuck them out at the time. I have now.'

Joe felt his heart sink with disappointment. 'You've thrown them away?'

'Why? Do you think they're important?'

'Pet definitely wrote down some addresses?'

'Yes. But I didn't think the stuff was worth keeping.' He thought for a moment. 'They might still be in the recycling. I'll have a look when I get home if you like.'

'That'd be great.' Joe handed over his card. 'You'll call me if you find them?'

'Sure.' Paolo yawned. 'Sorry, but I'm going home to get some kip before the evening rush.'

'Where do you live?'

'I've got a place near Queen's Square. Very handy.'

'Very,' said Joe, his mind working overtime. 'Where were you last Saturday night around eleven thirty?'

'On a Saturday I usually leave here around eleven thirty. I'd probably be on my way home.'

'And last night?'

'I was here all night . . . left around ten thirty. We close up a bit earlier on week nights.' Paolo stood up. 'If that's all, I'd better get out there and see if I've got a kitchen left.'

Joe knew when he was being dismissed. As he walked out of the restaurant it struck him that Paolo had shown little curiosity about how Pet had died.

Perhaps that was because he'd known all about it already.

Joe was on his way back to the police station when his mobile phone rang. He checked the number and his heart sank. Kirsten.

He stared at the phone for a few seconds then he cut off the call. He didn't have time for her right now.

His only consolation was that, as far as he knew, she was over two hundred miles away in the West Country.

He walked on past the Museum Gardens trying to focus his mind on the case. Was it a coincidence that Pet had been murdered so soon after she began investigating her mother's disappearance? He didn't believe in coincidences. And neither, he knew, did Emily.

When he arrived in the office he opened his desk drawer and took out the photograph Andy Cassidy had lent him, the one of the Yorkshire Schools and Youth schoolboys on their summer camp. He made a search of his desk and eventually he found a magnifying glass at the back of the bottom drawer.

He began to study the immature, earnest faces in the photograph. Cassidy was there standing by a much slimmer Den

Harvey; two men with such different lives but united by a common youthful experience. Or were they united by another kind of experience – the act of murder?

His eyes were drawn to the other figures on the edge of the picture, at the side of the wooden hut sitting on the grass near to the posed group. There was something vaguely familiar about one of them but, like the film of Jade Portright, the image would need enhancing. This would be another job for Scientific Support and he just hoped the budget would stand it.

After putting the photo to one side, he began to search his in tray for the still image of the person who'd been watching Jade from the bushes and the arm that was pushing back the foliage. When he found it he placed it squarely on the desk in front of him. He stared at it as he'd stared at the YSY picture, seeking inspiration. Only this time it finally came. It really was so obvious and he cursed his own stupidity.

Emily timed her entrance well. She hurried into the office looking stressed and solemn and Joe followed her into her office, armed with the photo, hoping what he had to tell her would cheer her up.

'Come in, Joe. Tell me some good news. You've cleared up the case and the murderer's down in the interview room just waiting to be charged.'

Joe smiled dutifully. 'Not exactly, boss. But I know who was watching Jade Portright from the bushes.'

He handed her the picture and the magnifying glass. 'Look at the arm parting the bushes. That's a tattoo. Portright's got a tattoo exactly like that.'

'So why didn't he say it was him when we showed him the picture?'

'Good question. Why didn't he want us to know he'd been watching his own daughter and her friend?'

'Messing about in bikinis.'

Their eyes met in understanding.

'Have we just got dirty minds, Joe, or . . .'

'I think we've just hit on a possible reason why Jade would want to disappear.'

'But what about Nerys?'

'Perhaps we'd better have another word with her family.' He paused. 'There is another possibility of course.'

Emily looked away. 'That Portright tried it on with both girls and things got out of hand. But that doesn't explain why he says he saw Jade.'

'He could be trying to put us off the scent. If he did harm the girls it must have really put the wind up him when the case was reopened.'

Emily yawned. She looked tired. 'Did you find Paolo Jones?'

'Yes. Pet went looking for him. She was trying to trace her mother. Helen Ferribie stayed with him for a while when she came up to Eborby but then she got her own place and they lost touch. I really don't think he knows anything but Helen left some papers at his place – mostly details about houses and flats she was looking at. He showed them to Pet and she wrote down some details. He's going to try and dig them out of the recycling for me. But I'm not hopeful that they'll be any help.'

'A dead end then.'

'Looks like it.'

There was a knock on the open door and Joe looked up to see Jamilla standing there. She looked serious. 'They've traced Anna's parents in Poland, ma'am,' she said. 'They'll be coming in on the next flight to Manchester.'

When Joe looked at Emily she turned away.

Zepper's hand hovered over the telephone. He could feel it shaking and he told himself to keep calm.

He picked up the receiver and dialled Cassidy's number. He didn't altogether trust Cassidy but he had little choice in the matter.

Cassidy picked up after the fourth ring and said a wary hello.

'I've got Pet's notebook. I think we should meet.'

There was a long silence at the other end of the line. Then Cassidy spoke. 'It's difficult at the moment. Anna's dead.'

'She wasn't the girl near the hospital . . . ?'

'Yes. They say it's the same killer.'

It was Zepper's turn to fall silent. He knew he had to choose his words carefully.

'Pet went into a lot of detail,' he said after a few moments. 'And it doesn't make either of us look good.'

'Are you going to take it to the police?'

'I don't know.'

'Maybe you should tell them about it. It might get them off our backs.'

'What exactly does kissing the demons mean?'

When Andy Cassidy slammed the phone down, Zepper was left listening to the dialling tone droning away like an angry wasp.

EIGHTEEN

Matt lay in bed listening to the noises, the scraping and thumps that seemed to come from the ceiling above him. He glanced at the glowing red numbers of his alarm clock. Twenty past midnight.

Before he'd put the light out he'd lain there on his back, staring at the cracks on the dirty white ceiling. Those cracks certainly seemed to have grown since he'd looked up at them the previous night. It was as if something was up there, weighing on the joists. And he hardly liked to think what that something could be.

He knew Jason and Caro had heard the sounds too but Jason made a joke of it, saying that it was old Obediah come back to haunt the place. Caro dismissed it as sounds from next door. But the Quillans didn't seem the type to be shifting things around in the loft at midnight. Jackie Quillan looked like the sort of woman who'd panic if she broke a nail. And Rory always looked clean and immaculate. Besides, the activity wasn't in their loft. It was directly above Matt's room.

Matt had found George Merryweather's visit earlier that day reassuring and the fact that Caro and Jason hadn't been in had come as a relief. The last thing he'd needed was their scepticism. He hadn't really known what to expect when George did his bit; thunder and lightning, green vomit, screaming spectres or nothing at all. The reality had been closer to the latter but he did feel that the place seemed a little less hostile now. Or maybe that was just his imagination.

He recalled the prayer George had recited. Visit this place, oh Lord, and drive from it the snares of the enemy. He liked those words, 'snares of the enemy'. Number thirteen seemed full of them. But he wasn't quite sure whether the enemy in question was spirit or flesh and blood.

The noises were louder now as though something was being dragged across the ceiling above him. Matt covered his ears with his pillow but he could still hear it . . . shuffling and speaking in wordless whispers. Was it old Obediah in eternal torment, dragging the corpses of his victims across the floor? Or was it the dead clawing their way out of purgatory? He slipped beneath the duvet and shut his eyes tight, trying to summon the courage to get up and go downstairs. But that's where it had happened so maybe the terror would be even stronger down there.

He heard a crack, almost like a muffled gunshot, and he peeped out from the duvet, lying quite still. Something was in the room with him. Something unpleasant.

As he began to wriggle one hand towards the bedside light, there was a loud crash and something heavy hit the bed.

He jerked his body up and scrabbled for the light, and as his hand hit the switch the lamp fell over and lay on its side, its feeble bulb illuminating the scene. Above him through billowing clouds of dust he could see a yawning black hole in the ceiling. And he knew that someone or something was moving up there.

Then his eyes travelled down to the bed where a black bin bag lay, grey with powdery dust, weighing down his lower leg. The bag had split open and he could see something inside. Something that looked like matted hair.

Matt opened his mouth to call out but instead the sudden intake of dust into his lungs made him cough uncontrollably. He pulled his legs from under the bag and covered his mouth but the movement caused the bag to shift and the black plastic opened wider to reveal the thing inside.

He stared, horrified, at the mummified head with long, dusty brown hair clinging to the skull and brittle, desiccated flesh pulled back to show a set of grinning teeth.

Then he leapt from the bed and rushed out on to the landing as if the devil himself was after him, unaware of the murmuring voices in the roof space above.

*   *   *

Joe was asleep when the phone by his bed rang just before one in the morning. He had been dreaming about Kirsten. He had come across her body in undergrowth. She had been stabbed and her tongue had been hacked out like Pet Ferribie's, silencing her accusations for ever. While he had been bending over her body her eyes had flicked open and she had sat up, staring at him with dumb hatred. Then a fire alarm had gone off somewhere and he'd woken up to realize that it was the telephone. For once he was glad to have his sleep disturbed. It hadn't been a good dream.

It was Emily. She sounded as tired as he felt. 'A body's been found at thirteen Torland Place.'

Joe sat up, suddenly wide awake. 'One of the students?'

There was a pause. 'You're not going to believe this, Joe, but a bin bag containing a mummified body has just fallen through the ceiling in Matt Bawtry's room. Frightened the life out of the poor lad.'

Joe swore softly under his breath. He knew student houses could be pretty unsanitary but desiccated corpses in the attic seemed to be taking things a bit far.

'I've said we'd get down there,' Emily continued. 'Apparently the students are in a bit of a state.'

'Any idea who the corpse is?'

'Not yet. But the attic was sealed off on the students' side and the party wall up there had been partially knocked through. Next door were using it to store God knows what . . . including mummified corpses.'

'There's more than one?'

'They're still conducting a search. They've arrested the couple next door, by the way. The Quillans.'

'Then we'd better have a word with them.' Joe yawned. The initial rush of adrenalin was wearing off but he forced himself out of bed and stumbled towards the chair where his clothes lay in an untidy heap, cradling the phone between his shoulder and his ear as he reached for his trousers.

'And there's something else. A black BMW was spotted driving away from the Quillan's. All the traffic cameras in the area are being checked to see if we can get the registration number. A patrol car's coming round to get you in ten minutes so get your clothes on. And Joe . . .'

'What?'

'Doesn't Barrington Jenks drive a black BMW?'

Joe didn't answer. He was too busy buttoning up his shirt.

Both thirteen and fifteen Torland Place had been sealed off with police tape and when Joe arrived the scene was alive with activity.

When Emily met him at the door to number thirteen, she informed him that the Quillans were still next door under the guard of a couple of uniformed constables. She'd considered having them taken to the police station but she reckoned that they might be more talkative if they were there on the scene with the incontrovertible evidence. The students, too, were still in number thirteen, huddled together in the living room as if for comfort.

Joe made straight for the living room with Emily following behind. Matt, Caro and Jason were sitting around the table in their dressing gowns, empty mugs in front of them.

'I'll put the kettle on again,' Caro said, making for the kitchen.

Matt gave her a grateful nod. He looked as if he was in shock and Joe reckoned he needed something stronger than tea.

It was Jason who spoke first. 'So who was our unwelcome housemate?'

'We can't say for sure yet,' Joe replied. 'But whoever it is, she's been up there quite a while.'

Matt had been staring at his mug but he suddenly looked up. 'She?'

'According to our doctor it's a female. Probably an adolescent girl.' Emily caught Joe's eye. It was only a matter of time before the body was identified officially by dental records and what was left of the ragged clothing. But in the meantime, they were pretty sure of the dead girl's identity.

Caro brought the tea in on a stained plastic tray and Joe watched her, waiting for a suitable moment to begin the questioning.

'What can you tell us about your next door neighbours?' Joe asked once they had the steaming mugs in front of them.

'Not much,' said Caro. 'We called a couple of times to ask when to put the bins out and that sort of thing.'

'And we took a parcel in for them once,' Jason chipped in.

'They seemed quite . . . Well, I don't know if normal's the word. There was something a bit weird about them.'

Joe nodded. But he doubted if Jason would have delivered that verdict if the Quillans had proved to be upright citizens who didn't keep mummified corpses in attics. Hindsight is a wonderful thing.

'Well at least I know what the noises up in the loft were now,' said Matt quietly. 'I feel a bit stupid now . . . thinking it was . . .'

'The ghost of old Obediah Shrowton,' said Jason with a sneer. 'Really, Matt, you're so easy to wind up. Hang on, maybe the body belongs to one of his victims . . . one that was never found,' he added, his eyes glowing with mischievous enjoyment.

Matt took a sip from the mug Caro had just placed in front of him. 'Well he did kill those people in here. You can't deny that.'

Joe stood up. If the students wanted to start an argument, that was none of his concern. He looked at Emily who was listening in silence. She gave a slight nod. 'Right. We'll take a look upstairs,' he said. 'Has anybody told Cassidy about this? He'll need to know about the damage to his property.'

'We thought we'd tell him tomorrow,' said Caro.

Matt looked at Joe. 'That person dressed as the Grim Reaper . . . could it have been Quillan from next door?'

'We'll ask him,' Joe said before leaving the room and making his way upstairs. Emily followed him, hanging back as though she was afraid of what she'd see there.

When they reached the top of the stairs they saw Matt's door standing open and the unnaturally bright temporary lighting gave the scene inside the look of a stage filled with actors. The crime scene team were going about their business with quiet efficiency and in the calm centre of the action Sally Sharpe was bending over something on the bed. When she heard Joe's voice she swung round.

'Come and have a look.'

When Joe and Emily entered the room Joe noticed an aluminium ladder stretched upwards to a large jagged hole in the ceiling. The room was blanketed with dust and debris and a pair of dusty suitcases lay at a drunken angle on the floor at the end of the bed. They must have come down with the body, Joe thought as he stared at the thing on the bed.

He had seen mummified bodies from ancient Egypt in various museums during the course of his life but this one was different. Parchment skin and scraps of grey clothing clung to bones but the worst thing was the head, the empty eyes and the drawn back lips below the matted mess of hair. If it weren't for the head, the body would have looked like a bundle of rags. The head made it human.

'Any idea of the cause of death?' Emily asked.

Sally considered her answer while the police photographer began to ascend the ladder to get a few shots of the attic. 'My first impression is that she probably died of a head injury. Here.' She pushed aside some of the matted hair with a gloved hand. There was certainly a wound there. 'The conditions up there in the attic caused the mummification. Dry heat. She was probably near the hot water tank.'

'In a bin bag?'

'No. She's been put in that very recently. I'll do the post-mortem tomorrow. You're keeping me busy, Joe,' she added, with what could have been a wink. But he was too tired and preoccupied to notice for sure.

He felt Emily nudge his arm. 'Let's go and see what the Quillans have to say for themselves.'

They left number thirteen and made for next door, still wearing their crime scene suits. Emily had always claimed that she resembled a snowman in hers and Joe wondered whether she'd have made a more imposing chief investigating officer if she took it off. But he said nothing.

The Quillans had been separated on Emily's orders and they found Rory Quillan in the lounge perched on the edge of the sofa, looking far from comfortable. He wore jeans and an old, torn T-shirt and his clothes were covered in dust.'

'The woman's in the kitchen,' Emily whispered as they peeped round the door. 'Who do you want to start with?'

'Ladies first, I think.'

They made their way to the kitchen where Jackie Quillan was sitting at the glass breakfast table. Like Rory, she was fully dressed in what Joe's father would have described as 'gardening clothes'; torn jeans and a baggy sweatshirt. Her clothes too were covered in a layer of dust and debris, as was her hair.

'You look as if you could do with a bath,' said Emily as she sat down on one of the neighbouring chairs. 'Been up in the attic, have you?'

Jackie looked away. 'That attic hasn't been cleaned out since Rory's uncle lived here. We'd no idea what was up there.'

Emily leaned forward and put her face close to the woman's. 'Liar. You knew exactly what was up there. That's why you've been searching up there for the past week or so. The students next door have told us about the noises from the loft. There's a big gap in the party wall between the two loft spaces and you used next door's attic to hide the body. Handy that it was sealed off from the students' side so they couldn't take it into their heads to have a nose about.'

'We didn't do that. It was Rory's uncle Norman. He owned both houses at one time. You ask Rory.'

'Rory spent a lot of time here in Uncle Norman's day, didn't he?'

'So?' Jackie pushed her hair back from her face with a grubby hand.

'Tell us what happened tonight?'

'We decided it was time we cleared out the loft and when we moved a load of cases we saw it there in a bin bag. Rory must have stepped back with the shock and then the whole lot went through the ceiling. It's got nothing to do with us. We're as shocked as anybody.'

'Funny time to clear out a loft.'

'We're both at work during the day and neither of us go to bed early so . . .'

Her story seemed to make sense but Joe suspected that it was a lie. 'Only our pathologist reckons the body's only just been put in that bin bag. Hoping to get rid of it, were you?' He didn't wait for a reply. 'Mind if I have a look upstairs?'

Jackie looked at him. 'We haven't got any other bodies hidden around the place if that's what you're thinking.'

Emily gave him a nod and he marched out of the room and made his way upstairs, taking the stairs two at a time. He had a quick look in each room, flicking through wardrobes and opening drawers and by the time he'd finished he reckoned he'd seen everything he needed to see.

When he returned to the landing his eyes were drawn to the loft entrance. The hatch was open and Joe mounted the ladder and poked his head up into the roof space. The light was on and he could see that the loft of number fifteen was filled with neatly stacked boxes, suitcases and small items of unwanted furniture.

Through a gaping hole in the wall separating number fifteen's loft from next door's he could see a couple of crime scene officers working carefully under the lights they'd set up. The neighbouring loft looked dirty and cluttered. And it seemed odd that anybody in the Quillans' position should take any interest in it. Surely the sensible thing to do would be to block up the party wall again. Unless there was a good reason not to. Unless the Quillans knew there was something in there that had to be disposed of.

He returned to the kitchen and sat beside Emily, giving Jackie Quillan a businesslike smile. 'I see you and Rory don't share a bedroom.'

'So?' She was suddenly on the defensive. But if she thought he was prying into her private life that was hardly surprising.

'Rory's not your husband, is he?'

'He's my partner. We're not married.'

He saw Emily give him a questioning look. 'An arrangement of convenience, is it?'

'No. I . . .'

'What is it you do, Jackie?'

'I work in Nebula. It's a boutique near Coopergate.'

'And Rory?'

'He works for the local council. Housing office. Why?'

'How long have you been together?'

She suddenly looked wary. 'Must be about twelve years.'

'You must have been very young when you got together.'

'Childhood sweethearts, that's us. Now if you've finished, I need a shower.'

'We won't keep you much longer. I've seen you recently on CCTV.'

There was no mistaking it, she looked uncomfortable.

'A man thought he'd seen his long-lost daughter in Coopergate and he called us. We found CCTV footage of the area at the time he said he saw her and you were on it. Why did you change your name, Jade?'

He glanced at Emily and saw her mouth open and close as though she was about to say something then thought better of it.

'My name's Jackie.'

'Then you wouldn't mind doing a DNA test. Just a mouth swab. It doesn't hurt.'

As Jackie stood up the chair legs scraped loudly on the floor. 'No. Piss off. I'm not going on any DNA register.'

'What happened to Nerys, Jade?'

'I don't know what you're talking about.'

'Did you kill her?'

'No.'

'Why is Rory's wardrobe full of women's clothes?'

She suddenly looked shocked, then she rearranged her features into a bored expression. 'They're mine. I need more wardrobe space than him so I've taken over some of his.'

'So how come they're three sizes bigger than the ones in your wardrobe?'

There was a pause while she considered her reply. 'I've lost weight,' she said, gnawing at her fingernails. 'I was ill and I lost weight.'

'They're too long for you as well. I'd say they belong to someone a lot taller.'

Emily caught on quickly. She cautioned the woman and told her they were going to take her in for questioning.

Joe only hoped he had it right. If not he would probably make an almighty fool of himself. As Jackie was being led away by a policewoman, he began to walk towards the lounge. It was about time they heard what Rory Quillan had to say for himself.

Quillan stood up as he entered the room, Emily hovering behind him. She was leaving this one to him and he knew if he was wrong he'd have to take the flak.

'Hello, Jasmine,' he said as he sat down in the leather armchair.

Rory Quillan put his head in his hands and began to cry.

Emily arrived home at three in the morning, knowing that if she didn't get a few hours of sleep she wouldn't be in any fit state to sort out the Dead Man's Wood case the next day. And she'd need all her wits about her if she was to get Barrington Jenks to tell the truth.

Jeff had been asleep when she'd got in and, as it was Saturday, she left him in bed and got dressed as quietly as possible. As she looked at him lying there, hiding his head beneath the duvet, she felt a pang of guilt at abandoning him to see to the kids single handed again. Maybe Joe had it right and police work demanded a semi-monastic existence. But something told her that Joe too longed for the comfort of what passed for domestic bliss in the twenty-first century. Only for some reason it always seemed to elude him.

At eight thirty she arrived at the police station and gathered the team in the incident room for the morning briefing. The big news was that Jackie and Rory Quillan were waiting in the cells to be questioned about the body found at Torland Place. But, to her disappointment, there was no more news concerning the more urgent matter – the deaths she had started to refer to as the Grim Reaper murders for want of any better label. The killer was out there and there was every reason to suspect that he would strike again.

Sharon Bell had died years before, as had Roni Jasper. And Joe was convinced that Cassidy's sister, Grace, was killed by the same person. Cassidy had been convicted of that particular murder and he had known Sharon, Pet and Anna. All they needed now was solid evidence to put him away again. Surely it would only be a matter of time.

She looked around for Joe but he wasn't there and she was relieved when he appeared, creeping into the incident room with his coat over his arm like a naughty schoolboy trying to creep past the teacher to avoid a late mark.

He saw her and smiled apologetically. 'Sorry, boss. I overslept. Anything new come in?'

But before she could speak she was interrupted by Sunny.

'News, ma'am. Traffic camera picked up a black BMW speeding away from Bearsley at twelve forty-five last night and it's registered to one Barrington Jenks. Want me to pick him up?' he asked with a grin that verged on the wicked.

'No,' said Emily quickly. 'I'd better deal with it.'

Sunny strode off muttering something about friends in high places just as the phone rang on Emily's desk.

After a brief conversation, she looked up at Joe, a triumphant smile on her face. 'Rory Quillan wants to make a statement. He wants to tell us everything.'

Zepper's conscience had kept him awake all night. Pet had trusted him, confided in him. But had he betrayed that trust?

He climbed out of bed, standing naked on the well-worn rug. Pet had been so lovely and he had wanted her . . . just as he had wanted Grace Cassidy all those years ago. Pet had reminded him so much of Grace. And now both girls were dead.

He slipped on his towelling dressing gown and walked into the living room, the polished wooden floor cool beneath his feet. It was Saturday, a full week since he'd taken part in the Early Music Festival. A full week since he'd last seen Pet Ferribie alive, gazing up at him as he performed on that outdoor stage. Somehow it seemed so much longer.

Pet's little pink notebook lay on the coffee table. After making himself a coffee to wake himself up, Zepper opened it. He needed to read it again before he made a decision.

Once he was satisfied that there was nothing in there that might incriminate him, he picked up the phone and dialled the number for Joe Plantagenet's direct line.

'Zepper's coming in to make a statement,' Joe announced as he and Emily were walking down the corridor to the interview room where Rory Quillan was waiting for them.

Joe saw Emily's eyebrows shoot up. 'Voluntarily?'

'Voluntarily. But he wants his solicitor present. He said he has a notebook Pet Ferribie left at the university.'

'So why hasn't he told us all this before?'

'No doubt we'll find out when he comes in. He says it's mostly about her search for her mother. There's a lot in it about someone she refers to as The Great Chef. Paolo Jones, I suspect.'

'Mr Jones is another person we need to talk to again.'

'I thought he was being quite open.'

'Oh come on, Joe, I reckon his relationship with Helen Ferribie was a lot more interesting than he was letting on.'

'Interesting?'

'Stormy maybe. Lovers' quarrels and all that. She left her

husband because he was boring and she wanted to become an artist. I reckon she would have been looking for a bit of passion in her life.' She grinned. 'As are we all.'

Joe opened his mouth to speak but thought better of it. He'd known passion and, in his experience, it only led to pain. Perhaps it had led to pain for Helen Ferribie . . . or even to death.

When they reached the interview room Joe took a deep breath before pushing the door open. As they entered Rory Quillan looked up, his eyes anxious.

'I want to tell you everything,' he said.

'A wise decision,' said Emily as she sat down.

'Jackie's not my wife. In fact we've never even . . .'

'You mean it's a platonic relationship?'

'Yeah, something like that.'

'Tell us how you met.'

'It was twelve years ago. She was only a kid and she needed help.' He fell silent for a while but Joe and Emily waited for him to gather his thoughts. 'I was staying at my uncle's house. He was away at the time so I had the place to myself. I went out to this bar . . . Anyway, I picked up this bloke . . . some posh estate agent.' He looked Joe in the eye, challenging him to criticize. 'That's how I am . . . how I was made. I've always felt more comfortable as a woman and . . .'

'You've never thought of making it permanent . . . having – what do they call it? – gender reassignment?' Emily asked.

'That takes some courage . . . having operations and all that. It's not something I've been able to face but . . . maybe one day.'

'What happened on the night you met Jackie?' Joe knew they were in danger of becoming sidetracked.

'Like I said, I picked up this bloke in a bar.'

'Barrington Jenks?'

'Barry, yes. He was a businessman; an estate agent. Very smart. Nice clothes. Big shiny car. I thought my luck was in.'

'He said you asked him for money.'

'I might have asked but I didn't get it. Events rather overtook us.'

'Tell us what happened.'

'We went back to the student house next door to my uncle's place because the students were away and I had the spare key my uncle had given me in case of emergency. But it was a lovely summer night so we decided to go into the woods. I got hold of a sleeping bag and . . . It seemed exciting; a little bit dangerous. Anyway, we were . . . when we heard this sound; a bit like sobbing. I said to Barry we should check to see if there was someone there. He was very worried about people finding out, you see – said he was married and had a lot to lose. Anyway, we got ourselves dressed and followed the sound. We got to this clearing and saw this girl lying on the ground. Another girl was bending over her sobbing. She got the shock of her life when she saw us. I rushed over to see if the girl was OK but Barry held back because he didn't want to get involved. I was in women's clothes and I guess the girl was a bit taken aback – or even scared thinking she'd met a pervert in the woods. Or at least that's what she told me later. Anyway, the girl on the ground wasn't breathing and there was blood on her head.'

'She was dead?'

'Yes. I asked the girl what had happened and she kept saying she'd killed her. I asked her why and she said she had to stop her. Barry said he had to go. He was scared stiff and he kept saying he couldn't afford anyone to find out. I told him to get the police and the ambulance and when he rushed off I thought that's what he was doing. Anyway, I took Jackie back to the house to wait but it turned out that Barry had buggered off and the police never came. Then I started to have second thoughts. Jackie was in a real state and she kept insisting that it had been an accident.'

'I thought she'd confessed to killing her.'

'Yes, but she was really upset and she wasn't thinking straight. She pleaded with me not to call the police but I didn't know what else to do.

'Did she say how this accident happened?'

'She said they'd been messing about and the other girl fell and hit her head.'

'What about her claim that she had to stop her doing something? What did she say about that?'

'Nothing. And I didn't ask. I just assumed she wanted to stop her getting hurt . . . I don't know.'

'What did she tell you about the dead girl?'

'Only that her name was Nerys and she was a friend from

school. She seemed very upset at first but then she came to her senses, like someone had flicked on a switch. She said she couldn't face it if the police started asking her questions and she couldn't face going home. She said that if we hid Nerys's body nobody would know. It was a stupid thing to do but I went along with it. I got a wheelbarrow from my uncle's garden and we took Nerys back to number fifteen. Then I thought of the loft. Nobody ever went up there and it'd give us time to think of what to do. I knew my uncle had sealed off the loft hatch next door because some bricks were missing in the party wall and you could get through to his loft that way. He said he didn't want the students getting up there and into his house. He was paranoid like that. We put Nerys at the far end of the loft next to the water tank hidden behind some old trunks, well away from number fifteen and we left her there.' He buried his head in his hands. 'I'm so sorry. It was a dreadful thing to do but . . .'

'And Jackie moved in with you?'

'She said she was in trouble and that she could never go back home because something terrible had happened. I let her stay in my flat and it just became a habit. Then, when I moved into my uncle's place, she moved with me. We never mentioned Nerys lying up there in the loft. It was as if we'd put her out of our heads. Blanked it out of our memories.' He hesitated. 'What'll happen to us?'

'That depends on how exactly Nerys died.'

'She said it was an accident.' Tears began to stream down his cheeks. 'And I believe her.'

'What about Barry?'

'What about him?'

'You've kept in touch?'

Rory's moist cheeks turned red. 'That was Jackie's idea. After a couple of years we kept seeing his face on election posters – your parliamentary candidate. Whiter than white. Big house and wife with a plastic smile. Jackie said he was a smug bastard and if only people knew what he really got up to. She made me contact him again . . . ask for money to keep quiet. Then we met up again a few days ago in a hotel. He paid up quite happily. Honest.'

'And he helped you move the body?'

'When that girl next door got murdered, me and Jackie

thought things were getting a bit hot. What if the police decided to break into the loft and search it? We asked Barry to help us with the move. We needed a bigger car to move her cause I've only got a little Fiat and I reckoned he owed it to us. We had to put her in a bin bag so she wouldn't make a mess all over his precious boot.'

'And I bet you threatened to go to the press.'

'Jackie did. It was all her idea. Everything.'

It was an old story, one that Joe and Emily had heard so many times before.

Zepper felt nervous as he was led into the interview room by a young female PC. But he had time to notice that she had very good legs. Out of uniform she'd be a stunner.

Once she'd left him he was kept waiting in that uncomfortable chair for what seemed like an age. But he supposed it was just another police tactic. Psychological warfare.

By the time DI Plantagenet entered the room, Zepper was starting to regret his decision. But Pet's little pink notebook sat there on the desk before him. If he played the cooperative citizen now, he'd be home and dry.

Plantagenet was with a young Asian woman, the sensible type but quite attractive. Zepper gave her a smile to establish a rapport. She didn't smile back.

The first thing the DI asked him was why he hadn't come forward sooner. He had his answer ready.

'I only found it yesterday. She'd left it in my room at the Music Department and it must have got hidden under a load of papers.' There was no way he was going to admit that he'd found it a couple of days ago and hung on to it so that he could see what, if anything, she'd written about him.

'Do you know what kissing the demons means?' the inspector asked as he finished flicking through the book.

'Pet used the phrase from time to time. She said it was something her mother liked to do. I presume it means doing something dangerous . . . taking a risk. Or maybe doing something forbidden. Your guess is as good as mine.'

Joe nodded. Den Harvey had used the title for the computer file hiding his secret stash of porn, which certainly fitted Zepper's interpretation. Something risky. Something taboo.

'A man called "The Great Chef" features quite a lot.' Zepper leaned back, more confident now the spotlight was focused elsewhere. 'She thought he knew what had happened to her mother. In fact she suggests that he might even have killed her. Any idea who he is?'

The inspector didn't answer the question.

'There's also "the landlord" – I presume that's Andy Cassidy.'

'Any idea who "the slob" is?'

Zepper shook his head but Joe thought he knew the slob's identity. Cassidy had used the word to describe Den Harvey.

'I presume you're "The Tutor". Very flattering some of this . . . suggests she'd like to – how does she put it? – explore new possibilities. And she says she wants to lose what has become burdensome to her.' Joe looked Zepper in the eye. 'Does that mean her virginity, do you think?'

Zepper nodded.

'And she mentions someone called "Suit Man". Says her mother might have gone to him before she disappeared. Know who he is?'

'No, sorry.'

'Cassidy thinks you killed his sister.'

'There's no way I'd ever have harmed Grace.'

'But she was under-age and you were sleeping with her. Did Cassidy find out? Is that why you killed her and got him locked up? And what about Pet? I bet she was a tease. I bet she drove you mad blowing hot and cold.'

Zepper felt a sudden pain in his chest. The room began to spin around and he heard blood rushing in his ear. He clutched at his shirt. It was too tight. Crushing him as he slid off the chair and landed heavily on the floor. Then he heard a loud alarm as the inspector hit the panic strip that ran around the walls.

Then he heard nothing more until a young nurse in intensive care asked him if he was comfortable.

'Do you want the good news or the bad news?' Joe stood in the doorway of Emily's office.

'Start with the bad news. I always like to get it out of the way.'

'Zepper's had a suspected heart attack . . . when I was questioning him.'

'Bloody hell. Hope he's not going to accuse you of police brutality. How is he?'

'Don't know yet. They've taken him straight to hospital.' He paused. 'Just when it was starting to look promising. He brought in a notebook belonging to Pet Ferribie – said he found it under some papers in his office, not that I believe that for a second. It's mostly notes she made about her mother's disappearance. I think Pet had a close relationship with Zepper . . . just like Grace Cassidy did.'

'She was a virgin.'

'So it was only a matter of time.'

'He hasn't got much of an alibi. But did he kill Sharon Bell and Roni Jasper? And what about Anna Padowski?'

Joe shrugged. Somehow he wasn't convinced. Zepper might have seduced his fifteen-year-old student. He might even have killed her to shut her up when she threatened to tell her father what had been going on. Maybe Pet too was becoming a nuisance. But Joe couldn't really see him killing Sharon and Anna in cold blood. That would take a different sort of monster. A demon.

'According to the notebook, Pet thought Paolo Jones had something to do with her mother's disappearance. But I don't see it myself.'

'Always keep an open mind, Joe,' Emily said with a small smile that verged on the smug. 'Anyway, it's time I had a word with Jade Portright – or Jackie as she likes to call herself these days. I'll take Jamilla with me – the woman to woman approach.'

'It'll be interesting to see whether she confirms Rory's version of events. Do you believe him?'

'Yes. I think I do.'

Sunny poked his head round the door. 'Jenks has been picked up, ma'am. He's on his way in with his lawyer in tow.'

'There's something I need to do before we talk to him,' said Joe.

Emily gave him an enquiring look.

'Got the number of the House of Commons?' he said lightly as he left the office.

After a few phone calls he found out what he needed to know. Barrington Jenks had taken part in a parliamentary debate on the night Roni Jasper had died. And it had finished an hour before her estimated time of death.

He sat at his desk, waiting for the call that would tell him Jenks was waiting for him in one of the interview rooms. But when the phone rang he heard Sally Sharpe's voice.

'Joe. I've had a good look at this mummified body. I know I'm doing the autopsy later but I wondered if you wanted to hear my preliminary thoughts.'

'I always like to hear your thoughts, Sally.' Somehow distance was making him feel bolder as far as Sally was concerned. Face to face he always felt a little embarrassed.

'Well I found some wood splinters embedded in the head wound. I think someone hit her very hard with a lump of wood from behind. Is that any help?'

'We've got a statement that says she had a fall and hit her head.'

'Crap . . . if you'll pardon the expression. There's no way that injury was the result of a fall. Will I see you later?' It sounded like an invitation to something more pleasant than a date at the mortuary.

'Probably.'

As soon as he ended the call the phone rang again. Jenks and his solicitor had arrived and had started kicking up hell downstairs.

NINETEEN

Jenks had hit upon a simple tactic, aided and abetted by his smartly dressed solicitor. Every question was answered with the words 'No comment'.

However, on the evidence of Rory Quillan, Jenks was charged with concealing the death of Nerys Barnton. When Joe warned him that it might only be the beginning, for the first time he saw the politician's confidence drain away.

Joe had passed a note detailing what Sally had said about Nerys's injuries into the interview room where Emily and Jamilla were questioning Jade Portright. Now he was waiting for Emily in the incident room to see what she'd managed to find out, but no sooner had he settled down to catch up with some paperwork when he had a call from reception telling him that somebody wanted to speak to him.

Joe picked up his jacket off the back of his chair and made his way downstairs, full of curiosity and when he pushed open the door which separated the sharp end of the police station from the outside world he saw Paolo Jones sitting on the bench at the far end of the foyer. He seemed to be staring at a crime prevention poster, deep in thought, but when he spotted Joe he stood up and took a sheaf of papers out of the leather bag he was carrying.

'I searched through the recycling like I promised and I found these.' He held the papers out to Joe as though he was anxious to get rid of them. 'They're mostly letting agents' details about flats and houses. I suppose she might have rented one of the places and didn't bother to let me know.'

'Thanks,' said Joe as he relieved Paolo of his burden. 'By the way, we've found a notebook belonging to Pet Ferribie. She reckons you know more about her mother's disappearance than you let on.' He watched the man's face for a reaction.

But Paolo shook his head. 'I tried to tell her but I don't think she believed me. I can't add anything to what I've told you already. Helen disappeared and I've no idea what happened to her.'

Joe was about to make his way back to the incident room but he saw Paolo Jones shifting from foot to foot as though he was reluctant to leave. 'Was there something else?'

Paolo hesitated for a moment before speaking. 'I was wondering . . . I just wondered how your investigation's going. And . . .'

'Go on,' Joe said quietly.

'Do you think Helen might still be alive?'

Joe thought there was no harm in giving him an honest answer. 'I'm sorry, I just don't know.'

Paolo slung his bag across his shoulder. 'I'd better get back to the restaurant for my shift. Promise you'll let me know if you find out where she is.'

Joe nodded. Although it was a promise he knew he might not be able to keep.

When he returned to the incident room he found Emily in her office. He gave a token knock on her door and walked in. She looked up but didn't smile.

'How did you get on with Jade?'

She sat back in her chair. 'Don't you find that there are some questions you wish you'd never asked?'

'What happened? What did she say?' He sat down on the chair opposite her, sensing she wanted, or needed, to talk.

'I hate anything to do with kids, Joe. I don't know if it's because I've got kids of my own . . .'

'You don't have to have kids to feel that way.'

She looked up. 'Oh Joe, I'm sorry. I didn't mean . . .'

'That's OK.' The fact that he and Kaitlin hadn't had children, that it was something they'd planned for a future that never happened, had bothered him a lot after her death. He'd always thought that a child would be a little bit of her still left on earth and for a while he'd grieved about it. Over the years the grief had faded. But sometimes it returned at the most unexpected times. 'What did she say?'

'Her father abused her. It started when she was about nine and went on until she couldn't stand it any more. When she had the chance to disappear she took it and she built up some sort of relationship with Rory Quillan – not sexual which probably came as a relief to her after what she'd been through. More like brother and sister. She changed her name – became Jackie Quillan. And of course they were bound together by their shared secret.'

'Nerys's death.'

'She claims that her desire to get away from her father was behind her unwillingness to report the so called accident.'

'I take it you told her about Sally's findings?'

'I did but she stuck to her story that Nerys fell. Said she must have hit her head on a log. But she did admit that she had a quarrel with Nerys that night. They'd planned to run away to London – they'd even left their rucksacks in the wood to pick up – but Nerys changed her mind and wanted to go home. And she said she'd tell Jade's parents where she was.'

'So Jade lost it. She'd thought she was going to get away from her father once and for all but Nerys let her down so she lashed out. I take it she hadn't told Nerys about the abuse?'

'She says not. Her story matches Rory's exactly. She met the two men in the woods and Rory helped her. Later, when she knew who Jenks was, she hit on the idea of blackmail.

I told her he'd been questioned and I think she assumed he'd told us everything. And I wasn't going to enlighten her.'

'And Rory went along with the blackmail?'

'Yes. But I don't think his heart was in it. If you ask me, Jade was the brains behind it all.'

'We'll have to tell Nerys's parents.'

Emily rubbed her eyes. 'Yes. But what about Jade's parents? What about Steve Portright?'

'He could face charges for what he did to his daughter.'

'It's her word against his and he's bound to deny it. Jade doesn't want us to tell her parents but I don't know how we're going to keep them in the dark once the news of Nerys's death becomes public.'

'What about her mother?'

'She blames her for not putting a stop to the abuse. She doesn't want to see either of them again, Joe. She says she's happy living with Rory. She says that he's her family now and she seems very protective of him.'

'It's a kind of love, I suppose,' said Joe. He understood the need for another human being to share things with; the trivialities and the big events of life. Someone to confide in; someone who was there.

'Yeah.' Emily said. Joe saw her glance up at the children's paintings she'd pinned up on her office wall.

'Paolo Jones has just been in to see me,' Joe said. 'He found those papers Helen Ferribie left at his place.'

Emily looked relieved at the change of subject. 'You think Helen Ferribie might be another victim?'

'Pet was looking for her. Perhaps she was killed because she was about to stumble on the truth.'

'Do you see Jones as a suspect?'

Joe shrugged his shoulders. 'Not really. But I don't think we can rule anything out at the moment.' He stood up. 'I'll go and have a look through the stuff he brought in. Who knows, it might be useful.'

Joe returned to his desk. They'd cleared up the case of the two missing girls but the murders of Pet Ferribie, Anna Padowski and the rest still remained stubbornly opaque. And whenever Joe thought they were clearing the fog away, it seemed to form again, thicker than ever.

He cleared a space on his desk and placed Paolo Jones's

papers there in front of him. He turned them over one by one. The most interesting and poignant item was a sheet of paper on which was written a poem in what looked like a young child's best handwriting. The poem was about a fairy. *Over lakes and over ponds, I skip to leafy bowers. My wings are made of spiders' webs, my dress of lily flowers.* The rest of it continued in a similar manner and Joe suddenly felt that he was intruding on something precious: a remnant of the time when Petulia Ferribie's childhood had been happy. Before her mother abandoned her to find whatever it was she was looking for. Helen Ferribie must have taken the poem to Eborby with her – a keepsake of the daughter she'd betrayed. But had that betrayal anything to do with her ultimate fate?

Most of the papers Paolo had given him were printed details of flats and houses for sale or rent and Joe flicked through them, making a note of all the addresses so that they could be checked out. Then suddenly he spotted one that made him look twice. On a sheet bearing the logo of a city centre estate agent he saw the printed details of a ground floor flat off Boothgate: one bedroom, lounge, kitchen, bathroom with access to a small courtyard garden. But it was the name and phone number scrawled and circled in blue ink that caught his eye. The number was unfamiliar but he knew the name alright. Andy Cassidy.

It was about time Pet Ferribie's landlord answered a few more questions. He looked at his watch. It was three o'clock already and he hadn't eaten a thing. He contemplated bringing Cassidy in again for questioning but he changed his mind. If he called on the man it would get him out of the office and he'd just have time to pick up a sandwich.

As soon as he'd taken his coat off the stand in the corner Sunny hurried in and made straight for him like a homing missile.

'I asked someone to contact all the local carpet companies,' Sunny said. 'Three places in the city centre have been carpeted in blue and red wool mix carpet – some people have no taste.' He smirked. 'A posh jewellers in the Fleshambles, a bridal shop in Coopergate and a staff recruitment agency in Boargate. I've sent someone round to check them out.'

Joe thanked him but somehow he couldn't see any of the premises mentioned being used as the location for two gruesome

murders. No doubt the officers Sunny sent would have a good
sniff around for anything that seemed suspicious but he wasn't
getting his hopes up.

The enclosed, busy atmosphere of the incident room was
rather oppressive and as he walked through the streets he felt
a welcome sense of freedom. After buying a sandwich, he
took a short cut through the Museum Gardens, sitting on a
bench to eat at leisure and feeling like a naughty schoolboy
playing truant.

When he'd finished eating he walked on past the abbey
ruins, imagining how the place would have looked in its heyday.
The magnificence of the great abbey church must have rivalled
the cathedral itself and the abbey buildings would have
stretched across the park almost down to the river.

He walked beneath the old abbey gate and out into the
street. It wasn't far to Cassidy's place and he used the time
to think. Wherever they looked Cassidy's name kept cropping
up and his connections to the victims – with the possible
exception of Roni Jasper down in London – was impossible
to ignore. And he couldn't forget that the man was a killer,
tried and convicted.

Cassidy didn't look at all surprised when he answered the
door, almost as if he'd become resigned to visits from the
police. He stood aside to let Joe in.

'I've got some news,' Joe began. 'Ian Zepper's in hospital.
Suspected heart attack.'

Cassidy said nothing for a few moments and when he spoke,
his voice sounded hoarse, as though he was suppressing some
strong emotion. 'How is he?'

'They think he'll live.'

'Good.' The word sounded half-hearted, almost as though
the news came as a disappointment.

'I want to talk to you about Helen Ferribie.'

'Who?'

'Pet's mother. You met her a few years ago when she was
looking for a flat.'

'I meet a lot of people. I can't remember them all.'

'She'd written down your name and phone number on the
details of a one-bedroomed flat not far from here.'

'I own a flat on Boothgate Close. Is that the one?'

Joe nodded and took the sheet of paper out of his jacket

pocket. He'd put it in a protective plastic cover and folded it carefully. When he handed it to Cassidy he studied it and nodded.

'I only had a couple of properties back then and I was letting them through these estate agents at the time but I sometimes showed prospective tenants round. She'll have called me for an appointment – that'll be why she's written my name and number on here.' He handed it back to Joe. He seemed confident, as though he knew Joe could prove nothing. 'And before you ask, I don't remember her.'

'Did Pet mention this to you?'

'She asked if I'd met her mother and I told her I didn't think so.'

'Did she tell you her mother was missing?'

'Yes. But I got the impression she'd run off. I mean there's missing and missing, isn't there? It sounded like her mother didn't want to be found. Not that I told Pet that. I thought it was best to let her live with her illusions.'

'I think her mother was murdered,' said Joe bluntly, watching Cassidy's reaction.

But he was disappointed. 'Sorry to hear that but it's nothing to do with me. I never killed my sister and I never killed this Helen woman . . . or Pet or Anna for that matter.'

'Dr Zepper brought in a notebook belonging to Pet. It's mostly about her search for her mother. You get a mention.'

'So I believe. He rang me last night and told me all about it.'

'How did you feel about Zepper sleeping with your fifteen-year-old sister?'

Cassidy began to walk towards the kitchen. 'Don't know about you but I need a coffee.'

Joe waited patiently while the coffee was made – properly by a flashy machine with elaborate spouts and dials. It tasted good and he sipped at it while he waited for Cassidy to speak. He looked as if he was in the mood for confidences. The only trouble was Joe didn't know whether to believe a word he said.

'OK,' said Cassidy as he sat down. 'Zepper was screwing my little sister. He could have lost his job . . . gone to prison, I don't know. But he knew exactly what to say to make me keep my mouth shut.'

'What do you mean?'

Cassidy sighed. 'He'd caught me with a woman . . . one of my teachers. She was married and she said that if anybody found out it would ruin us both. I was infatuated with her and I couldn't bring myself to betray her. Anyway, it didn't seem to have anything to do with Grace's murder. It didn't give me an alibi or anything like that so I kept quiet. I wish I hadn't now but I thought I was doing the right thing at the time. You do make some daft decisions when you're young and romantic, don't you.'

'Do you still think Zepper killed your sister?'

'He had an alibi and he's always denied it but . . . Look, if I could prove he killed Grace and clear my name, I'd be a happy man. But he keeps coming out with crap about loving her. Love? He was in a position of trust and he abused her. He should have gone to jail.'

'I can see why you're angry. Did you take that anger out on your sister?'

Cassidy turned away, fists clenched, and Joe knew that if it weren't for his job he'd probably have a bloody nose by now. He changed the subject. 'Who's the slob Pet mentioned in her diary? Could it be Den Harvey?'

'I suppose so.'

'And the Suit Man? Someone her mother might have seen before she vanished?'

'Haven't a clue. Could be anyone.'

'What about kissing the demons?'

Cassidy swung round. 'It was just something we used to say – me and my mates. It just means living dangerously. Kicking over the boundaries.'

'Pet used the phrase.'

'She might have heard me saying it. Or Zepper might have picked it up from Grace. Grace used to hang round sometimes when we were talking so she'd have heard the phrase. I've forgotten who first used it but we liked saying it. It made us feel . . . I don't know . . . daring maybe.'

'Do you possess a Halloween suit – the Grim Reaper?'

'You're joking.'

'I'd like a list of properties you own.'

Cassidy hesitated for a moment then disappeared. He returned a couple of minutes later with a printed list of addresses which he dropped on the coffee table.

'Are all of these occupied?' Joe asked as he picked them up.

'The address in Mungate's empty at the moment.' He pointed to one address. 'And this one in Bacombe's being renovated so it's crawling with builders.'

'Got the key to the Mungate flat?'

Cassidy disappeared for a minute or so and returned with a Yale key which had a cardboard label attached to it by a piece of string. Joe thanked him and promised to return it as soon as possible before taking his leave.

As he reached the door Cassidy spoke again, his voice subdued. 'Have Anna's parents arrived yet? I'd like to . . . I'd like to pass on my condolences. And I've put all her belongings in suitcases so . . .'

When Joe turned to face him he could have sworn he saw tears in his eyes.

When Joe arrived back in the office he found a brown envelope waiting on his desk. But before he opened it he asked somebody to check out the address Cassidy had given him – the vacant flat that didn't have builders crawling all over it. It was situated near the city centre in the new Mungate development. From the willingness with which Cassidy had provided the key, he didn't expect to find anything incriminating. But he couldn't help wondering about blue and red carpets.

He opened the brown envelope and found that there were six photographs inside, each a blown up section of the YSY group picture. When he laid them out together the image almost filled his desk. A number of new faces that had been distant blurs in the original were now sufficiently well defined to be recognizable but Joe was quite sure that he hadn't seen any of them before. It had been a long shot which had turned out to be a waste of time.

He looked at his watch. It was five o'clock on a Saturday afternoon. The time when most people were enjoying a weekend away from the demands of work. There was a time when he'd have wondered how soon he could get away. But as it was, he didn't have much to go home for. There were times when he wished Maddy was back in Eborby and not down in London – and this was one of them.

*   *   *

Death knew it was important to do things properly. He had thought up these rituals all those years ago during the times of terrifying darkness when he could neither see nor hear nor speak nor see nor touch nor taste. Before the mask of normality had been put on, so firmly that nobody could see behind it.

In those days he had only had the ghost of a murderer for company; a murderer who had owned the house he lived in and whose shade dwelled there still; breathing in the night, half seen in the shadows. The ghost of the murderer had visited in those dark times and he'd whispered to Death in that blackened room under the stairs.

This time the victim would be deprived of the sense of touch. Fingers were easy to sever and they made splendid souvenirs to treasure, to keep safe and precious to relive the sensations of killing. Death checked the knife he had sharpened on the electric machine in the kitchen and he knew that the blade would cut through flesh like butter.

Death wanted more than anything to return to the scene of Jacob Caddy's crime. He had been watching the woman who lived there from the trees behind the house and he'd seen her undressing at her uncurtained bedroom window, confident that she couldn't be seen. But Death had been there watching.

Recently the place had been crawling with police so Death knew his careful plans might have to change. Perhaps it would be amusing to claim one of the enemy as a victim; or somebody whose loss would cause them pain. Death knew that surprise was on his side. And besides, taking risks made you more powerful.

It was so good to kiss the demons.

TWENTY

At six o'clock Emily strolled over to Joe's desk. 'Anything new?'

He shook his head. 'There's no forensic evidence to match Andy Cassidy, Den Harvey or Ian Zepper to the crime scenes. I'm beginning to wonder whether the killer's invisible. There's nothing on CCTV or . . .'

'He'll slip up sooner or later.'

'You don't think he's going to stop now he's got a taste for it, do you?'

When Emily didn't answer he picked up a sheet of paper Jamilla had just left on his desk. It was a list of past staff at a firm called Harby's, one of the letting agents Helen Ferribie had dealt with. When he scanned the list of names, he saw one he recognized. He allowed himself a small smile of satisfaction as he handed the sheet to Emily.

'Look at this. Barry Jenks. Managing Director. This was in the days before he stood for parliament.'

'So he could have shown Helen Ferribie round properties?'

'If he was the boss he probably would have delegated but it's possible. Shall we get him in again?'

Emily nodded. 'Tomorrow, eh.'

Joe was about to say that if Jenks was the killer he should be locked up before he had a chance to strike again. But the fact that he was in charge of a letting agent used by a woman who may or may not have been a victim of crime was hardly evidence. Perhaps his instinctive dislike of the man was shading his judgement. He had helped cover up a crime when he hadn't called the police upon discovering Nerys's body, but that didn't mean he was a murderer.

Emily was about to return to her office when she spotted the blown up photograph, now stacked neatly into sections in his in tray. She picked the photos up and began to look through them. 'Any luck?' she asked.

'I don't think so. But it was worth a try.'

Suddenly she froze. 'I'm sure I've seen one of these lads before but I can't remember where. Of course he's much older now but . . .' She leaned over and pointed out a figure, a boy in shorts and T-shirt who was standing a few yards away from the main group posing for the camera.

Joe frowned. 'Yes, you're right. Of course it might not be him. Maybe if we had another word with Andy Cassidy . . .'

Emily nodded and Joe picked up the telephone receiver. If their luck was in, this was something that could be settled by a quick phone call.

Cassidy wasn't in. Neither was Den Harvey. The latter's mother had answered the phone and had been quite rude, accusing

Joe of harassing her son. Hadn't he been through enough when Sharon, that girlfriend of his, was killed? Joe left a message on Cassidy's answer phone and asked Mrs Harvey to tell Den to get in touch.

As soon as he put the phone down it rang again and he picked it up, hoping that it was Cassidy. But instead he heard an unfamiliar voice.

'Hello, this is Victor Smith from the Cosy Carpet Warehouse. Someone was in asking whether we'd fitted any blue and red wool mix carpet recently in the city centre.'

Suddenly Joe felt a thrill of hope.

'It's just that somebody bought a roll end of that carpet recently. It wasn't on our fitting records because she took it away with her in a van, said she'd get it fitted herself.'

Joe's heart was beating a little faster now. 'It was a woman?'

'That's right. Very smartly dressed.'

'Do you have a name?'

'Yes. There's a signature on our copy of the receipt.' He paused. Joe could just see him squinting at the handwriting, trying to make out the name. 'It looks like Carla Vernon. And there's an address. Do you want it?'

'Please.' Joe sat with his pen poised over his note book. When he'd written it down he thanked Victor Smith profusely and rushed to Emily's office.

But before he could get there he was waylaid by Jamilla who had yet another list in her hand. 'One of the house agents Helen Ferribie used was called Duttons. I thought you'd be interested in this.' She handed the sheet of paper to Joe and he read it with a smile.

'Thanks, Jamilla,' he said before resuming his journey to Emily's office. Then he turned back and picked up one of the blown up sections of the YSY photograph on his desk: the one featuring the unknown but familiar boy. 'Jamilla, can you keep trying Cassidy's and Harvey's numbers, then can you show whichever one you get hold of first this picture and ask them if they know who it is?'

Jamilla took the picture and when Joe entered Emily's office somehow he knew that he was going to make her day.

From where Death stood on the fringe of Dead Mans Wood he had an excellent view of thirteen Torland Place. The students normally went out on a Saturday night and sometimes the girl walked home from the city centre alone. The van was waiting at the end of the street and it wouldn't be hard to get her in there. She'd feel safe so close to home. Until the tape tightened around her wrists and ankles and she saw the knife descending.

He strolled away from the woodland and down the narrow alleyway at the side of the house. The rotting wooden gate leading to the small back garden of number thirteen was the way Jacob Caddy would have gained access all those years ago. It was more than a hundred years since Obediah Shrowton had been hanged for those murders he didn't commit. Caddy was a humble butcher but he'd been so clever – a genius – and nobody had suspected his guilt for a moment. And even though Shrowton knew the truth, nobody had believed him. Caddy had written down the story for his son who had passed it on to his son and so on, until this dark flame had been passed on to Death. Until Death had sat senseless in that blackened cupboard, conscious only of that terrible, triumphant story pouring into his brain.

As he walked down the alley and out into Torland Place, he passed a man out walking his dog but he didn't give Death a second look. Then he saw his quarry, strolling with a young man by her side, one of her housemates – the one called Matt. They were walking close to each other in silence as if they were trying hard to avoid any kind of physical or social contact. But from what Death had heard that house affected people like that, setting friend against friend, husband against wife and brother against brother.

Matt's presence meant that Caro was out of reach for now. But there'd be other nights, other times. And, besides, it might be an ideal opportunity to put the alternative plan into operation.

When Death walked past them they didn't even notice. But why should they?

The mask of normality had always served him well. And now it was time to go home and consider the next move in the game. The greater challenge. Kissing the demons.

TWENTY-ONE

Emily put the phone down. Jeff had had a hard day entertaining the kids after a week spent teaching a class of adolescents who weren't particularly interested in the history of the Industrial Revolution but he seemed to take the news that his wife wouldn't be home until after midnight philosophically. She'd told him it couldn't be helped. This new lead might well come to nothing but all her instincts were telling her to follow it.

She'd arranged to meet Joe in the car park and as she left the office she glanced at herself in the small mirror that hung on the wall, her one concession to vanity. She saw dark smudges beneath her bloodshot eyes and she knew she looked a wreck; but then she always seemed to look that way when there was a major murder enquiry on.

Joe drove them to Carla Vernon's address in Bacombe, a new block of flats on the main road out of Eborby. Just as he was about to press the button with the name 'Vernon' printed neatly below it, his mobile phone began to ring and he answered it quickly.

Emily listened to the conversation. Joe rarely sounded angry and her curiosity was aroused.

'You're drunk,' she heard him saying. 'Just leave me alone, will you?' Then he seemed to change tack. 'OK, you can stay at mine tonight. But only one night. My neighbour's got a key. Number five. Let yourself in and have a black coffee. I'll see you later.'

When he ended the call, Emily couldn't resist asking the obvious question. 'Who was that?'

Joe seethed for a couple of seconds before answering. 'Kirsten. My sister-in-law. She arrived back in Eborby this afternoon and she claims she's lost her credit cards so she can't book a hotel room. She says she's got nowhere to stay.'

'That's not your problem.'

'She sounds as though she's been drowning her sorrows all

afternoon. I felt I had to offer her a bed for the night, the state she's in.'

'I hope you're not giving her yours.' Emily was beginning to feel rather indignant on Joe's behalf. In her opinion, the Sister-in-Law from Hell was taking advantage.

'I can hardly let her sleep on a park bench, can I,' Joe replied.

'You're too bloody soft. I'd tell her where to go. Go on. Ring the bell.'

Joe did as he was told and after a few moments a breathless voice answered and they were buzzed in. The flat was on the third floor and Carla Vernon met them at the door, her arms folded defensively. When Emily had last seen her at the offices of McNeil and Dutton, she had been dressed for the world of business in formal suit and high heels. Now she wore jeans and a black long-sleeved T-shirt and her feet were bare. Emily noticed a pair of muddy trainers in the corner of the hallway as they followed her in. The mud looked fresh.

'Have you been out?' Emily asked, trying to sound friendly.

'I went out for a walk. Why?'

'You got a car?'

'Yes,' was the wary answer.

'You'll have needed a car to transport the carpet, I suppose,' Joe said.

'What carpet?'

'The roll end you bought from the Cosy Carpet Warehouse. Where is it now?'

'I'm not sure.'

'You can't just lose a roll of carpet.' She smiled, trying to hide her impatience. 'Do you mean you bought it for someone else?'

'It was for Ethan's office. He knows someone who's going to lay it for him.

'Is it still in the office?'

She hesitated. 'I think he might have taken it home. I'm not sure.' She didn't sound convincing.

'Have you got a key to the office?'

'No. Ethan keeps the keys.'

'What's his address?'

Carla hesitated. 'I don't know if he'd like . . .'

'His address.'

Carla thought for a few moments. Then she went over to

the telephone and picked up a tattered address book. 'Thirty-four Bamford Road, Hassledon.' She looked at her watch.

'Anxious to be somewhere?' Emily asked sharply.

'No. It's just that I planned to go out later and . . .'

'Well we won't keep you.' She looked at the phone. 'And I'd be grateful if you didn't contact Mr McNeil to tell him we're on our way. We like to surprise people and there's an offence called obstructing the police.'

Carla stood there with her arms folded and her expression gave nothing away. As Emily left she glanced through into the kitchen. The light was on, reflecting off a set of lethal looking knives arrayed against a magnetic strip on the wall. There was a space in the middle as though one was missing. But she dismissed the idea – for all she knew it could be in the washing up.

Kirsten's head was thumping. She'd thought a few drinks would take her pain away but she'd been so wrong.

She'd lied about losing her credit cards but he'd believed every word, so now she'd have him there alone and she'd get him to slip up and admit his guilt. And even if he didn't, there might be some evidence there in his flat, something that would give him away. She'd had no real luck in Devon but she was determined to prove somehow that her sister's death had been no accident.

Although her last drink had been a while ago and the effects had started to wear off, she still felt a little unsteady. Getting the key from Joe's neighbour as instructed hadn't been easy. She'd had to concentrate hard on getting the words out without slurring and betraying the state she was in. The neighbour had looked at her suspiciously at first but it seemed that Joe had rung on ahead to warn of her arrival. She had hardly expected him to be so cooperative. Perhaps he was up to something. She'd have to be on her guard.

She had aimed the key carefully at the lock and opened the door of his flat. It was dark and still in there and she didn't like the way the small block of flats stood so close to the grey, oppressive walls that guarded the old city.

After helping herself to several glasses of water to slake her raging thirst, Kirsten lay on the sofa and switched off the light. She kept her eyes open because whenever she closed them the room started to spin round and she felt a little sick. But after a while she couldn't fight sleep any longer and she lay there, unconscious and snoring, unaware that the front door she had left slightly ajar was being pushed gently open.

The small detached houses in Bamford Road had been built in the 1960s in the nadir of house building and no effort had been made to blend in with North Yorkshire's vernacular building style. Somehow Joe had expected an estate agent to have chosen something more architecturally inspiring.

There was no reply at number thirty-four although a light was on behind the closed blinds in the front room downstairs. Joe hoped Carla Vernon hadn't ignored Emily's warning and called to warn of their arrival.

After the third attempt he decided to try the neighbours.

With Emily by his side, he walked up to the front door of the neighbouring house and their knock was answered by a middle-aged woman dressed from head to toe in beige who gave them a glare that would have stopped a charging lion in its tracks. 'Before you start I don't buy anything at the door.'

'Quite right,' said Joe as he presented his warrant card. 'We're trying to get hold of your neighbour at number thirty-four and there's no answer. Do you know when he'll be home?'

'I don't, I'm afraid. His car's not there.'

'There's a light on. Is his wife likely to be in, do you know? She might not like to answer the door to strangers after dark . . . some people don't. But if you know her . . .'

'Oh I never see her. They keep themselves to themselves.' She leaned towards him and lowered her voice. 'They've got a baby but it never seems to cry. But some babies are like that, aren't they? Not that mine ever were.'

Emily stepped forward. 'You've seen Mr McNeil with the baby?'

'I see him taking it out in a pram from time to time. When they moved in he said the baby was a girl but I've not had a proper look at her and you can't see their garden from our house 'cos it's surrounded by that huge leylandii hedge. I asked him to get it trimmed and he said he'd do it. But nothing's happened yet.'

'You wouldn't have a key to the place by any chance?'

The woman shook her head. Then her round face lit up as though she'd just remembered something. 'Hang on.' She disappeared into the house and returned a few minutes later with a Yale key in her hand. 'I used to look after it for the Gibsons who lived there before and I forgot to give it back when they moved out.'

'May we borrow it?'

There was mischief in her eyes as she handed over the key, as though she was enjoying being part of a conspiracy against her stand-offish neighbour. 'Go on. But you'd better let me have it back.'

'We're a bit worried about the family. We'll just have a quick look to make sure everything's OK,' said Joe, taking the key. That was the official line and, from the ghost of a wink the woman gave him, she understood the situation.

'I wonder if she's had a look round the place already,' Emily whispered as they made for number thirty-four.

'It wouldn't surprise me.' He paused. 'But if she has she might have been playing a dangerous game.'

Emily inserted the key into the lock and the door swung open silently as she called out 'hello' in a confident voice.

When there was no answer she stepped into the cramped hallway and flicked on the light switch.

Joe looked around. The hall was painted in bland magnolia and there were no pictures on the wall, or anything else that marked it out as someone's personal space. If he hadn't been told that Ethan McNeil had a wife, he would have said it lacked the feminine touch. A baby's pushchair was folded up in the space under the stairs but this was the only sign of youthful life.

'So we're looking for a roll of carpet?' Emily said as she began to wander from room to room.

'If it was still in the office, surely Carla would have known. I think he took it home for some reason.'

'Or she did,' said Emily quietly. 'There was something odd about her, don't you think?'

Joe didn't answer.

The living room was sparsely furnished and lit by a standard lamp in the corner of the room. There were oatmeal coloured vertical blinds at the windows which gave the place an insti-tutional look.

Even the pile of brightly coloured plastic toys in the corner of the room looked wrong somehow. Too neatly arranged, perhaps or too shiny and new.

After a swift look in the kitchen, noting the bare worktops, Emily led the way upstairs. The wardrobe in the master bedroom contained men's and women's clothes but Emily observed that she'd never known a woman to have so little clothing . . . or so few shoes.

In the smallest room a night light glowed in the distant corner and Joe could see a mobile hanging over a cot. This was where the unusually quiet baby slept. He crept over to the cot and looked inside. But what he saw there made his heart almost miss a beat. A baby lay there on its side, its little face hidden in shadow. It lay quite still and seemingly fast asleep. He tiptoed out and found Emily on the landing. 'The baby's asleep in there. McNeil and his wife have left it on its own.'

'We'd better call Social Services then,' she said as she pushed past him into the small nursery. She bent over the cot and Joe saw her touch the baby's head with gentle fingers. When she swung round to face him he knew something was wrong. 'She's cold, Joe. Put the light on.'

Joe obeyed and hurried over to the cot, hovering anxiously behind Emily who had stripped the bedding off the tiny body.

'Oh God no,' he murmured as he watched Emily's fingers work quickly, feeling for a pulse, searching for signs of life.

Then suddenly she let the baby go and Joe saw her lips form a grim smile.

'Is she alive?'

Emily didn't answer. Then, to his alarm, she picked the baby up by its left foot and when she threw it to him he caught the small body in his outstretched hands and stared down at it in horror.

'Creepy or what?'

It took Joe a second or so to realize the truth. What they'd both assumed was a baby was in reality a very lifelike doll. It would fool most people at a distance and it had certainly fooled them in the dim glow of the night light.

Emily took the doll from him and flung it back into the cot. 'Good job we didn't make fools of ourselves by getting social services out. But what I want to know is why.'

Suddenly Joe's mobile rang and he fumbled to answer it. After a quick conversation he turned to Emily. 'That was Jamilla. She's just been round to Den Harvey's and he identified the boy on the photo as Ethan McNeil. He said he used to hang around with him and Cassidy sometimes – trailed after them, was how he put it. And he reckoned there was something odd about him. He used to act oddly around girls and Sharon Bell thought he was creepy.'

'That figures,' Emily said, looking down at the doll. 'When I saw McNeil he talked about his wife and baby – even had a photo of them on his desk. The family man. Is that what's behind all this, Joe? Is he playing a part so women will trust him? And if there is a wife where is she now?'

'Where is he for that matter?'

When they got downstairs Joe looked round again. This time he spotted something he'd missed the first time. A photograph on a shelf at the far end of the room amongst an assortment of paperbacks that looked unread.

Joe picked it up and looked at it. It was of a woman in a wedding dress but she wasn't the woman whose picture had stood on the desk in McNeil's office. When he examined it carefully he could tell that the picture had been folded over so that whoever was next to her – the bridegroom – had been cut out of the picture. Joe took the picture out of its frame and spread it out so he could see the whole image.

Paul Ferribie was instantly recognizable as the hidden bridegroom, even though the photo had been taken when he was in his twenties. And if Paul had been the groom it meant that the bride in the picture was Helen, Pet's missing mother. But why did Ethan McNeil have a photograph of her in his house? He showed it to Emily and she gave a puzzled frown. It didn't make sense. Yet.

'Get the crime scene people to give this place a going over. And I want that office searched as soon as possible. We'd better keep looking for that carpet and we'll get Carla Vernon down to the station for questioning while we're at it. She knows something, I'm sure of it.'

But there was no sign of the carpet in the house or the shed and a search of the office drew a blank. Carla Vernon claimed she had no idea where it was. Not that Joe trusted a word she said. In his opinion she was more than capable of lying to put them off the scent.

But he knew one thing for certain: once they found that carpet they'd find the killing place.

Kirsten opened her eyes. She felt as if someone was hacking pieces out of her brain and her mouth was dry. She needed more water. But at least now she'd sobered up. She didn't know why she'd got herself into that state and she swore it wouldn't happen again. Maybe once she'd avenged her sister she would start to live again.

After their parents died she'd neglected her sister, Kaitlin, to lead a life of arid selfishness. Men and drugs had been her priority when she and Kaitlin should have been a comfort to each other. She'd gone away and left Kaitlin to her fate; to a man who, in spite of an impressive royal name, came from a large Catholic family crammed into a small terraced house in a Liverpool street. He'd tried the priesthood but that hadn't lasted. Then after Kaitlin died he'd joined the police – a fine career for someone like that, a man who had let her sister die.

The thoughts swirled in her head as she tried to justify her actions and convince herself that she was in the right. When the doubts sometimes crept in she suppressed them rapidly. She wasn't falling for Joe Plantagenet's lies like her sister had done.

She heard a door open and close somewhere in the flat. He was back. She closed her eyes for a few seconds and sighed. She had intended to speak to him, to discover the truth, but her mind was fuzzy and there was no way she could muster the concentration to catch him out. She cursed herself for being so stupid. But intoxication of one kind or another had always been her weakness. She hadn't even grasped the opportunity to search for evidence as she'd intended to do.

She closed her eyes tight when she heard footsteps coming down the hall. There was no way she wanted to talk to him now as she knew that he might take advantage of her vulnerability to convince her of his innocence and that was something she couldn't face.

She thought he'd just peep in, see that she was asleep and go. But she heard his footsteps creeping towards her muffled by the carpet. She kept her eyes shut. She was in no state for conversation, polite or otherwise.

Then she felt something on her face. Something heavy and sticky sealing her eyelids together. And her mouth. She tried to scream but it was impossible to get the sound out. Her arms were pinioned behind her back and she felt herself being dragged off the sofa. But the more she struggled to resist, the tighter she was bound. Then she felt herself being flung on the ground and rolled over into something that smelled of damp and mothballs. Then she heard a zip being fastened and felt herself being moved at crazy angles so that her bruised limbs hit the floor. She felt as if she was being wheeled in some sort of large holdall, bound and disorientated.

Joe Plantagenet had gone too far this time, exposing her to a terror she hadn't experienced since childhood when the bad demons came to her in nightmares.

A few phone calls lured the team from the Saturday evening comfort of their homes and a thorough search was being made of McNeil and Dutton's offices. The motive behind the murders still baffled Joe. Why had the killer deprived each of his victims of one of their five senses? Maybe he'd explain when he was caught.

A patrol car had been sent to pick up Carla Vernon. Joe needed her to make a list of all the properties on McNeil and Dutton's books. Then it would be a matter of waiting for the search teams to do their bit.

Emily was pacing up and down the office gnawing at her nails and Joe knew how she felt.

Cassidy had been out when they'd tried him earlier but Joe tried his number again and this time he was in luck.

'You're a friend of Ethan McNeil's . . .' he began as soon as he heard Cassidy's voice.

'More of an acquaintance really. Ethan's a family man and he doesn't go in for male bonding.'

'You said he was with you on the night of Pet's murder?'

'That's right.'

'What time did he leave? And I want the truth this time. Think carefully.'

There was silence at the other end of the line. 'I said midnight, didn't I?'

'If you tell us it was earlier, you won't be incriminating yourself. I promise.'

'You sure?'

'Yes. We need the truth now. The exact time he left.'

Cassidy hesitated. 'I might have exaggerated a bit because I knew I needed an alibi. I wasn't watching the clock but I think he left around ten thirty. Why?'

This was a question Joe didn't want to answer just at that moment. 'I need to know if he owns any properties in Eborby.'

'He's got a house in Hassledon. Bamford Road.'

'Have you been there?'

'Once.'

'Was his wife there?'

'She was away at her mum's. She spends a lot of time there. He met her down in London and they only came back to Eborby eighteen months ago. Come to think of it, I've never actually met her.'

Somehow this was what Joe had been expecting to hear. 'Does he own any other properties? Please think carefully.

'I don't know whether he's got rid of his parents' place. I came across it recently when I was looking for properties to develop – it was in a bit of a state so it was perfect for what I wanted. I contacted the Land Registry to find out who owned it and when I discovered that it was Ethan I was a bit surprised 'cos he'd never mentioned it. When I asked him he said he'd inherited it from his parents and he hadn't decided whether to sell it or not.'

'I take it his parents are dead?'

'His mum died years ago and I think his dad died just before he came back to Eborby but I couldn't swear to it. Why are you asking all these questions?'

'Where is this house?'

'Flower Street, just south of the city centre. It's a detached Victorian place – looks a bit "house of horrors" 'cos nobody lives there. But with a full refurbishment . . .' Cassidy hesitated for a moment. 'Does this mean I'm in the clear?'

'Thanks for your help, Mr Cassidy,' Joe said.

As he ended the call Jamilla hurried up to him. 'Carla Vernon's been taken to McNeil and Dutton's office. Want me to come with you?'

'Yes. But I've got a call to make first. McNeil owns a

property in Flower Street and I want to get someone over there.'

Once he'd informed Emily about the Flower Street development and arranged for a patrol car to check the house for signs of life, he left the police station with Jamilla. Carla was waiting for them in her office, sitting at the desk she normally used, arms folded defiantly. 'It's all nonsense,' she said. 'Ethan wouldn't hurt anyone.' There was aggression in her voice. And something else – uncertainty perhaps.

Joe pushed her in tray to one side and perched on the edge of the desk, his eyes fixed on her face as though he didn't want to miss any telltale change of expression. 'You seem very loyal.' He saw her blush. 'Are you having an affair with Ethan?'

She looked away but Joe continued. 'Correct me if I'm wrong but I think he's promised to leave his wife for you when the time's right.'

'They have a young baby so he won't leave her in the lurch. I know that's no good for me but it shows that he's a decent man. He hasn't done anything. You're making a big mistake.'

Someone had to break the news and he reasoned it might as well be him . . . especially as a dose of truth might make her more willing to talk. 'We don't think Ethan's wife exists, Carla . . . and there's certainly no baby. It's all a charade.'

She shook her head violently. 'You're lying.'

'When one of our officers went to Ethan's address to confirm Andrew Cassidy's alibi for the time of Pet Ferribie's murder, he spoke to a woman who said she was his wife. Was that woman you, Carla?'

'His wife was away at her mother's with the baby so he asked me to stand in for her because he really couldn't afford the time to cope with all the intrusive questions the police ask people. He was at home but he didn't have anyone to vouch for him so I stepped in. You do understand, don't you? I was helping him.' She looked at him with pleading eyes and Joe couldn't help feeling a little sorry for her.

'Did Pet Ferribie visit Ethan?' He took Pet's photo from his pocket and pushed it towards her. 'She was trying to trace her mother who disappeared in Eborby some years ago.'

Carla hesitated. 'Yes. She came to the office. She was going round all the estate agents. We couldn't help her.'

'She saw Ethan?'

As Carla nodded Joe was sure that he now knew the identity of Suit Man.

'We need a list of any properties he has access to in or near the Fleshambles area.'

For a moment Carla looked as though she was about to refuse. But after a few seconds she stood up and walked over to a filing cabinet near the door. She took out a file and handed it to Joe. 'These are details of all the office premises we're handling round there.'

Joe handed the file back to her. She'd be able to do this quicker than he would. 'Just make a list.'

As she began work Joe's mobile rang.

When he answered it he heard Sunny's voice on the other end of the line. 'We're at that house in Flower Street. He's not here but a window was open round the back so we let ourselves in . . . just to check that all was well of course.' Joe could imagine Sunny giving a meaningful wink as he said the words. 'You should come down here and see the place. It's seriously weird.'

'How do you mean?'

'You'll have to see for yourself. I've let the boss know and she's on her way.'

'Any sign of McNeil?'

'A neighbour saw him driving up in a van earlier. He went into the house then came straight out again, as though he'd changed his mind.'

'Thanks, Sunny. Get the place sealed off and I'll be there as soon as I can.'

As he ended the call he heard Carla's voice. 'There are only two places. One in Queen's Square and one on the Market Square.'

'Are you sure that's all?'

He suspected that she was lying so he took the file from her but when he looked through it, it seemed that she was right. Only two office properties fitted the bill.

His mobile rang and this time it was his neighbour, Shirley; a sensible and rotund woman in her sixties and owner of several cats. He'd told Kirsten to ask her for his spare key and he assumed that was the reason for her call.

'Sorry to bother you, Joe, but I found your flat door wide

open. I gave that lady the key like you said and I went inside to check she was alright but . . .'

He realized that Shirley sounded worried. 'What is it, Shirley? What's the matter?'

'When I went in there was nobody there. And it looked as though there'd been some sort of struggle. I really think you should come back and have a look.'

He turned to Jamilla. 'Sorry, I've got to go. You see what else you can find out here and get someone to check out those premises.'

Jamilla followed him to the door. 'Everything OK?' she asked, lowering her voice.

'My neighbour's just called to say there's a problem at my flat. I'll get round there then I'll join Sunny at Flower Street. You OK here?'

Jamilla nodded, glancing at Carla who was sitting at her desk staring ahead, her lips set in a stubborn line. 'I'll try and get her talking.'

Joe thanked her and rushed off. If Kirsten was playing silly games at a time like this he'd be very angry.

As Kirsten was driven away she felt as though she was about to suffocate. She was trapped in what she assumed was a large case or holdall with soft canvas sides and her whole body felt as though she'd been thrown from a great height. She tried to call out but her mouth was taped shut. There was tape over her eyes too, and over her ears, and she couldn't move her limbs. She was in a dark unsteady world without sensation. When she'd accused Joe Plantagenet of killing her sister, she'd never thought for one moment that he was capable of anything so cruel, so calculating. It took a lot of hatred to take revenge like this.

She hadn't seen her assailant's face but she'd had the impression of someone tall, probably somebody Joe had paid to get rid of her. It must have been organized by her brother-in-law; nobody else knew she'd be there in his flat.

Everything she knew about Joe came from what Kaitlin had told her . . . and that had all been good because Kaitlin had been blinkered by infatuation. Kirsten, however, had built up an alternative picture as she'd constructed the case against him. She'd persuaded herself that he was a deceiver – a failed priest on the make, ready to take advantage of a wealthy and unworldly young woman. But when she'd met him the contrast between her expectation and the reality had shocked her and she'd had to struggle to convince herself that Joe was a good actor: a purveyor of lies wearing a false mask of honesty. There was no way that the man she'd found in Eborby was the real Joe Plantagenet.

The vehicle she was in had come to a sudden stop and when she tried to struggle in the confines of her trap she found movement impossible. She was at somebody else's mercy and for the first time doubts began to creep in and she hoped she was right about the identity of her captor. If Joe had organized it to teach her a lesson and get her off his back, then he wouldn't go any further. He'd given her a shock and that would be that. Surely.

Joe found Shirley flapping around like a worried hen.

'I didn't hear anything,' she said, full of apology. 'But then I had Strictly Come Dancing on rather loud and . . .'

'Don't worry about it,' Joe said, placing a reassuring hand on her arm before venturing inside his flat.

Shirley was right about the disturbance. The sofa had been pushed to one side and a lamp, still lit, lay on its side next to a pool of cold tea from an upturned mug on the wooden floor. Joe looked round, taking in the scene. Then he knelt down and picked something up from the floor. A tiny piece of fluff, possibly from a newish carpet. He couldn't be sure from such a small sample but it seemed to be red, maybe with a fleck of blue. He rushed out into the passage where Shirley was still standing.

'Did you see anyone come in or out this evening?'

'I don't think so.'

'Or anybody hanging around the flats?'

Shirley thought for a while. Then she raised a finger. 'I did have a peep out of the window just before Strictly started. A van was parked outside. I saw the driver get out and go round to the back. He took out one of those big wheelie holdalls and wheeled it towards the front door.'

'Was it big enough to hold a person?'

Shirley looked a little shocked. 'I suppose so, yes.'

'Did you see this person enter the flats?'

'Sorry. I didn't see anything else after that because Strictly started.'

Joe bent forward and gave her a quick kiss. Shirley looked rather gratified and touched her cheek. 'What kind of van was it? Can you remember?'

'It wasn't as big as a Transit. It was more the size of an estate car . . . only with no windows at the back if you know what I mean.

Joe knew alright. He called in the details. Soon all police patrols would be on the lookout for small dark-coloured vans.

'And the driver? Did you get a look at him?'

'No. He had his hood up – I thought it was a bit odd because it wasn't raining.'

It was as Joe expected. Whoever had abducted Kirsten – if she had been abducted – would have been careful not to be identified. Joe thanked his neighbour, locked up his flat and rushed out into the night air.

He'd promised to join Sunny and Emily at Flower Street. There was always a possibility that McNeil would return there with his prey – if indeed he had got Kirsten. There was a strong chance that she'd made a mess and gone of her own accord as some kind of twisted joke. However, Shirley's sighting of the van, the tiny shred of carpet fluff and the hooded figure with the holdall, big enough to hold a human body, indicated otherwise. But he wondered why, amongst all the women in Eborby, McNeil had picked on Kirsten.

He drove too fast to Flower Street and as soon as he turned the corner he saw an unmarked car and a patrol car parked outside the house at the end of the cul-de-sac.

He climbed from the car and looked up at the house. It was an ugly building, set on its own and separated from its neighbours by tall laurel hedges each side. There were lights on inside and he could see the old-fashioned interior through dirty, uncurtained windows. The front door was ajar and when he pushed it open he saw Emily standing in a narrow hallway with nicotine coloured walls. He thought she looked a little shocked, not her usual self.

'What have you found?' he asked.

'Come and see for yourself.'

As Joe followed her upstairs he outlined what had just happened; Kirsten's disappearance and the state of his flat.

At first Emily made sceptical comments – until he told her about the holdall and the carpet fluff. Then she looked worried.

'Why target Kirsten?' she asked, puzzled, as they stood on the landing.

'Perhaps he's been watching my place.'

'And if he's been watching your place, he's probably been watching mine,' she said softly. He saw her suppress a shudder.

The thought that a killer had been spying on him made Joe uncomfortable. And Emily was right. If he was playing a game of cat and mouse with the police why wasn't she a target?

'Perhaps I should warn Jeff . . . The kids . . .'

'If he's just interested in young women they hardly qualify.'

'Oh God, Joe, I hope you're right.' It was nine o'clock now but she made a quick call to Jeff, just to tell him not to let the kids out of his sight at any time. She finished the call and touched his arm gently. 'Joe, you'd better see this.'

She opened the door to the back bedroom slowly and carefully. He could see she was wearing her crime scene gloves and he fished in his pocket and put on his own before following her into the room. There was no bed in there, just a large mahogany desk standing on a threadbare rug and a chest of drawers in the corner. The curtains were thick and half eaten by moths. The room smelled of decay and death and Joe had the uneasy feeling that he was being watched from the shadows by unseen, malevolent eyes.

There were sheets of paper around the walls, stuck to the faded flowered wallpaper with rusty drawing pins and, on close examination, he found that they were pages from old newspapers, yellowed with age. As he began to read he discovered that they dated from the eighteen nineties, the far off days before papers carried photographs. On each sheet an article was circled. The Shrowton murders.

'There's a book on the desk,' said Emily. 'A kind of diary.'

Joe walked slowly over to the desk and picked up a book that was lying in its centre. It was heavy and seemed to be bound in some sort of leather – pig skin perhaps. Joe opened it up.

'Good job you've got those gloves on, Joe. Read the first page.'

He did as she suggested and instinctively dropped the thing back on the desk.

'This book is made from the skin of Obediah Shrowton, hanged at Eborby prison thirteenth October 1896.'

He could see the pores in the tanned flesh and it made him feel a little nauseous. But he forced himself to open it again. He had to know what was written inside. In the light of the bare bulb dangling overhead he began to read.

'I Jacob Caddy have the power over life and death. I am Death. The Reaper of souls. I have kissed the Demon and she urges me to kill.'

He turned to Emily. 'Have you read this?'

She nodded. 'I talked to the neighbours before you arrived. They've been here for years and they remember Ethan McNeil's parents . . . said they "kept themselves to themselves", which I took to be a coded way of saying they were odd. They hardly saw Ethan when he was growing up but they often heard him crying and they said he was unusually quiet. I suppose these days someone would have called in Social Services.'

'Anything else?'

'The house has been in the same family since it was built in the 1880s so if that's true it means that McNeil's a descendant of Jacob Caddy.'

'Keeping up the family business,' Joe said almost in a whisper as he began to read the next page of the horrible journal.

It was an account of the murders of Obediah Shrowton's family and servants. A cold-blooded narrative outlining each blow. The fact that he had split the skull of Obediah's wife open so that he could see her brain seeping out of the broken skin. And there was more about demons. The demons Caddy embraced who urged him on to terrible acts. He wrote dispassionately about how he despised Shrowton whose high-handed attitude to him as a tradesman had rankled. As Joe turned the pages he discovered that other people who had offended Caddy, either in reality or his imagination, had died too. Some of these murders went unsolved, others blamed on somebody amongst the victim's family or close associates. Caddy himself, he wrote, had never come under suspicion. His demons had protected him . . . and the fact that he wore the mask of the harmless, jolly butcher. Caddy's business had prospered and he had settled in this house. His demons had seen him right.

'Was his demon real, do you think?' Emily asked unexpectedly.

This possibility had never occurred to Joe. He had assumed that the demons were in Caddy's head. 'He refers to the demon as "she" and talks about kissing it. Maybe it was a woman urging him on. But why? It doesn't make sense.'

He moved slowly round the room. There was a dusty book-case filled with notebooks. He picked one out but the lists of times, numbers and scribbled notes they contained didn't make much sense. The name written neatly on the covers was Prof. G. McNeil. Presumably a relative.

Suddenly he heard a voice shouting from downstairs. 'Ma'am, we've got that door open.'

'They've been trying to open the door to the cellar,' Emily explained. 'It was locked and it seemed to be reinforced with something. I'm not looking forward to seeing what's down there.'

They made their way down the stairs in silence. When they reached the hall Joe saw that the door under the stairs was ajar and the uniformed constable was standing next to it with a solemn expression on his face.

Joe knew the question had to be asked. 'Has somebody had a look down there?'

The constable nodded but he said nothing. As Joe descended the narrow stairs he expected to see more dust and cobwebs but it looked as though the stairs had been recently cleaned and when he reached the bottom he found himself in the cellar with brick walls and a roughly cobbled floor. The bare bulb overhead was lit but there was darkness in the corners.

'There's nothing here,' he heard Emily say. He had almost forgotten she was there behind him.

'There's another door.' Joe strode across the cobbled floor and when he tried the door he found it locked and swore softly under his breath.

'Is this any good?'

He turned and saw that Emily was holding a large iron key. 'It was hanging on that hook over there,' she said, pointing to an old rusty hook protruding from the wall.

Joe took it from her and put it in the lock. It was stiff but it turned eventually. 'Go on,' Emily said impatiently as the door creaked open.

He took his torch from his coat pocket, glad she was close behind him. No outside light penetrated into that small, brick-lined room, empty apart from a filthy mattress against the far wall and a bucket in the corner. The place smelled dank and musty. And it smelled, Joe thought, of suffering.

'Oh God,' Emily muttered. 'This must be where he brought them.

Joe shook his head. 'That door hasn't been opened in years. He doesn't bring them here, I'm sure of that. He uses this house but this isn't where he takes his victims.'

'So what's this room for? Oh bloody hell, Joe, it makes my flesh creep.'

'I've no idea,' Joe said quietly. 'But I'm sure it's been used to imprison someone at one time.'

'Who?'

'It's an old house. It could have been used at any time.'

He walked forward into the dank little chamber, eight foot square. The mattress looked ancient, as did the old enamel bucket with the nasty stains in the base. On the wall next to the door was something Joe hadn't noticed at first glance. A pair of hooks, rusty like the one in the main cellar. From one hung a length of fraying rope. From the other dangled something that looked like part of a medieval helmet. But this was no protection for a human head, just a cage with a piece of iron protruding inwards where the tongue should be. Both the rope and the metal contraption were encased in cobwebs and once the door was shut, the place would be completely dark.

He heard Emily draw in a sharp breath. 'I've seen one of those before in a museum. It's a scold's bridle.'

'It's rusty. And look at the cobwebs – it hasn't been used for years.'

'Certainly not on our victims but there's a theme here, Joe. No light, soundproof room, hands tied together with the rope so you can't feel your way around the walls. And that thing to imprison your tongue.' Joe saw her shudder in the torchlight. 'Let's get out of here.'

Joe followed Emily out of the cellar, leaving the door to that dreadful room wide open. Being in there had disturbed him, as though demons had been concealed there in the shadowy corners. Something terrible had happened in there.

But none of the evidence pointed to it being the scene of the murders of Pet Ferribie or Anna Padowski. They had died in another place.

When they reached the hall Emily addressed the half dozen officers who'd been waiting there in case McNeil returned. 'Right, I want a couple of you to get this place sealed off so the Crime Scene people can have a good look round . . . with particular attention to the cellar. Everyone else I want out looking for McNeil's van. He might be somewhere in the city centre.'

Joe saw one of the newer detective constables looking at her curiously. 'Am I right in thinking, ma'am, that he's got another victim?'

Emily gave the lad an appreciative look. 'Let's just say we need to find him urgently. There is a possibility he might have picked up someone else.'

'Who, ma'am?'

'Just let's find him, eh.'

As they left the house Joe whispered in her ear. 'You don't reckon Kirsten could have arranged all this? If she had a look at my case notes and . . .'

'Bit of an elaborate charade just to get back at you. But from what you say . . .'

Emily didn't have a chance to finish her sentence before her mobile rang. After a short conversation she caught hold of Joe's arm. She looked excited, as if the breakthrough they'd been waiting for might just be in view.

'That was Jamilla. She decided to use her initiative and compare the list Carla provided with the details on the office computer. She found another address – an empty office on the Fleshambles that belongs to McNeil and Dutton. When she asked Carla why she hadn't included it on her list she claimed that it wasn't a property they rent out on behalf of clients so she'd completely forgotten about it. The bitch was lying, of course. Come on.'

Joe drove, switching on the blue flashing lights built into the unmarked car, while Emily sat in the passenger seat calling for back up.

It took ten minutes to get to the heart of the city and when they neared their destination Joe drove down Coopergate and turned left down a pedestrianized street, making for the market square behind the Fleshambles. He drove slowly, receiving curious stares as the wandering tourists parted to let him through. He negotiated the narrow street leading on to the square and brought the car to a halt in a space next to a small navy blue van parked well away from the nearest street lamp.

'Do you reckon that's his van?' he asked as they got out of the car.

Emily didn't answer. Then, as if by mutual agreement, they dashed towards the narrow snickleway that led on to the Fleshambles. The passage was too cramped for them to walk two abreast so Joe, the faster runner, went first.

'What number?' Emily snapped, following close behind.

'Fifteen.'

They reached the street and rushed along its length. Most of the little shops weren't numbered but finally they found a souvenir shop that bore the number nine. They counted along. Nine, eleven, thirteen. Fifteen was a jeweller's shop and any other time Emily would have taken an interest in the expensive items glinting in the window. But when she could see no obvious way up to the jutting storey above the shop, Joe saw her clench her fists and ram her right hand down on the wide windowsill.

'Round the back.' Joe sensed that their quarry was near.

As they rushed back down the snickleway towards the jumble of back yards behind the shops, a maze of rickety gates, fire escapes and outbuildings, Joe stopped running and tried to get his bearings, suddenly plunged into despair. Then he felt Emily's guiding hand on his arm.

'Come on,' she said as she rushed along the row, counting to herself as Joe followed. Then she stopped abruptly and he almost cannoned into her. 'This is it.'

Joe saw a battered wooden gate, half falling off its hinges, bearing the number fifteen scrawled in faded white paint.

Emily gave it a hefty push and when it gave way they both stumbled into a back yard full of junk: defunct office chairs, wooden crates and even an antiquated desk top computer. Half the yard was sheltered from the elements by a corrugated roof but this hadn't protected the items dumped there from damp. They picked their way through a narrow gap and found themselves facing a half glazed back door.

'Do we go in or do we wait for back up?' Joe whispered.

Emily froze, listening for the sound of approaching sirens on the night air. 'Let's go in.'

Joe put his hand on the door and to his surprise it opened silently. They stepped inside a small lobby, dimly lit by the tall street-light standing just outside the yard. On one side Joe could see a solid steel door which, presumably, led into the jeweller's shop. Ahead of them was a narrow staircase. He took his torch from his pocket and shone it upwards. In the torch beam he could see a white painted door at the top so he began to climb, Emily following behind. When they reached the small landing at the top he doused the torch. The last thing they wanted was for whoever was in there to see the light under the door.

They stood there listening for any telltale noises but all they could hear was the sound of sirens, distant at first then getting nearer. Then very near as though they'd burst into the market square. 'Now,' Emily hissed.

Joe put a tentative hand on the door handle and felt a frisson of satisfaction when he discovered that, like the back door, it was unlocked. He gave the door an almighty shove and it banged open. He fumbled for a light switch by the entrance and the cramped hallway was flooded with light, revealing three closed doors.

Emily gave the first door a kick and when it burst open they saw a tiny, shabby kitchen. 'Stay there,' she hissed to Joe as she opened the second door. Joe watched her, tensing his body in case he needed to rugby tackle a fleeing murderer. Emily switched on the light but all he could see in the watery light of the overhead bulb was an empty, unremarkable office, carpeted in grey.

He marched towards the third door, their last option, kicked it open and reached for the light. But again the room was empty. Joe swore under his breath.

'What do we do now?' Emily muttered.

Joe didn't answer. The van was outside and McNeil owned the premises, a fact which Carla had gone to some trouble to conceal from Jamilla. He wasn't going to give up yet.

He stepped into the first office and looked around. But he saw nothing that might conceal a hiding place. The second office was the same.

'He's not here, Joe.' Emily sounded despondent. 'The back up's arrived so I'll get them to seal off the area.'

Joe didn't reply. He made for the tiny kitchen and switched on the light. It too was empty, the stained worktops bare of even the most basic equipment. Joe began to shut the door when he spotted something: another door that had been hidden when the door was wide open. Emily had come up behind him to investigate and when she saw it their eyes met.

'It'll be a cupboard,' she said in a whisper. 'But we'd better have a look.'

Joe counted to three before he put his shoulder to the door and it gave way with a crash.

Instead of the expected cupboard or larder, the door opened on to a large, low-ceilinged room with a subdued light in the corner. There was no tell tale glow of a window to the outside world and he guessed that it might once have been part of an attic in the higgledy-piggledy building. As his eyes adjusted to the dim light, he saw a figure crouching at the far end like a wild beast guarding its prey.

'Hello, Ethan,' Joe said quietly, watching the figure as he felt for a light switch. But the wall was bare.

'We've got back up downstairs. You can't get away now.' As the killer straightened himself up, Joe spotted a shape on the floor, lying quite still. And he could make out something in Ethan's right hand. Something long and slim. A knife.

As Joe crept closer, he could hear Emily breathing behind him and he was strengthened by the knowledge that he wasn't alone.

'Is that Kirsten?'

There was no answer and the shape on the floor didn't stir.

'I've seen the cellar in Flower Street, Ethan. I know why you're doing this.'

Joe could almost feel the killer's body tensing.

'They kept you in there, didn't they?'

Joe heard a strangled cry of pain, swiftly cut off. He thought it came from the killer rather than his victim.

'Why don't you come outside? We'll look after Kirsten.' He couldn't be absolutely sure it was Kirsten but he thought he'd take a chance.

All of a sudden he heard a howl, the desperate sound of a cornered, wounded beast, and the figure dropped to his knees, shifting Kirsten's body on to his lap. He sat there quite still, forming a shadowy tableau that reminded Joe of the carved

Pietas he had seen during his years when he'd thought of giving his life to the church. But this was no mother mourning her son: this was a killer mourning, if not his victim, then his own damaged life.

Joe shook off Emily's restraining hand and began to walk slowly towards him, bowing his head because of the lowness of the ceiling. He could hear the killer sobbing as he held Kirsten close. But he wasn't sobbing for her. He was sobbing for himself.

Joe had reached him now. He knelt down on the square of carpet – thick piled and still smelling of fresh wool – and took Kirsten in his arms, hardly daring to check whether or not she was still alive. He could hear a commotion downstairs. Their back up had arrived.

There was little resistance when he took the knife from Ethan's hand and flung it away into a far corner of the room. Emily had been hovering by the door but now she moved swiftly to summon help.

Joe didn't take his eyes off Ethan but he was aware of Emily returning a minute or so later with more officers who entered almost silently, as if they were unwilling to break the spell.

'Take her out till the ambulance arrives,' he said in a loud whisper, his eyes still fixed on the killer who was kneeling, perfectly still, on the carpet in front of him. Before a large uniformed officer took Kirsten's dead weight from him with surprising gentleness, Joe felt on her neck for a pulse. He couldn't find one but he was no expert. All he could do was to say a swift prayer that she'd live; that she wouldn't die cursing him as her sister's murderer. He had felt blood, warm and sticky on his hands, but he hadn't dared to look too closely. That horror could wait.

Then finally he found himself alone with the killer. Facing him there in the semi darkness.

'Tell me about the room in the cellar, Ethan.'

He waited but Ethan said nothing. If the room in the cellar had anything to do with why he'd killed all those women, he was keeping his secret to himself.

'You'll have to come with me now,' Joe said softly.

To his surprise the man struggled to his feet and stood there with his head bowed. Joe took his arm, ready to lead him out of that low attic room. But as he touched the sleeve of his shirt he felt it was damp and sticky. He led him out into the light of the small kitchen and then into the hallway where the others were waiting. Emily was there and he saw her eyes widen in horror as she stared at the prisoner.

He had been so concerned with getting Kirsten and the killer out of that room safely that he hadn't bothered to look at Ethan's face. But now he did he saw to his horror that blood was bubbling from the man's mouth and that his clothes were covered in sticky, shiny red. And when Ethan McNeil opened his mouth to speak the only sound that emerged was a low animal moan.

He had cut out his own tongue.

TWENTY-TWO

There was no way McNeil was in any state to give any sort of statement and Kirsten was still in surgery. The knife had just missed her heart but she was still in danger. Joe tried to pray for her but it was difficult. The woman had accused him of murder and made his life a misery. But forgiveness takes more guts than loathing and he still felt some obligation to her. She was Kaitlin's closest relative after all.

When they returned to the police station through the quiet streets it was almost midnight and the first thing Emily did was to hurry to her office to ring Jeff – to let him know I'm still alive, she joked. But if things had gone differently it might not have been a joking matter.

He waited for her in the incident room. There was somebody they needed to talk to. Jamilla had questioned Carla Vernon and, according to her report, the woman knew more than she was telling. Now that Ethan had been caught, there was a chance that Carla would understand that she couldn't protect him any more.

There was a hush over the whole building as he walked down the dimly lit corridors to the interview room with Emily at his side. Even though they'd caught the killer, nobody felt much like celebrating. Maybe things would be different in a couple of days.

Carla was waiting for them. During their absence she'd acquired a solicitor, a slim, horse-faced young woman in a grey trouser suit who looked as though she'd rather be somewhere else.

Carla looked exhausted. Her eyes were bloodshot and her hair was a mess; she looked so different from the businesslike woman they'd first encountered at the offices of McNeil and Dutton.

Joe sat down beside Emily and switched on the tape machine that sat at the end of the table. He outlined everything that had happened that evening at the office above the Fleshambles jewellers, leaving nothing out. Then he gave a vivid account of Ethan's injuries, telling her he would be charged with the murders of at least three women, probably more, and the attempted murder of Kirsten . . . if she pulled through.

Carla bowed her head but there was still a hint of spirit, of defiance, in her eyes.

'Is there anything you want to tell me, Carla? Did you know what he'd done?'

She shook her head vigorously.

Then he told her about their visit to the house in Flower Street and Carla looked up.

'He took me there once,' she said, almost in a whisper. 'He told me about his stepfather. He told me what he did to him.'

'What did he do?' Joe thought he knew the answer but he wanted it confirmed.

Carla was silent for a few moments and when she spoke her voice shook a little. 'Ethan's real father died when he was three. His mother married again but the man she married liked to experiment. It was just trivial things at first. Cutting his hair and seeing how long it took to grow back. Then finding out how well he could see in the dark after he'd eaten certain foods.'

She hesitated.

'Go on.'

'Then his mother died and that's when the tests got really cruel.'

'He imprisoned him in the cellar?'

There was no reply. Joe repeated the question.

'He told him he wanted to see what would happen if he couldn't see. He said he was interested in what would happen when he was let out. Then it was hearing. He tied earphones on him and transmitted white noise so he couldn't hear. Then he put padded gloves on him and tied his hands behind his back so he'd be deprived of the sense of touch. And he had a horrible bridle he put on him so that he couldn't move his tongue to stop him making a noise or even taste anything. And he recorded it all. He wrote it all down.'

'Who was this stepfather? What did he do for a living?'

'He was a professor at the university. He was researching the effects of sensory deprivation. He published papers on it. Ethan showed them to me.'

'Professor G McNeil. I think I found his notebooks at the house.'

Joe looked at Emily, imagining the terrified child in the darkness. 'I presume this man is dead?'

She nodded. 'He died a couple of years ago. That's when Ethan inherited the house. He came back from London and bought Dutton out.'

'In an upstairs room there's a lot of material about a Victorian murder case – a man called Obediah Shrowton who was supposed to have murdered his family.'

Carla nodded again. 'That was another of Professor McNeil's interests. He'd found stuff up in the attic. There was even a diary covered in Shrowton's skin. Ethan showed it to me. Professor McNeil discovered that the real killer actually lived in that house . . . His name was Jacob Caddy and Ethan was his direct descendant. His real name's Caddy, you know, but his stepfather made him take his name. McNeil used to tell Ethan that he had bad blood. Evil blood. That there were demons inside him. How can someone say that to a child?'

Joe sat quiet for a while. It disgusted him that a grown man could treat a child with such icy, sadistic cruelty. When people thought of abuse these days, they tended to think of the sexual kind. But the calculated torture of a child for supposedly scientific purposes was just as evil.

'Weren't the neighbours ever suspicious?' Emily asked.

'Professor McNeil was a highly respected man, an academic. Nobody asks questions of respected men, do they?'

The face of Barrington Jenks leapt unbidden into Joe's mind. Carla was right. The mask of respectability can conceal many dark sins.

'Why do you think Ethan told you all this?' he asked.

Carla looked up at him, suddenly defiant. 'Because he loves me and he wanted me to know everything about him. Because he was going to leave his wife for me. I can't believe he killed those women. He'd been through hell when he was a kid and he'd been hurt so much himself that he'd never put anybody else through that.'

Joe was reluctant to tell her that it often didn't work like that. Carla was deluding herself. But she wouldn't be the first woman to do so and she, no doubt, wouldn't be the last.

Emily gave him a gentle nudge with her elbow and he announced that the interview was over for the benefit of the tape.

'I'll send someone along to take a formal statement,' he said to Carla. 'Then you'll be able to go home.' He looked at the solicitor who seemed anxious to be on her way to salvage what remained of her ruined Saturday night. 'I'm afraid there may be charges . . .'

'I need to see Ethan,' Carla said pathetically.

Joe followed Emily out of the room.

Joe had returned to his flat at two in the morning but he hadn't been able to sleep because his head was filled with images of that dreadful little room in the cellar at Flower Street and Ethan McNeil's twisted, bloody face. Eventually he fell into a restless half-sleep and awoke at six a.m. to find himself tangled in his sheets, trapped in cotton and unable to escape. In that half waking moment, he felt a sudden flurry of panic. But then when he woke properly he disentangled himself and lay down again, closing his eyes in an attempt to get some more rest. But it wasn't long before his thoughts returned to the horrors of the night before and by eight he was more than ready to get up.

It was Sunday but this Sunday wouldn't be a day of rest. They had interviews to conduct and they would have to see Kirsten and McNeil if the doctors judged them well enough to receive visitors.

After the swiftest of showers Joe was about to put on the clothes he'd been wearing the night before but he noticed that they bore smears of blood. He rushed into his small kitchen wearing only his boxer shorts and threw the clothes straight into the washing machine. He'd see to them later.

He put on the only shirt that wasn't in his ironing pile and a pair of trousers he found hiding in the dark depths of his wardrobe, before leaving and making for the police station. As he walked he called Emily's number on his mobile. Although it was nine o'clock she was already at her desk. Somehow he knew she would be.

She told him that the doctors hadn't given the go-ahead for either Kirsten or McNeil to be interviewed but they were going to review the situation later in the day. Joe felt a pang of disappointment because he'd been looking forward to getting the whole affair cleared up. Then he had an idea. There was something he wanted to do. And this might be the right time to do it.

'I'm going to see Pet Ferribie's housemates. Then I think I should have another word with her father.'

Emily considered the suggestion for a few moments before saying 'fine'. Soon they'd be fully occupied with tying up all the loose ends of the investigation so he should grab the opportunity to give the victims' friends and relatives some police attention while he had the chance. He borrowed a pool car from the car park and drove to Bearsley through deserted streets.

Thirteen Torland Place had been on Joe's mind and he wondered whether the gaping hole in the ceiling above Matt Bawtry's bedroom had been fixed. He'd been a little concerned about Matt and how the traumatic experience of having a mummified corpse landing on his bed had affected him.

The curtains at number fifteen next door were all shut against the feverish press attention of the past couple of days. But with the advent of more dramatic fare in the form of last night's police activity, it seemed that the fourth estate had lost interest in the tale of the MP and the schoolgirls; a story which would surely have provided front page material for days in happier times.

The curtains at number thirteen were closed too but that didn't stop Joe ringing the doorbell twice. He wasn't surprised when he had a long wait. But eventually his patience was rewarded when Caro, wrapped cosily in a long towelling dressing gown, answered the door. As she stood aside to let him in he thought she seemed more friendly today, more relaxed.

'The news said you've arrested someone for Pet's murder?'

'That's right.'

'It wasn't Cassidy, was it?'

Joe shook his head. He was about to say that it was nobody they knew but then he remembered that Cassidy had called in Ethan when he needed a valuation on number thirteen. He had been there, in the sanctuary of Pet's house, probably after marking her out as a victim when she'd visited his office in search of her mother. He had infiltrated the party dressed as the Grim Reaper to watch his prey and the thought made him shudder.

When he told Caro the identity of the killer, she nodded as though she'd known it all along. Then he asked her whether Matt was in and she said she'd heard sounds from his room – now cleaned out and repaired by Cassidy – and when she offered to go upstairs and chivvy him out, Joe thanked her.

He entered the living room and was surprised to find that it no longer felt oppressive, almost as though some sort of curse had been lifted. But Joe told himself not to be so imaginative.

He waited there five minutes before Matt appeared in the doorway fully dressed in jeans and a T-shirt proclaiming the virtues of a certain local brew.

'Hi, Matt. You OK?'

Matt nodded.

'Recovered from your shock?'

'Suppose so.' Matt gave a coy grin. 'I went out last night and I'm finding it rather a good chat up line.'

Joe looked round, wondering what had changed since his last visit. 'I get the feeling there's something different about this place. I can't think what but . . .'

Matt sat down heavily on one of the old wooden chairs arranged around the table. 'Even Jason commented on it last night. It's like . . . like there was a sort of atmosphere of misery but now it feels normal. Does that sound really stupid?'

'No, not at all.'

'It seemed to happen all of a sudden. When we got back last night the place seemed different – like it wasn't the same house. Do you think it was something to do with that girl in the loft? I feel stupid thinking about presences and all that . . .'

Joe hesitated, wondering if what he was about to say would sound foolish. But he said it anyway. 'Last night we discovered for certain that Obediah Shrowton was framed for the murders that happened here. He didn't do it and we've proved his innocence once and for all.'

Matt looked astonished. Then he smiled. 'Maybe that's it. Old Obediah's cleared his name.' He glanced upwards. 'Caro said you've caught him . . . the man who killed Pet. She said it was that mate of Cassidy's who came round to view the place. Do you think Cassidy knew?'

Joe shook his head. 'I think he was as fooled as anyone.'

Then someone else spoke. 'If I get my hands on the bastard I'd rip his throat out.' Jason was standing in the doorway, his fists clenched by his side. He looked angry. And Joe could hardly blame him.

Matt frowned. 'Why did he have to go and kill Pet?' He bowed his head. 'She was lovely. Like an angel.'

Joe stood up. He'd broken the news and his job was done. 'Never forget her, will you,' he said quietly.

Matt shook his head. 'I won't forget. She'll stay with me forever.'

TWENTY-THREE

McNeil couldn't talk but he could write. At first his account of his crimes had been coherent and had provided the solution to all Joe's unanswered questions. But now nothing he wrote made any sort of sense. It was as if his mind had been taken over by some chaotic force. Madness maybe. Joe sat by his carefully guarded hospital bed and watched him scribbling words on a notepad. In times gone by, he thought, people would have assumed that he was possessed by some sort of demon. But in the rational age of reason and mundane explanations, no doubt the hospital's psychiatric department would claim to have the solution to the riddle that was the killer's mind.

He seemed almost unaware of Joe's watchful presence and from time to time he'd tear sheets of paper off his notepad and chuck them on the shiny linoleum floor. Joe picked them up and read the scribbled words. Demon. Kill. Grace. Laugh. Punish. Demon. He folded them carefully and put them in his pocket.

If you knew the truth about the murder of Grace Cassidy, Andy's sister who laughed at her brother's socially awkward friend, there was a kind of logic behind the words. Grace had offended him and she was punished. As was Sharon Bell, Den's girlfriend who used to object when he stared at her, who used to urge Den not to see him because he gave her the creeps. She'd been his enemy so she'd had to die and he'd put out her eyes – those big blue eyes with the long lashes he'd found so fascinating. Then there was the whore in London who'd asked for more money. Then there was Pet who'd asked those awkward questions about her mother and who'd looked so tempting at that party when he'd watched her, dressed as death. And Anna who'd seen him leave Cassidy's house early and suspected the truth. She'd called him, wanting money to ensure her silence and her fate was sealed.

These women had offended him and each time he'd used their offences to justify taking their lives. The demon in his head provided the perfect excuse.

But in all McNeil's ramblings there had been no mention of Pet's mother. And yet he'd been in possession of her photograph. The leaflets Paolo had given him suggested that McNeil had shown her round a number of properties before she disappeared. Had he killed her too because she rebuffed his advances? There was no evidence either way. Perhaps it would remain one of those unsolved mysteries that frustrate the police from time to time.

McNeil was so engrossed in his writing that he didn't even look up when Joe's phone rang. Joe took the call outside the room, nodding to the constable who had been given the tedious task of guarding the prisoner.

The call was from Emily and she wanted to know whether McNeil was in any condition to provide a formal statement. Joe said he didn't think so but Emily seemed unfazed. They had more than enough evidence now, she said.

And there was something new: the search team who were taking the Flower Street house apart had just made a discovery in the garden. When they'd dug up an area near the house they'd found a body buried about three feet down. The body was that of a woman in her thirties and, obligingly, her handbag and a holdall had been buried with her.

The name on the bank card found in the handbag was Helen Ferribie.

Kirsten was in Eborby General Hospital for a week before the doctors reckoned she was well enough to be discharged. Joe visited her whenever he called in to see how McNeil was doing. It seemed like the right thing to do.

And when she was discharged he told the ward sister that he'd be willing to look after her. She was Kaitlin's sister after all, his only link with the woman who'd been most precious to him. And besides, he wanted the opportunity to convince her once and for all that he had nothing to do with Kaitlin's death.

However, he was hardly surprised when she refused his offer and told him that she was going back down south. They parted at the hospital entrance, crowded with visitors and outpatients unaware of the little drama going on a few feet away.

'You're still not well. You should stay,' Joe said, trying to sound sincere.

She looked at him, puzzled. 'I don't know why you didn't let that lunatic kill me.' Then the defiance appeared in her eyes and Joe saw he had failed. 'You would have done if other people hadn't been there to see.'

Joe looked away. 'You're talking rubbish again.'

But Kirsten leaned towards him, talking in a whisper. 'I still think you had something to do with Kaitlin's death. I haven't found enough evidence yet but one day . . .'

Joe said nothing. There would be no happy ending and tearful reconciliation. Even the fact that he'd saved the woman's life had made no difference.

'Good luck,' he said. Then he walked away.

TWENTY-FOUR

'The students moved out three weeks ago and you can see it's in need of decoration.' Cassidy attempted a sincere smile. It was late July now and he had hoped that the events of the spring would fade in his mind. But they hadn't.

Now he was desperate to be rid of thirteen Torland Place and he was finding it hard to find a buyer; a combination of the national financial situation and the house's grim history. But he'd keep on trying.

The woman hadn't said much but she certainly seemed interested. Too interested, perhaps. However, he knew that she wasn't a journalist after a juicy story. He knew who she was: their paths had crossed professionally on several occasions but he wouldn't have classed her as even an acquaintance.

'I'll take it. I'm disposing of some property on behalf of my husband so the price you're asking isn't a problem.'

'I'm letting it go cheap because of the condition of the place and . . .'

'And the history? It's the history that attracts me, Mr Cassidy. And my husband. When he . . . when he comes out of hospital I want him to have a proper home to return to.'

Cassidy felt the blood drain from his face. He'd heard that there'd been an odd sort of wedding in the chapel of the secure hospital but he had no idea that a release was on the cards. The news disturbed him but he tried to keep his expression neutral. 'But I thought . . .'

'He'll get better. That's why he's in a secure mental hospital and not a prison. His condition's treatable and he won't be there for ever.'

Cassidy saw a smug smile on the face of Carla McNeil, née Vernon. Then the image of his dead sister's face flashed across his mind and he remembered the years he'd spent incarcerated for the crime committed by Ethan McNeil.

But money was money so he shook the woman's hand.

Don't miss out on the next
Joe Plantagenet mystery ...

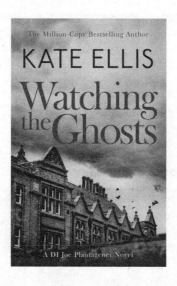

The Million-Copy Bestselling Author

KATE ELLIS

Watching the Ghosts

A DI Joe Plantagenet Novel

Boothgate House is a recently converted apartment building with a sinister past. Once an asylum for the insane, known as Havenby Hall, it was where serial killer Peter Brockmeister was sent on his release from prison.

Detective Inspector Joe Plantagenet is drawn into the house's history when the daughter of a solicitor, who was investigating Havenby Hall's closure, is kidnapped.

Joe wonders whether there may be a connection between the cases and the building's disturbing past.

But as secrets come to light, Joe is forced to face an evil that threatens those closest to him.

Don't miss Kate Ellis's
DI Wesley Peterson novels

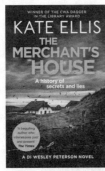

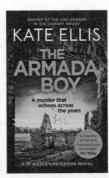

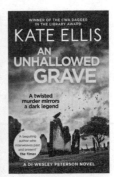

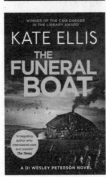

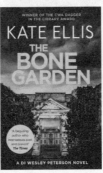

For a full list of the novels and to find out more
visit Kate Ellis online at:

www.kateellis.co.uk
@KateEllisAuthor